WHEN the BOWL FILLED

a novel

ALLISAN BECK

RIVER GROVE
BOOKS

Published by River Grove Books
Austin, TX
www.rivergrovebooks.com

Distributed by River Grove Books

Design and composition by Greenleaf Book Group and Mimi Bark
Cover design by Greenleaf Book Group and Mimi Bark
Cover image by © CPD-Lab/Shutterstock Images

Publisher's Cataloging-in-Publication data is available.

Print ISBN: 978-1-966629-56-6

eBook ISBN: 978-1-966629-57-3

First Edition

CONTENTS

CHAPTER ONE

OUTSIDE BOUNDARIES

"The movers are here!" I heard Nick call up to me from downstairs. My heart skipped a beat—the journey we'd been planning for months was about to begin. I left our second-floor bedroom and walked down the hall, dragging my hand along the wood banister I'd dusted numerous times over the past three years. Slowing to pass by the large bay window, I looked out at the huge tree that stood next to our beautiful Victorian house. There, at its base, bloomed the flowers I'd planted around it last year. The view tugged at my heart. I started down the stairs, inhaling a long, calming breath that I hoped would ground me for the next few hours.

Nick stood at the bottom of the stairs, about to unlock the heavy wooden front door, but he hesitated, looking up at me standing on the landing. Our eyes met and I knew we were thinking the same thing—this had been our first home together, our first big adult purchase. Now we were selling it, closing the fun newlywed chapter of our lives and starting another. At twenty-five,

I knew I was overdue for leaving the comfort and security of my home city and should explore the world. Butterflies did somersaults in my stomach as I descended the stairs and walked into the dining room.

"Oh, excuse me," I said, my daydreaming abruptly interrupted as I bumped directly into one of the movers and ricocheted off.

"Where do you want us to start?" the seemingly unmovable large man said, looking annoyed as he stood there holding his tape and boxes.

I looked for Nick and saw him busy guiding another man armed with paper and tape into the kitchen.

"Oh, uh, upstairs is fine," I said, moving out of the way as he brushed past me. I headed over to find Nick, only to see more movers throwing boxes together effortlessly in the kitchen, rapidly wrapping all our newly acquired wedding gifts, cookware, Nick's grandmother's antique wine glasses, my grandmother's antique serving trays, and my beloved cookbooks. Those frequently used books had been through my many attempts at recipes and their pages were dog-eared and stained from messy, furious cooking. I thought of the first time I made a meal for Nick in this kitchen—macaroni and cheese from scratch—only to have him say to me in a disapproving tone, "You made me macaroni and cheese for dinner?"

I'd smiled, giving him a pinch on the cheek and reminding him it was from scratch and pretty damn good too, thank you very much.

As the large mounds of thin, rectangular tan wrapping paper disappeared, surrounding our stuff in a protective cushion, I noticed that conserving paper didn't seem to be a priority for these movers. I was just in the way most of the time as I moved from one room to the next, trying to find a small corner to stand in that wasn't being used for bundling up our possessions. Everything in this house had a story behind it. My Uncle Fredrick, who was a boatbuilder, had made the beautiful oak dining table. The bookshelf had been my mother's when she was a kid and still had the carving of her name in it, which had gotten her in lots of trouble with my grandmother.

"Oh please be careful with those oil paintings, they were my husband's great-grandmother's," I said to one worker, who was on the floor flipping the painting over and wrapping it in paper and tape. He gave me a frustrated smile.

"We'll be very careful, ma'am."

I'd never been called ma'am before, but knew it was his way of saying "back off." Getting the hint, I walked into the office, where the tornado of packing hadn't hit yet. I stood for a moment looking at the delicate antique flower pendant light hanging in the office. Nick and I had found it a few years ago while antiquing together. It was a pastime that we both loved. The light was perfect for the space, and it complemented the house so well that people thought it was an original fixture. It was one of the many small touches we made when we decided to fix up an old Victorian house. *Not an endeavor I want to undertake again*, I thought, still musing at the light. It had kept us busy enough, but I was done with remodeling a house. I hoped the next one we found wouldn't need much work at all. I wanted to spend my time going out to eat or seeing live music—exactly what New Orleans was all about.

"The light has to stay," Nick said with a smirk, seeing me standing there looking up at it.

I gave him a wry smile.

"Don't worry, Cole, moving will get easier—you'll see. Every new place comes with its own set of challenges and excitement. And if the new location stinks, you know it's only temporary," Nick declared proudly.

"Easy for you to say, Mister 'moving is easy!' You've adapted seamlessly to moving to a new city every three years. This is my first move away from everything I've known and loved, my house, my gardens, friends, family—"

"Nonsense! Not *everything*; you still have me!" He paused, then he grabbed my hand and twirled me around, singing, "We are family . . ."

I couldn't help but laugh.

"Cole, you always said you wanted to travel more. Now you can and you don't even have to pack your own stuff, you lucky gal." Nick finished our dancing by guiding me into a deep dip and a kiss.

"New Orleans," I said, looking up at Nick, still in my dip. "It wasn't even one of the places that we asked to go!"

"Okay, Collette." Nick guided me back upright. "I'll explain one more time—it's called a 'dream sheet' for a reason. We put all the possible places we dream of going, then someone else picks for us!" He said, laughing, "The military likes to keep you guessing! It's going to be a great opportunity for my career and for us. We'll work hard and play hard. Remember how shocked you were to learn that there was a Coast Guard base in Cleveland?"

I laughed in embarrassment, remembering how he'd pointed out that the Great Lakes were part of their Area of Responsibility (AOR). I hadn't considered that the Coast Guard could be in Ohio too until after we first met. AOR was just one of the many acronyms I'd been picking up throughout the first few years of our marriage.

"Well, Cleveland wasn't first on my list," Nick said, "but I'm so glad I was stationed here and met the love of my life." He gave me another kiss and led me out of the room, which was now getting crowded with packers.

Four months earlier, when we found out that we were heading to New Orleans, Nick and I visited the Rock & Roll Hall of Fame. "To give you inspiration," he said. There on the large first floor was a section about New Orleans artists: Professor Longhair, The Meters, Fats Domino. I put the headphones on that were connected to the wall and transported myself through the music to New Orleans. My feet were stuck to the ground as my brain was trying to process the rhythms I'd never heard before. The sounds were making new neuronal connections in my brain. I stood transfixed in front of the small screen displaying the album covers. Track after track played while droves of people passed me, traveling in blur, like a scene from a busy train station. I was excited I'd be spending three years immersed in such a fascinating city, but now that moving day had arrived, I was terrified.

"You sure do have a lot of stuff," huffed one of the workers carrying a large box. He stacked it in the growing pile with the others.

"It's mostly wedding gifts," I said apologetically, and then I chastised myself. Why did I have to apologize? Weren't they getting paid to do this?

"Hey, Collette, I'm thirsty. How about you?" Nick had a twinkle in his eyes. He must have noticed me overseeing the packing process and following the movers around the house.

I knew he was up to something. "There are some soda cans in the fridge, but you can't use the glassware—it's packed already."

"Well, since we can't get a drink here, let's get one at José McBagpipes one last time."

"I thought we had to stay and watch the movers," I whispered.

Nick shook his head. "No, let them do their jobs. We already packed the important valuables with the other things that we have to move ourselves. Plus, we won't be that long. C'mon." He tugged at me. "We probably won't find a Mexican-Irish bar in New Orleans. It'll be our last time going there." He had a way of pushing his agenda. Luckily for me, it was usually a fun one.

Hours later, the house was finally quiet: just Nick and me and more than three hundred boxes.

"It's a bit embarrassing to have this much stuff," Nick said as we ate the pizza we'd brought home from the bar. We were sitting on the floor, eating it right out of the box. "Let's aim to reduce this by ten percent. Before our next PCS move."

"Permanent Change of Sanity . . ." I said with a mouthful of room-temperature pizza.

"Permanent Change of Station," Nick said between bites, rolling his eyes. "Every three years."

"Right. Anyway," I continued, "I wouldn't know what to get rid of." I was already mourning the things I hadn't sold yet. I then added quickly, "We could start with your things!"

"Let's just make it a goal for our next move," Nick said, ignoring my comment. "We'll have time to sort things out when we unpack."

"Oh my. That might take a while," I said, searching for one of the last precious napkins we'd brought back from the bar. By then, there was absolutely nothing else to use.

Nick gave me a knowing glance and said, "I'd like to get that done quickly once we get settled." Then he continued. "We should get to bed soon so we can be ready for tomorrow."

"I can't believe this is all happening," I said, the realization finally hitting me. "I just want to call my mama to say goodnight. Do you mind?"

Nick shook his head. "Meet you on the air mattress," he said, planting a kiss on my lips.

I gathered the remaining cheese pizza and stuck the whole box in the fridge. With no wrap or Tupperware to use, cleaning up was a breeze.

I picked up the phone and walked among the stacked boxes to the front room. I found a spot on the floor near the window that had a sliver of light coming in from the streetlamp and looked out the large windows.

"Hi, Mama!"

"Hello, sweetheart. How are you doing? How did the movers do today?"

"We have a *lot* of stuff," I said. "I don't know how long it's going to take me to unpack it all."

"Oh, well, I'm sure Nicholas will help out, honey. Don't get yourself all worked up. Whatever you don't get to, I'll help when we come to see you next month!"

"That would be wonderful! Wait, next month? We don't even have a place yet!"

"Honey, you'll find one, I know you will. I've been praying for you."

"Thanks, Mama—I know we'll find one with you on the red phone to the Big Guy." I took a breath. "I'm not going to say good-bye yet. I'll just start to cry."

"Sweetheart, embrace this new change. You've always said you wanted to travel. You get to really see the country now! And you can call me anytime, day or night, you know that."

"I know that. It's just now that it's happening . . ." I trailed off, not wanting to say out loud that I didn't want to move.

"It'll be fun, Collette. You have a new life now with your husband—embrace it."

"Okay, I'll try to be more excited and less terrified. Thanks, Mama, you always know just what to say. I love you. I'll talk to you tomorrow."

"Have a good night, honey."

"Goodnight." I hung up the phone, walked upstairs, and crawled onto the air mattress with Nick, displacing his body left and right as I tried to carefully place my body down next to his. Eventually I calmed my nerves down enough to fall asleep.

I got up early the next morning and arranged our things for our drive down south. I walked over to the row of five-gallon buckets and peeked into them to see our fish swimming around happily with the air stones bubbling away. "Good morning, little fishies," I said. "Are you ready for your big trip?"

Nick answered for the fish in a squeaky little voice: "Yes." He followed me into the bathroom.

"My little fishies don't talk, Nick. That's what makes them better than my patients at the hospital," I said to him. "Though I do miss all of them already."

"You'll find another nursing job in New Orleans, Collette. Don't worry. You're lucky that you have a job that relocates easily—a lot of military spouses have a hard time finding new jobs with every move. That being said, we have seventeen hours to chat about how lucky you are, among other things. Let's get rolling," Nick said and gave me a little smack on my butt.

I guess he was right. Finding another job shouldn't be too difficult, I told myself. "The movers weren't too thrilled to crate up our big fish tank," I said as Nick was getting dressed.

He paused and poked his head into the hallway. "Well, they *are* getting paid extra to crate it. But yeah, I heard one mention that he never saw anyone with a 180-gallon tank before! Go big or go home, right?" Nick laughed.

My Uncle Fredrick had custom made the poplar wood stand for the tank so that it stood four feet off the ground. It felt as if we were standing at an aquarium display, peering into the large tank of fish. Our Discus, Plecostomus, Cory Cats, Zebrafish, Platies, and Angelfish had moved around the tank in a happy fish community. Dracula, our nine-inch-long Plecostomus, would only come out at night to clean the tank of invading algae. We'd spot him hanging upside-down on the glass acting as our quiet aquatic vacuum cleaner.

"Well, I can't wait to set it up again and watch our Fish Channel," I said to apparently no one as Nick, I realized with the click of the front door, was now outside loading up the car.

"Let's wait on packing the fish until we're ready to go," I called to him from the open bedroom window. I saw the moving truck rumble up the street and come to a stop in front of the house. *Here we go*, I thought, and I took a deep breath and quickly got dressed.

There was a flurry of activity this time, calling out box numbers as the boxes were wheeled out and put onto the truck one by one. One man holding a roll of numbered tape was checking off the boxes on the many sheets of carbon copy paper as the dollies carried away boxes and stacked them high in the truck.

When the last of the boxes were loaded, Nick signed the multiple pages of paperwork and the movers got in their truck.

"See you in New Orleans!" the driver called back to us as they slowly pulled away.

"Have a safe trip!" I yelled back, and Nick and I waved as the truck drove out of sight. I found a broom and dustpan mistakenly left behind and started to sweep my cherrywood floors to remove all the dust and debris left over from the move. I just couldn't leave my house for the last time in a dirty state. It seemed unfair to the beautiful floors.

As I threw the last pan of dust bunnies out, I heard Nick say to me from the patio, "Bad news, Cole."

"No way? Already? We haven't even left yet!" My heart started to race.

"It's not *that* bad! It's just that Hercules won't fit in the car. He'll have to stay here, but it'll be a nice housewarming gift for the new owners."

A smile crossed my face realizing what he was referring to. "Are you sure? I love that plant. We've been through so much together. That aloe has been used on all my cuts."

"We'll get another when we get settled. Speaking of, let's hit the road!"

Reluctantly I walked away, staring at the huge aloe plant sitting on the front step seemingly watching us leave it behind.

Nick held my hand and escorted me to the car. The 1988 brown Lincoln Town Car wasn't my choice as the car we'd buy together, but it was affordable on our tight budget and it had air conditioning, which we would desperately need down south. The car was loaded down so much from the weight of the fish buckets in the trunk that the tail pipe was almost hitting the ground.

"Oh my gosh!" I exclaimed as I saw the car in its current state. "Is the car okay to drive like this?"

"It's all good, Collette. Ready for your big adventure?"

I looked back at my beautiful house with freshly painted gingerbread, my colorful gardens brimming with flowers, my familiar neighborhood, and Hercules, then faced Nick. "Yes," I said, convincing him but not myself.

The plan was to drive all seventeen hours, only stopping for food and breaks so that we could get down there, unpack the car, and immediately start searching for a place to live. Nick took the first leg of the trip. We drove out of town waving to our neighbors as we left, leaving a trail of sparks flying from the rear muffler as it bounced down the street.

Driving at night didn't help much for sightseeing. I started to doze off, instructing Nick to wake me when it was my turn to drive. Car rides, no matter how short, always made me sleepy if I was the passenger, and this was definitely not going to be a short drive.

⁓

I felt the car come to an abrupt stop and woke to the unnaturally bright fluorescent lights of a gas station. "Where are we?" I managed to say in a sleepy voice.

"Louisville, Kentucky. I'm still good to drive. You go back to sleep," Nick responded in a caffeinated and convincing voice.

He didn't need to tell me that twice! I was back asleep, probably drooling on my pillow, before he managed to get back in the car again.

The next time I awoke it was from the heat inside the car. The windows were down, letting in the hot, muggy air. The breeze was hitting Nick's face, which looked determined but now exhausted. "Good morning!" I said, maybe a little too refreshed.

"Good morning, Collette. Did you sleep well? I've got some fun news—we're only two hours from New Orleans!"

"Whoa! That's amazing! Do you need me to drive?" I offered.

"No, I got this. You can start searching for hotels to stay at while I drive."

I was so relieved—as it was, I had no idea where we were anyway. I thought of calling my parents to let them know, but decided to hold off and call once we officially arrived. I grabbed the New Orleans travel book my parents had given us before we left and started calling up hotels. I first called the ones rated with three stars. I called hotel after hotel, only to be told each time that they were fully booked. Nick, overhearing every discouraging phone call as we drove on, gave me a quizzical look. I offered him a determined smile of reassurance. Turning the page, I called the two stars, then the one stars. *For goodness' sake!* I thought. *What is going on down there?*

I finally got a hotel that had a vacancy. "I'll take it!" I said, so relieved.

I looked at Nick after I hung up. "Finally. No guarantees on how nice it is, but at least they have a room. It seems we're arriving during something called Essence Fest, and all the rooms in the city are taken."

"That's a relief! Good job, Cole!"

We pulled into the parking lot of the hotel and got out. The full magnitude of the humidity hit us immediately. I felt as if I was moving in slow motion to try to make my way through the thick air. The lobby was a large, open-air room with lazy fans moving the heat around. We rolled the suitcases with us to check in, leaving the rest of our house in the car.

The lady working the front desk greeted us nicely enough. She escorted us to our room down a long, worn, red-carpeted hallway. Scattered on the ground were dead bugs. They looked like huge cockroaches, but I didn't say anything, as I seemed to be the only one to notice or care. We came upon a door directly below an Exit sign. "Is this a joke?" I was about to say, but before I got the words out, the woman unlocked the door to reveal a small makeshift additional room. The space must have had a large enough landing to enclose it and designate it as another hotel room. There was another door inside the room that had an Exit sign I assumed led to the stairwell, though I didn't open it up to check. The room was L-shaped, so the bathroom must have been on the main hotel side. I wasn't sure how they'd managed to turn this arrangement into a room with a bathroom.

"Thank you very much!" Nick said with a smile.

"Are you insane or just really tired?" I asked. "Are we really staying here?"

"Yes. I'm exhausted and just want to sleep for a few hours before we need to start the process of looking for places to live," Nick said and collapsed on the bed. "Can you unload the car? There's not much left in there," he asked from the pillow.

My stomach rumbled, but I didn't say anything about it. "Sure," I said, reminding myself that he just drove the entire way without my help. I left to search for a luggage cart to get the rest of our things, including our fish. Once back at the room, I started to unpack the toiletries while Nick snored away. I saw the cracked plaster walls and noticed ferns growing out of one of the cracks near the window. What had I gotten myself into? I fought back the anxiety. I wasn't just in a new place—I felt like I was in a whole new world.

I pushed the luggage cart with the fish buckets, trying not to slosh the water too much, toward the bathroom. I hit an uneven transition in the floor and the cart gave a jerk, which stopped my forward progress, and I nearly fell. "Shit," I whispered, but thankfully I didn't wake up Nick.

I pulled the buckets the remainder of the way into the bathroom and peeked at the fish. "I'll change your water soon," I whispered to them. They were swimming away happily through the bubbling air stones.

I decided to go for a walk to collect myself. It was about time I called home anyway. I knew my mother would be worrying and most likely praying her second rosary by now.

Looking for a secluded place, I came upon the courtyard. I imagined it had once been a beautiful spot with clean, white, ornate wrought-iron balconies, cobblestone pathways, and a beautiful sparkling pool, but now with apparent neglect, the balconies were speckled with red rust, weeds were growing up through the stone path, and the pool resembled more of a pond. This, however, didn't seem to faze the handful of people floating on inflatable tubes and indulging in libations. *It's not even 9 a.m.*, I thought incredulously.

I found a chair under a torn awning and took my phone out of my pocket.

"Good morning, Mama!" I said, my voice wobbling only a bit.

"Oh praise Jesus, you made it! I was praying you would call me. Wait a minute. Are you there already? I've been so worried."

"Yes, yes. We're here. I called as soon as I could."

"Oh that's wonderful to hear! So, how is New Orleans?"

I paused. *How do I describe this place?* I wanted to remain positive, as it was only my first few hours here and I really only had seen this hotel. "Well, it sure is different, Mama."

She laughed. "Of course it is, sweetheart, you're in the South. I want to know all about it!"

"It's very muggy and hot and it's only still morning! The few people we met so far seem nice. Nick is asleep after driving the whole way, but I'm going to wake him soon so that we can get something to eat and start searching for a place. I'm starving."

"I'm so glad you got there safely. I can't believe he drove the whole way! Go and get yourselves something to eat and call me again with another update. God bless. Don't forget to call me! I love you."

"I will, Mama, I love you too." We hung up and I went back to the room to change the fish water in the buckets. I needed something to do to keep my mind off of my present situation. I slowly scooped out about one third of the water and carefully tested the temperature of the new water, so as not to startle the fish with abrupt temperature changes. As I poured the first large pint into the bucket, the fish began swimming frantically around in distress, and some immediately went belly up. *Oh my gosh!* I stood up, horrified at what just happened to my beloved fish, trying to think of something quick to do to help them. I started retracing my steps trying to figure out what I'd done. It must have been the water. I hadn't even thought to check the chlorine levels in the water here. We never had that problem back home.

I immediately stopped adding more water, but it was too late. We had lost almost all the fish in the first bucket. I fought back tears scooping out the few remaining survivors and putting them in other buckets. *Well*, I thought, *now I guess I have an empty bucket to dechlorinate the water in first.*

I sat down and tears flooded my eyes. I scooped the dead fish out and flushed them down the toilet. It was overwhelming trying to remain stoic. I needed a hug.

At noon I woke Nick, hunger and the fear of venturing out alone getting the best of me. I decided to keep the sad and embarrassing fish incident to myself.

"Hey, babe, what time is it?" Nick mumbled as I laid next to him and rubbed his back.

"Noon. I was hoping we could get some lunch."

"Yes. Great idea. And thanks for letting me sleep." As Nick rolled over, he asked in an inviting, sultry voice, "What are you in the mood for?"

"Food, not funny business," I said, smiling, removing his hand from my hip. "Let's explore and see what looks good."

"All right, all right . . . let's walk to get some food, then we'll get the car and start looking at neighborhoods. We might have time for funny business later," he said with a smile.

We walked toward the French Quarter, passing street signs that either had French names or were Saint-something. Eventually, we meandered to this small deli that seemed as if it was built in a forgotten alleyway. Small white metal bistro tables with plastic checkered tablecloths were arranged outside. The menu, posted on a sign out front, was simple and inexpensive.

We sat at one of the metal bistro tables and a middle-aged man came outside to great us without much fanfare. He put the laminated menus on the table and impatiently waited for us to order. Nick ordered the Italian sub and I chose the egg salad sandwich, not really the food I was expecting to have in New Orleans, but I was happy we'd found a small place with charm and not a tourist trap.

"So, where should we start looking?" I asked Nick.

"I was thinking we start in Mid-City, then Bayou St. John or maybe Central City. I'd like to stay near the streetcar lines so that I don't have to drive far to work." He had clearly been thinking about this for a while.

"All right, sounds good," I told him. Though honestly I didn't have a clue as to where he was talking about. "Did you figure this all out on your own while we were in Ohio?" I said without thinking first. I softened and added, "I would have liked to have been included on researching areas to live for the next three years."

"Cole, I tried to get you to sit with me, but you were too busy finishing up the last weeks of work. There was always something that distracted you. Honestly, I thought doing some research on my own would save us some time. Plus, I really don't want to have a long commute."

"What about living in an area that'll be good for us both?"

"All these areas are close to hospitals, so don't worry so much. You're beginning to sound like your mother."

"Be nice, Nick," I said in a measured and cautionary tone.

"Just don't worry—we'll find something. Let's just enjoy the ride today."

"Okay," I said, staring at the remaining crumbs on my plate, trying to calm myself down.

The rest of that afternoon was spent driving around the different areas of the city. I was awestruck by the beauty of the houses. Nearly all the houses we drove by had wooden siding and were very long and narrow. Each house was more ornate and colorful than the last. I'd never seen anything like it. "This is amazing!" I said in excitement. "They're so large. And all so long!"

"They're called shotgun houses, because if you open up the front door and rear door and shoot a gun through it you won't hit a wall."

My face must have conveyed *Where did you get that fact?* The reference to shooting inside a house was not at all comforting to me.

"I'm serious," said Nick, smiling.

"How do you know so much about this place? I still think you're making stories up."

"Stick with me, kid, and I'll teach you things." He started humming the song "A Whole New World."

I flashed him a humoring smile. He was so arrogant and confident—qualities that had attracted me to him. I loved it, though it was humbling how little I knew about places outside of Ohio.

We were at a stoplight, admiring the lush ferns and plants framing the houses while scanning the area for the elusive For Sale signs, when a car slowly appeared next to us on the left side of a two-lane street. I could see it was filled with five people.

"Oh my gosh! They're in the wrong lane!" I said, tugging on Nick's shoulder.

He rolled down his window, and the two of us watched in disbelief as they passed us in slow motion and rolled up the curb. The car hit the streetlight, making a quiet *ping* and stopping its forward progress. The people inside the car were laughing hysterically, and just as slowly as the car had rolled there, they reversed off the curb and slowly drove down a different street, this time on the correct side.

"That has to be the slowest accident I've ever seen," I said, laughing in disbelief.

We found St. Charles Avenue and drove up the beautifully lush street framed by old oak trees. The olive-green streetcar lined with wood and brass on the inside clanked noisily by us, windows open and packed with people.

"These houses are so grand! I know we're out of our price range," I stated, but Nick was too busy taking it all in to acknowledge my price-tag concern.

One house—or rather mansion—after the next had grand white round columns, ornate double front porches, and large wooden front doors. I felt as if I was transported back to a time where wealthy Southern women wore hoop dresses and all their jewelry, just because they could. *Way too many layers of clothing for the heat down here,* I thought. Already I had beads of sweat forming on my brow and chest from the short time we'd spent outside eating breakfast. The beauty of the intricate gingerbread decorating the houses did not go unnoticed by me.

The gingerbread brought me back to our modest Victorian house in Ohio. Such a familiar sight made me long for home, but also jolted me back to current reality and our predicament of finding a place to live. "Hey," I said, "it's nice to be a tourist and all, but how about getting into an area we can actually afford?"

"Yeah, I know. I just wanted to see this side of town. Dream a little."

I hated to squash his wanderlust, but the sooner we found a place the sooner I could get out of that musty hotel room. We drove for a little while, passing people resting on their front porches with iced beverages. A large grass-covered hill caught my attention; it seemed to extend for miles and had water on the other side of it.

"What is that?" I asked Nick, pointing.

"It's the levee," Nick said, so excited to show me new things. "It blocks the river from flowing into the city. New Orleans is shaped like a big bowl—much of it is built below sea level."

"That's amazing," I said, wondering at the simplicity of its design. "Does it work?" I asked.

"I guess so," he said, followed by, "I hope so."

We continued to drive until we came to the Canal Street streetcar line. We passed the bustle of downtown; Bourbon Street, small shops, and a few restaurants nestled in between the houses. The area seemed to become quieter, more residential. The street dead-ended appropriately at a cemetery. The Canal Street streetcars were very different from the St. Charles line. The candy-red cars looked like they might have a smoother ride, since the noise of the clanging cars was less than that of their green counterparts. The most alluring attributes were the closed windows that kept the fancy air conditioning inside the cars. What luxury this line offered! The houses in this neighborhood were not as grand, but they still had charm, with gingerbread on the rooflines and columns.

"I haven't seen one For Sale sign, love. I think we're going to need to change our approach," I gently suggested.

"Don't worry. This is the Big Easy, remember?"

"Apparently not *so easy* when it comes to finding a place. I don't think you're as worried as I am about where we're going to live."

"Cole, it's our first day. Relax," Nick said. "We've been driving for a while now, and that breakfast was a bit small—are you getting a little hangry? Let's grab some food and figure this out. Maybe talk to some locals to get an idea of what the neighborhoods are like. How does that sound?" He smiled at me and gave my leg a squeeze.

I hated it when he got condescending.

We turned off Canal Street and, as luck would have it, found a restaurant that appealed to both of us. The large wooden sign that read Parkway Bakery and Tavern sat atop the stick building, which was right across from a large pond. It had picnic tables outside, with lazy fans circling and strange bags of water with a penny inside hanging from the roof overhang.

"What's with the bags?" I asked Nick through my smile, careful not to speak too loudly.

"I don't know," he said, trying to be discreet as he glanced at me sideways so as not to give us away as naïve tourists.

Walking up to the place, we quickly figured out that we'd gone to the pickup window by mistake. Some locals pointed to the order window around the corner and we embarrassingly walked around, cover blown. The menu had many different sandwich options, all labeled as po'boys. At five dollars each, I could understand the name. What a deal! We ordered: one fried shrimp for me and fried oyster for Nick, accompanied by two local Abita Amber beers. It was, after all, past noon, though I got the sense that time didn't really matter much here. I was still staring at the mysterious bags when the counter clerk followed my glance.

"They're for the flies, dear," said the blonde woman with the wrinkled t-shirt as she accepted the change. "You two new in town?"

I was completely caught off guard and a bit embarrassed as well. "Oh, us? Yes. Sorry, I've never seen that before. Does it work?"

"I honestly can't tell," she said dryly.

We thanked her and took a spot on one of the picnic benches. "Shit. Sorry Nick, there goes our cover."

He laughed. "I don't think we have a cover. We stick out pretty good here." He put the red tray carrying our sandwiches down and gave me a kiss on the cheek as I passed out our beers.

The plastic silverware, along with hot sauces, were at a self-serve station around the side where we ordered. People were talking everywhere, though I couldn't understand what anyone was saying. The dialect was one I'd never heard before: short, clipped words muddled together. I made sure to speak quietly so as not to draw any more attention to us. I took a bite of the gigantic sandwich loaded with lettuce, mayonnaise, pickles, and deep-fried shrimp that fell out the other side.

"Oh my gosh," I said with my mouth full, "this is so good."

"So good," Nick echoed.

I looked around at the old wooden houses surrounding this large pond-like body of water, the lush green grass and a few branching trees. "This seems to be an interesting part of town. Maybe we can explore it a little more," I suggested.

After eating we got back into the car and started driving aimlessly around the area. I kept my eyes peeled for houses with the elusive signs out front, though this method was seeming more and more like finding a needle in a haystack. We kept the large pond—which we were informed at Parkway was called the bayou—to our right and drove through the streets until we passed a large horse track that didn't seem to be in use. "I don't see any horses," I said. "Do you think they have horse races there?"

"Probably, though it might be too hot in the summer to run the horses. I think it's a thoroughbred racetrack."

"How fun that would be to see!" I pictured in my mind the well-known racetrack in Kentucky, where all the ladies wore hats during the Derby. I was still daydreaming when Nick drove us to a large, lush green park. The sign we saw appropriately displayed the name City Park.

We rolled into a parking spot and Nick pulled out a map of the city.

"This place is so neat. Do we have time to walk around?" I asked.

"Let's do it!" He refolded the large map in a haphazard way and threw it on the seat of the car.

I grabbed Nick's hand and viewed my surroundings like a little kid at a new park walking slowly with her parent. The huge oak trees were draped with Spanish moss and the air was thick with heat and the music of cicadas. I felt as if I'd stepped into another world. We walked up a path to where we found a weathered stone stage with steps leading up to it and grand columns surrounding it. There was a small pond behind it with lily pads floating motionless on the surface of the dark water. I didn't want to know if reptiles also took up residence there—like alligators. I kept a safe distance just in case.

"I'm going to sit down here a moment," I said as I knelt down on one of the steps with stone lions looking at the pond.

"Great," Nick said. "I see someone over there—I'm going to go over and ask about this area we're in." He walked in the direction of the one guy throwing a ball to his dog. I sat there and admired the strange mixture of palms, oak trees, and other trees that looked dead, imagining it as a movie set patiently waiting to be discovered, or a beautiful painting. A large white bird gracefully floated to the edge of the pond and tip-toed around carefully, peering into the murky water. The peaceful area was filled with animal chatter: the chirping of squirrels as they ran down a tree, their nails gripping and scratching the dry bark, a grunt from a frog, the sound of the palm leaves as they brushed each other as a slight wind flowed. Behind me I heard the sound of Nick talking to someone else on the path. After some time he came and sat down next to me.

"Okay, I got the scoop!" he said and flopped down, dangling his legs off the step.

My eyes widened, waiting for his next sentence.

"Turns out the guy I met has a friend who's looking for renters at his place in Mid-City. That's the area we just were. He said he's over there now and we can stop by." Nick sounded enthusiastic.

"Oh! I'm so confused. Weren't we only considering places for sale?" I thought for a moment and then added, "I guess buying a place or renting, I really don't care that much. I just want to be settled."

"Right! If we're lucky we can find something and close on it quickly. We're already cleared for a loan from the bank. We might have to rent a bit until a house opens up to buy. Either way, I'd rather not have our stuff in storage for too long. Let's try to keep all options open." Nick had clearly been thinking about all the options.

"Sure. I guess we can rent until we figure out something to buy like we did in Cleveland."

Nick put his arm around my shoulders. "Exactly. You get it now, Cole!" He laughed and I rolled my eyes. "When we get back to the hotel I'll search for places for sale online, now that we sort of have an area picked out, but we should get going to try to catch that guy about the rental."

We skipped back to the car, feeling silly and flush with hope. Back toward Mid-City we drove, windows down, letting the hot air blow my short hair around.

Somehow Nick found where the house was located. There was no For Rent sign anywhere to be seen. I was hoping it was the correct house, or we were going to be pretty embarrassed. The place was raised about eight feet off the ground with many large steps going up to the door.

"Wow, this place comes with a grand entrance and a workout," I said. Having to walk so many steps to only reach the front door didn't seem ideal.

Before we could get out of the car, we heard someone yelling out of a muffled megaphone.

"What was that?" I looked earnestly at Nick, big-eyed, and rolled up my window and locked the door.

We stayed in the car until we could figure out what was going on. The sound got louder, and then we saw the pickup. It was a beat-up old truck filled with fruits and vegetables stacked precariously in the back. It now made sense—in a low, melodious voice, the driver was saying, "I have onion, I have garlic . . . I have cucumbers, avacada . . ." Nick and I exchanged smiles as we got out of the car. Now that was something you didn't see or hear every day in Ohio! Then again, not much down here was like anything I'd ever experienced before.

We walked up the stairs and knocked on the door. An angry-looking man opened it, keeping the outside screen shut. "Yeah?" he said, looking out at us.

"Hello, sir," Nick started. "We're new in the area and heard from a friend that this place is for rent."

The man softened a bit. "This here's my son's house. He's eatin' down at Finn's. Come back in a few hours an' you can talk ta' him."

"Okay, thank you, sir," Nick said warmly. "Sorry to have bothered you."

"No bother at all, son." The man paused. "Finn's is right 'round the corner. Why don't cha stop in yo'selves to find him."

Nick had a real talent to get people to instantly like him—which

I had to admit wasn't a strong suit of mine. "Wonderful! Thank you, sir. Have a great day," he said.

The man smiled and shut the door. I waited until we were a safe distance away to turn to Nick and say, "What a charmer you are."

"It worked on you too," he winked.

He was right, again.

We went to the corner of the street and looked around, as the man's directions weren't very specific. Walking down Banks Street, we spotted many tired houses. Sidewalks were cracked and uneven, and lush greenery was growing everywhere. You could tell it was a working-class neighborhood, maybe even working-poor. A few blocks away we saw the modest hanging wooden sign that told us we'd made it to Finn McCool's. I couldn't believe we'd found it.

The side street was packed with cars and even had a cab parked there, though no one was in it. It seemed very much like the local neighborhood bar. The entry door stood kitty-corner to the building and opened into the dark room. Once my eyes adjusted to the low light, I saw that I was standing in front of an intimate bar with a few stools scattered around it. Gambling and XXX game machines were in abundance. Following the bar around the corner, the room opened up to a slightly larger one with tables and chairs, but not much else.

"Must be a liquid lunch his son is having," I said to Nick.

"What can I get you?" the bartender asked as she wiped off her hands on a bar rag.

"I'll take a Turbodog," said Nick, and I quickly scanned the taps and noticed the Abita Amber, which I recognized from earlier.

"I'll have an Amber," I told the bartender. "Thanks."

We sat at the bar, leaving a seat open between us and another guy at the end just finishing up a pint. The bartender came over with three pints. She put two in front of us and one in front of the guy at the end of the bar.

"You two visiting?" she asked.

"Actually, we're relocating here. We're looking for a place to buy or rent and we were just checking out the area."

"Oh, well, you should talk to John here, he's a cabbie. Knows all the areas." She motioned to the man with the fresh pint of beer.

John sat at the bar staring up at the television above him. He was wearing a well-worn New Orleans Saints hat that covered his long wavy gray hair tucked behind his ears. John glanced at us and held up his beer as a nod. "What parts you looking in?"

I just let Nick talk at this point, since I still had no idea where I was.

"We like it here in Mid-City," Nick said. "Feels like a neighborhood with lots of potential."

"Yeah, it's getting better, though the crime is still bad on the other side of Banks Street. Houses are really hard to come by, I will say." He paused and took a drink. "Places sell before they even hit the market. Just gotta be lucky or know someone." At that point John got a call. "Hey, Lisa, I'll settle up here. Got a customer. Good luck, you two," he said to us.

"Thanks, John," Nick replied, and I gave a smile as I leaned forward, making eye contact with John.

John finished his pint as casually and quickly as if he was pouring it down the drain.

Apparently, he was still on the clock. I had to laugh at the thought of drunk people stumbling out of a bar and calling a cab just to have their cab driver leave a bar to pick them up. I was getting the feeling that there was a very different set of rules for this city than there was at home. It seemed to be an anything goes kind of place.

"Remind me not to take cabs here," I quietly said to Nick, and we both laughed.

"The streetcar is just a few blocks away. How about we take it downtown and check things out?" Nick suggested.

The notion of visiting Bourbon Street and drinking more didn't especially interest me, but checking out the sounds and scenes of the rest of New Orleans did.

"Yeah, I don't think us asking all of the patrons here to find the one guy with the house for rent is going to get us anywhere," I said.

We decided to go back by the house and see if we might be lucky enough to see the owner out front or at least leave our number with the father. It was a long shot, but the only lead we had so far. "How often does the trolley run?" I asked Lisa.

She smiled. "We call it a streetcar here. *When* it comes, it's every twenty minutes, though honestly, it's not very reliable."

I could feel my face turning red with embarrassment. "Oh, right. Sorry about that!" I appreciated the honest and informative answer. We finished our drinks, paid, and opened the door, letting in the shocking daylight. Our eyes needed a second to adjust again.

"Let's just walk through the neighborhood, then down Canal. This way if we see the streetcar we can hop on instead of just waiting at the corner," Nick said and winked at me.

That was fine with me—I hated waiting. Especially since standing in the sun in this heat didn't sound fun.

We started to meander down the streets. A few blocks away from Finn's, we turned up a different street than the one we'd walked down—South Telemachus. At least that was one street name I could pronounce; earlier, while driving around, I'd seen a sign for "Tchoupitoulas" and made no attempt to say that out loud. In front of one house was a construction pole. A double shotgun house was being gutted. Nick and I exchanged glances, letting the other know we were about to do some investigation. We walked up the three cement steps and knocked on the door.

"Hello?" Nick called into the house. The place seemed quite large, but thankfully much lower to street level than the rental place we were looking at earlier. The floors—scattered with construction dust, tools, and wood—looked like they'd already been refinished. The ridiculously long floorboards stretched from the front room to the middle of the house and seemingly beyond. The first two rooms had grand unfinished fireplaces, and the whole interior needed to be painted.

"Hello?" a voice called back. A man peeked out from around the corner and approached us with a tool belt on carrying a measuring tape in his hand. "Can I help you?"

Nick explained our situation again and asked if he knew of any houses for sale or rent. The man's eyes lit up and a smile stretched across his face. He said: "Funny you ask. We were going to list this place soon. We're just making some final touches."

My heart skipped a beat, and I squeezed Nick's hand. I tried not to look too excited or desperate. "Mind if we take a walk through?" Nick asked.

"Not at all! I'll show you 'round," the man said.

The first two rooms led into a kitchen and family room. The kitchen was a huge space—the whole house was huge. The bedrooms were all on the right side of the house. The wall dividing the two original residences had been removed at the kitchen, creating a large living area. The doorframes to each room still had the original rectangular glass transoms that could be opened to allow for airflow. Huge baseboards snaked through the rooms, the largest I'd ever seen. A small porch out back opened up to a large, unfinished backyard. The walls had measurements scribbled on them with pencil, the cabinets were not yet hung, appliances were missing, and there was no landscaping anywhere. There were six fireplaces, three bedrooms, and two full baths. I felt like Goldilocks facing the "too big" option.

After a serious discussion with the builder, we found out the price, which was more than what we'd hoped. We exchanged names and numbers, keeping all options open.

"Thanks for the walk-through," Nick said. "We'll have to think about it. We'll be back tomorrow, if that's all right."

"Yup." The builder shrugged a noncommittal shrug.

As we left, I took a better look at the neighborhood. A supply warehouse was a block away and the rest of the street seemed to have a mix of races and ages. It wasn't unlike the Cleveland neighborhood we'd fallen in love with a few years ago. We were now walking with a lighter step.

"It's bigger than we need, and not exactly move-in condition," I said. "And can we even afford it?"

I could see the wheels turning in Nick's mind. Then he nodded slowly. "We can afford it," he said. "It'll be tight, but once you get a job it'll be doable. Plus, my housing allowance is better here than it was in Ohio. I'm thinking we'll offer them a deal that we'll take it as-is, if they come down on the price. We fixed up a house before! Remember, he did mention that they want to sell quickly. They might be motivated." After a pause he added, "It *is* big."

"What about our stuff?" I asked.

"Well, it's going into storage, because we didn't have an address to ship it to yet. It's not a big deal. We'll just have it delivered when we have a place, and we'll work around the boxes."

"Right, all *three hundred* boxes," I said, thinking of working on a house in the middle of all those unpacked boxes.

"We'd have the space to store them with that house," Nick answered. He was always looking on the bright side of things—I was the worrier. I guess I did get it from my mother, though I'd never admit that.

As we walked down the street, we continued talking about what we could do next, potential plans going forward if it were to work out, and backup options if it didn't. The house was a long-shot, but who knew—maybe we'd get lucky. I could feel drips of sweat roll down my chest. We had to step over a large banana tree blocking our path that had fallen over and had its roots exposed, perhaps from some bad weather.

We turned onto Canal Street and continued to walk down the sidewalk, keeping an eye out for the streetcar. We were almost at Bourbon Street when it finally came. It was then that we realized that we should have been walking in the middle of the large grassy area in between the streets—"the neutral grounds," as we later came to find out they were called by the locals—so that we could wave one down and catch a ride. Streetcar stops apparently didn't really exist.

We had made it to the French Quarter and we were greeted with sensory overload. Music was on every corner, small bands making big sounds that flooded the air with brass instruments. The sound was raw and traveled for blocks, filling the air with musical notes. I could tell the players had talent, but not the kind that was stifled with musical rules. The notes blended and took their time coming to settle on the desired one. Kids with overturned five-gallon buckets banged on them with drumsticks, creating amazing rhythms that got everyone around them dancing and moving. Other kids had cans out, collecting money while they clapped and danced using improvised tap shoes. When one of the kids did a back flip into the air, I saw that his sneakers had metal bottle caps stuck to the bottom, making tap shoes out of them.

The natural raw musical talent in these kids was amazing. It was electric, touching everyone around. It transported me—and in that moment my worries melted away. The rhythm surrounded and penetrated me, immersing me in the fun and carefree attitude of the other people here. The nagging anxiety of finding a place to live fell away, replaced with a renewed sense of freedom and happiness that I hadn't felt since we'd left Ohio. It suddenly felt more like vacation and less like we were homeless.

Just then Nick grabbed my hand, spun me around, and started dancing with me in the middle of the street. We laughed together, holding hands, seeing only us among the crowds of people.

It was a magical night—a treat for every one of my senses, filled with neon lights, music, and dancing. Nick and I walked around with our fingers intertwined, holding drinks we bought along the way at the bars where you could walk up and get a beer or a daiquiri to go in a big plastic cup or boot. We must have looked like tourists. I felt like one, but I also had an insight no one else knew: in just one short day, something had changed. I was absorbed by this city. I could be walking through these city streets anytime I wanted to, without having to be concerned about the return plane flight home. This was going to be my city now.

CHAPTER TWO

THE BIG EASY

I awoke the next morning to a throbbing headache and that familiar disoriented feeling. The heat, the mugginess, the dampness of the room . . . all of it closed in, surrounding me. As the morning sun filled the room, I felt an emptiness slowly fill me. Vacation was over. I woke up conflicted. Though last night had been fun, I regretted it—not only because I was hungover, but now I was disappointed as well. Our fun had gotten us nowhere closer to figuring out where we were going to live. It was so hard to remain strong for Nick, for my mother, and for me.

What were we doing here in this crummy hotel room? What was *I* doing here?

Nick had his job. Life was easy for him. It was almost automatic—move, report in, wear the uniform, do the job. Sure, the people and responsibilities would be different than his last station, and I knew that was hard in its own way, but it was also vastly different for me, the military spouse. I needed to find a job, orient myself to this new place—and above all, be flexible. These were all things I'd never had to do all at the same time before.

The gravity of my situation made me feel more exhausted than the heavy air in the room did. I stared up at the crumbling popcorn ceiling and sighed. How did people with kids live this lifestyle? The thought of adding more responsibilities to moving every three years—like registering kids for new schools, finding new pediatricians, and supporting little people through separation from friends and their familiar way of life—to the long list of things to accomplish was dizzying. I never truly appreciated all that military families had to go through until I married into one. I would have to hold off on making our family bigger. I couldn't worry myself about the additional needs of my fictional family right now.

Time was ticking. We needed to go see if the builders would take our offer or if we'd need to resume house hunting again today. *What a curious phrase that is*, I thought. I imagined us dressed in camouflage sneaking around hunting houses. Although moving every three years was truly a skill honed by military life, my stomach turned when I realized that it wouldn't be the last time we would have to do this. Nick seemed completely unfazed by this whole process. I supposed that someday I'd become immune to it as well. It was an acquired life skill, one of many that I needed to work on.

I crawled out of bed, shuffled to the bathroom, and splashed some water on my face.

I wet a washcloth with cold water and laid it on my forehead. I wanted to call home, but didn't have the energy. Just then my phone rang. I ran to it and immediately picked it up, stepping outside the bedroom so it wouldn't wake Nick.

"Good morning, sweetheart! I just made your father the fried egg in the bread you both like and was thinking of you. What did you call it again? And how are things going?"

"Hi, Mama," I said. "The bullseye. Oh, that does sound perfect right now." I couldn't answer the second question yet. Though I did my best to hide my feelings in my voice, she already knew.

"Are you all right? You sound horrible."

"Oh, I'm fine. We had a New Orleans experience last night." I tried to play off my worry as being hungover.

"Ooh, was it fun?" Mama had a knack to get me to talk even when I wasn't in the mood for conversation. She paused and quickly said as an afterthought, "You're not going out by yourself at night, are you?"

"No, Mama, why would I do that?"

"Okay, good, I just want you to be safe there. It's dangerous for a young lady to be alone in a big city."

Ignoring the dire comments, I continued to tell her about the night we'd had. "It was so fun last night. I can't wait until you come here to show you and Dad around. The music is unbelievable. I don't think there's a single untalented person down here."

"How fun! How's the house hunting going?"

My stomach churned. "Say a prayer, Mama. We have a lead, but it's a fragile one. I'm really stressed out by this whole process."

"I know, love, I can tell. I'll say a prayer for you. Don't you worry. Everything will turn out just fine. Nicholas has done this before, so I'm sure he knows what to do. You'll find a house, I know you will."

Her voice was like a hug I really needed. "Thanks, Mama."

"Love you, honey. Drink some water today, okay?" she said with a laugh.

"Yes, Mama," I said in a knowing voice. "Love you too." I hung up the phone and heard Nick stirring in bed.

"How's your mom doing?" asked Nick sleepily when I came back in the room.

"Better than me right now. I wish this place had a breakfast restaurant. Do you think we can find some coconut water and an early lunch spot? We have to meet the builder soon!" I needed to get rid of this headache—and pace myself today.

I showered and changed, feeling slightly better. Nick found some coconut water at a small corner store and I was so excited I kissed him.

"We also have to pick up the car!" Nick said, which I'd completely forgotten about.

Thankfully, we had the builder's cell number and coordinated a time to meet to talk about the details. He couldn't meet up until after lunch, which gave us some free time. We stood in the heavy heat of the morning sun at the streetcar stop.

"You want to wait this time?" Nick asked.

I had no energy for a long walk before I ate, and the humidity prevented me from moving. I nodded a slow, tired *yes* and put my head on his shoulder. By some luck of the Big Easy, the streetcar came fifteen minutes ahead of schedule—either that or it arrived really late. Climbing aboard, we settled in and melted in the air-conditioned ride. We were whisked down Canal Street, passing some of the houses, streets, and shops we'd seen the day before. The streetcar stopped occasionally to exchange passengers or slow down to angrily blow the horn, warning cars to get out of its way. I felt separated from reality, as if I was observing all of this action in a video game.

Thinking about our present state of affairs and being that it was Sunday, my Catholic guilt tugged at me. I leaned over to Nick and whispered in his ear, "Do you think we could find a church to go to this morning? There has to be one around."

Nick looked at me and smiled. "Sure, I don't think I'll burst into flames. We'll probably have to ask for directions." I was pretty sure Nick's only time spent in church had been for our wedding.

I noticed a middle-aged woman dressed nicely and wearing a fancy hat. I figured these had to be church-going clothes.

"Excuse me, ma'am, I don't mean to bother you, but we just relocated here and are trying to find a Catholic church to go to this morning. Is there one you know of nearby?"

The woman turned toward me and gave a warm smile. "Where y'all coming from?"

"Ohio," I said. "It's my first city I'll be living in—other than my hometown."

"Well, you picked a good one to start! There's plenty of churches to choose from, but my favorite is Our Lady of Guadalupe on Rampart Street. It's the oldest church building in the city. There's a service at eleven you can still make." She gave a warm smile. "Welcome to New Orleans."

I thanked her and looked at Nick, hoping he'd know how to get there. "We'll get off in a few stops and walk there. It shouldn't be too far." He leaned over and squeezed my knee. I was very grateful for his superhero skill of somehow already having an internal map of the city in his mind—I, on the other hand, still couldn't determine right from left or north from south. So far this Crescent City had me completely disoriented.

We walked up to the modest white church that welcomed us with its three arches holding up a small spire. I opened up the heavy wooden door and spotted a wooden pew that we could squeeze into. The happy glow of the yellow walls and sun shining through the stained-glass windows radiated throughout the diverse congregation. Off to the side I spotted the band for the mass, heavy with a variety of instruments: trumpets, slide trombones, a saxophone, and drums. I had never seen those instruments in a church service. I thought back to my church at home with its white walls, a serious, almost somber service, with occasionally a choir and a piano.

The mass service began—and it was completely sensational. The band that played throughout the service was amazing. This wasn't my typical solemn white Catholic service like back home—this had life and joy to it. Everybody sang loud, everybody participated. It was refreshing and vibrant.

There was a little hop in our step after the service.

"That was amazing! I may even want to come back next week," Nick joked.

I smiled at Nick, who genuinely seemed to have enjoyed it. He was never much for attending church with me back home. "Let's walk back to the Quarter to find some food. All that singing has made me hungry," I suggested.

"I love that idea; are you up for some oysters? I noticed the Acme Oyster House that looked fun to try."

"Yes! Perfect!"

When we arrived, every table was taken, but we spotted two open seats at the small oyster bar. The hostess said those seats didn't require a reservation, but a table was an hour wait. We happily bellied up to the bar, sitting next to each other and watching the workers in front of us shuck the oysters. Three shuckers furiously and efficiently opened and stacked oysters on ice-covered plates. They made it look so easy.

Many of the workers didn't even bother to look at what their hands were doing. One hand gracefully picked up oysters from a pile, while the other split the shell and loosened the meat in one clean motion, all while carrying on conversations with the staff or customers. There truly was entertainment everywhere we went.

After we each devoured a dozen oysters and a cold beer, we were off to meet the builder at the house.

The streetcar wasn't anywhere to be seen, forcing us to walk off our lunch. Turning down South Telemachus Street after our sweaty walk from the French Quarter, my heart started to race. Thankfully, our car was still there on the street and we saw the workers inside the house. *So far, so good*, I thought.

We walked up the steps and Nick called inside.

The guy we'd met yesterday came out to greet us. "Hey, you two!" He waved. "Come on in. Johnny, by the way." He held out his hand for us to shake.

He escorted us to the back of the house and we sat at an old wooden picnic table on the patchy lawn. The cement steps of the porch looked freshly poured, and Nick made it a point to compliment them. After the initial prerequisite niceties, Johnny got right to the point. "As I said yesterday, we're pretty close to listing this place, but I wouldn't mind not dealing with listing agents and all that hassle. I'd prefer to close a deal sooner than later. That being said, I need to get some of my investment back and I'm not looking to lose money in this sale. I'm sure you know it's a sellers' market down here and houses are hard to come by. We're planning on listing the house for three ten."

A lump formed in my throat—three ten, as in 310,000 dollars? As in, *way* too much money for us.

I thought, *Okay, this was a big waste of time, let's move on*, but then it was Nick's turn to play this game. He told Johnny about our situation without making us sound too desperate to buy. He then laid out the deal he and I had discussed the previous night, of taking the house as-is and doing a quick close so our stuff could be delivered. I was impressed, as always, by how smoothly and calmly he operated. Nick countered at two sixty—a whole fifty thousand less than what Johnny was asking—reminding him that he'd also be saving on listing agent fees as well. I was curious to see how the very different counteroffer would come across. Witnessing Nick haggle in real-time was interesting.

There was the give-and-take that usually occurs in these deals, with the typical "I have workers and loans to pay," countered by "we're just a young couple trying to find a place to live." I let Nick do the talking, even though I thought of a few good points he'd missed and was tempted to chime in. I bit my tongue, as I was well aware that there was some respect lost if a woman, especially a transplant, came on too strong in these deals.

Nick had mentioned on the way over that he wanted to speak with Johnny about the price. "This town is mostly a blue-collar port city town. Let me make the deal, it'll come across better." His words echoed in my head, so I kept quiet by his side, like a good, proper lady.

Some time went by and I couldn't take the stress of the situation anymore. We needed a breather. I asked the men if I could have a few minutes to speak with Nick privately. Johnny nodded gratefully—he seemed as happy to take a break as I was. Nick and I got up and walked through the vast house again.

"What are you doing?" I asked Nick quietly.

"Buying us a house!" he continued. "Babe, the bank already approved us for a loan of 320,000. I don't understand how they think we can afford that, but anything under three hundred is a steal! I think we're close to closing this deal. It'll be great to be settled and start our life here."

"It's more than we planned on spending."

"Yes, but wouldn't you like to live this close to downtown? It's a great location for me to commute to my work. Don't you like it?"

That was a loaded question, and I needed a moment to process all of the information. I too wanted more than anything to be settled and get on with life. I certainly wanted to move out of the roach hotel as well, but to buy this place so quickly seemed to be a rash decision. And spending something in the range of 300,000 dollars? That was just insane.

"I just think maybe we should look at other options so that we know what the going rate is here. This place is almost a hundred thousand more than what we sold our Cleveland house for," I said, trying to bring Nick back to reality.

"It's not that far off. It's okay. I think I can get him to come down on his price a bit. It's a different market here; houses are really hard to come by. I've been watching them appear and disappear off the market in record time over the past few months. That's why I thought coming here and making offers before houses go on the market would be our best chance to buy one. Unless you want to rent for the next three years, this is the best thing for us."

I peered up at the fourteen-foot ceilings and stood at the place where the kitchen met the master bathroom. The flow of the house was really nice. I could see our stuff fitting in here easily. I took a breath—*I'd give anything to be settled*, I decided. "All right," I said. "Let's make a deal."

We walked back outside to meet Johnny. I got the feeling everyone knew this deal was going to be made. Still sitting at the picnic table, he looked at us as we came back down the porch steps, smiled, and waited for us to make the first move. Nick started to speak. "Do you want to forgo the back-and-forth and meet in the middle?" he said. "I'm not going to haggle over five thousand here or there. How about two-seventy five?"

"You're offering two seventy-five?" Johnny said incredulously.

Nick nodded.

"Meeting in the middle would be two eighty-five . . ." Johnny shook his head slowly and examined the ground, pausing to think. "Listen, I understand where you're coming from, but I need to pay off debts on my end. I can meet you at two eighty-seven five."

What a strange price, I thought—so specific. Was he just playing with us at this point? "Nick, we can always leave and think about it," I said, trying to put a little fear into Johnny.

We all just sat there staring at each other. It felt as if time had stopped, everyone waiting for the other person to talk. Maybe it was the heat of the day filtering into the backyard combining with the conversation making everyone uncomfortable, or maybe it was only me.

"Johnny, at that price, you'll need to put up cabinets of our choosing and all the appliances. Or you can walk away with a closed as-is deal for two seventy-five."

Johnny cleared his throat and looked around. "Fine. Two seventy-five it is. You have a deal. Come over tonight and let's sign the documents."

"Sounds great!" Nick said, all smiles.

We all shook hands and I couldn't believe we had just bought a house. What a day! I wanted to skip around the neighborhood. But I also realized now we were once again stuck with finishing up a house. My dream of a turnkey house vanished in front of me. We left the house—*our* house—jumped in the car, and started driving.

"Where are we going?" I asked Nick.

"To celebrate! Congratulations, Collette—you just bought a house!"

That night, we returned to our soon-to-be-permanent residence to take care of the formalities. I was hoping Johnny wouldn't have a change of heart and raise the price, as what we had thus far was only a gentleman's agreement. We met the other, somewhat unpleasant co-owner and I could see the tension between the two—maybe Johnny was ready to be done with him and that was the driving force for closing the deal. I didn't really care though; I was just excited to have a house. They could deal with their relationship after we signed the paperwork. The deal was good to go. We signed all the many papers and made it official. Saying goodbye to the two men, we walked through the house admiring the layout with excited eyes and a new perspective. The bank transfer would take place tomorrow, and then the keys would be ours.

I called home immediately to tell of the good news.

"Mama! Guess what? I'm calling you from outside our new house!" Nick was simultaneously on the phone with his dad, and I could hear the congratulations coming over from his phone.

"Praise Jesus!" my mama shouted. "How wonderful, honey! Oh, I was praying that you'd find something right away. Chuck!" She yelled to my dad through the phone, as she had a habit of doing when excited. "The kids bought a house!"

As I was telling my parents about our good fortune, I began to notice a gang of around ten kids, teenagers and tweens, talking loudly and meandering down our street. Viewing them horsing around, a few pushed the short kid into a parked car. He bounced off and spun around, hitting the kid who'd pushed him in retaliation. As they passed our new house, one of them flicked a cigarette butt onto the lawn and another kid dropped an empty fast-food cup onto the street. I looked at Nick and felt a chill go through me: I'd heard that the kids here were dangerous and unpredictable, and that the gangs had young, impressionable kids carry out all the illegal stuff because they couldn't get charged as adults. I kept up my excitement on the phone to my parents, but I cut the call short so as not to call attention to us in the car. Once they passed, unaware of us sitting there quietly in the dark, we started the car and drove to the hotel, hoping that was just an odd occurrence rather than a bad omen.

CHAPTER THREE

MY LITTLE OLD HOME DOWN IN NEW ORLEANS

We pulled up to our new house, our car once again packed to the limit with the five-gallon buckets and their air stones bubbling away. "We're home!" Nick said and smiled to me. "Just leave the stuff in the car for a minute. Let's go inside together." We strolled up the sidewalk past the banana tree growing on the lawn—the only thing in the front of the house besides the ugly utility pole—and walked up the concrete steps hand in hand. Nick unlocked the door and, before I knew it, whisked me up in his arms. "Whoa! What are you doing?" I giggled.

"Carrying my wife across the threshold, of course." He carried me into the first room and gently set me down.

"I still can't believe this is our house," I said. "It's going to be so fun figuring out what to do with all of these rooms." I paused. "And picking out our new appliances! I didn't get to do that in our old house."

"It's going to be fun making this house ours, Cole. You can get some stuff from your own dream list."

Nick and I got right down to business over the next few days. We went together to the hardware store and chose our appliances, paint colors, and tools to fix the rest of the house. Multiple annoying back-and-forth trips for forgotten items helped me memorize the quickest alternate routes to take. For someone who is directionally challenged, this was a big accomplishment.

Wash, rinse, repeat. Our days were beginning to become very similar to each other. I woke up one morning feeling more excited than usual. We'd made significant progress and I was eager to get up and start the day. Only a few weeks left until the multitude of boxes were scheduled to be delivered and fill our currently cavernous house with our beloved stuff.

Waking up daily in our new house on the tired and well-worn air mattress we took with us from Ohio was getting old. I leaned over to see Nick was already awake. He rubbed his eyes and let out a big yawn.

"Hey," I said. "Good morning! How long have you been awake?"

"Not long. It's getting harder to sleep in. The combo of this uncomfortable air mattress and our looming delivery date wakes me up nice and early."

"I was just thinking about that. Only a few weeks to go. We'll need to change our mantra to 'Get up early, work hard, play hard.' I'll make the coffee." I rolled off the mattress, sending the familiar tidal wave of movement over to Nick, who just moaned. "At least it's not too hot and humid outside yet," I said, trying to start the day off on a positive note while bending over to fill the coffee pot with water.

Though he grumbled now and then, I could tell Nick was enjoying putting the finishing touches on the house. He bought a new tile saw that afternoon and began the monumental task of retiling the hearths of all six fireplaces. I got the fun task of picking out the tile—though my first two choices got vetoed. The third time was the charm, and I found one that we both liked: red, gray, and white, the Ohio State colors.

Our new fridge, stove, dishwasher, and washer and dryer—all shiny and new—came within the week. It was so exciting and satisfying peeling off the protective tape on everything. Each new addition made life that much easier. I found the local grocery store about a mile away—a modest store, but with all the necessities. With our fridge now stocked with alcohol and food, we were an unstoppable force.

"It's coming together, Cole. We may even be able to get everything fixed and hooked up in time for you to unpack our boxes!" Nick mused.

"Oh, is that my job now?" I stopped painting and came out of the guest bathroom, covered in speckled white paint from rolling paint on the walls, to meet his gaze from down the hall.

"Well, not officially, but realistically, it's getting close to my check-in date for work. Usually it's a task the wives do, setting up the house, but I'll help you when I get home. You can decide where you'd like things to go," Nick said, still facing the wall and fumbling with the dryer hose.

I rolled my eyes, not liking that I needed to unpack the entire house myself—or that there were assumptions made without asking. "I guess I should have my mother visit sooner to help out!" I shouted back down the hall, but the comment was either not heard or selectively ignored.

The outside of the house didn't have any curb appeal whatsoever. Construction dust, wood pieces, cardboard, and empty paint cans lined the porch and spilled lazily into the front yard. Taking a break from painting, I stood on the front porch, gazing at the mess in disbelief. *I hope cleaning up outside isn't my job as well*, I thought. The grass was growing in between dirt patches and the only sign of life was the sad-looking banana tree. A large hole in the middle of the yard now replaced the ugly utility pole that once stood there. It was my job to figure out all the utilities and have them put into our name. My list of partner to-do's was getting longer by the day.

Since I was now organizing everything, I took it upon myself to meet with a security salesman to get an alarm set up in our house one day when Nick had to run back to the hardware store. Showing Nick the fancy booklet I was given and explaining all the new system options to him, I felt that I was now the salesman. Nick was patient and humoring, as if talking to a child showing him their crappy school artwork.

"And the pamphlet is free," I said, adding one last embellishment. "We pay just a small monthly fee for all of this!"

"Cole, it's a bit ridiculous to have a security system installed. We never had one in Cleveland," Nick remarked.

"I know, but it's a different city, different area . . . and this house is gigantic!"

Nick rolled his eyes and gave me a placating smile. "And what will you do if the alarm goes off?"

"Oh, that's easy. I'll probably scream bloody murder, or be frozen in my spot, too terrified to know what to do. But I still want one."

Nick chuckled, then sighed. "If getting this is what will make you happy and comfortable here, that's fine. As long as we're not paying too much."

I thought of the salesman stating that this was an "up and coming" area. I was glad Nick finally caved and agreed to let them install the system.

Hours passed and I decided to take a break from the endless painting. I went searching for Nick to see if he wanted me to make us a late lunch, but couldn't find him anywhere in the house. *This house is too big for us*, I thought. Though it made sense that Nick would want that—he always loved hosting parties with lots of people in Cleveland. Our house was a revolving door between friends and family. Amid my inner grumblings I heard my name being called from outside.

"Collette! Hey! Come on out here!" Nick bellowed.

By this time I was almost in the back of the house near the kitchen and had to break into a sprint to get to the front, since I didn't know how long he'd been calling my name. I was breathing hard when I opened the front door. "What is it?" I said, looking around trying to find him.

"Hey, there you are! I want you to meet some of our neighbors!" he called out.

He was standing in the neighbors' front yard, smiling at me. I was so relieved it wasn't an emergency that I wanted to kill him for making me worry. I walked next door to meet him at our neighbors' front porch. The house was smaller and older than ours—it was a legitimate single shotgun house, not a double made into a single like ours. It had the old asbestos siding on it, and it appeared as if our neighbors had been there for a very long time. The door opened a crack and a short woman appeared, fending off three gigantic Great Danes. She wiggled her way through the loud slobbering dogs and stepped outside on the front porch, followed a few seconds later by her large husband, who was wearing a dirty white t-shirt and still holding the television remote absentmindedly.

"Oh, hello! You must be Collette," she crooned. "Nick told us all about you. Welcome to the neighborhood!" She smiled at me and brushed away some loose hair hitting her face from the slight breeze.

"Thank you," I said, waiting for her to give her name. The dogs were barking so loud I couldn't tell if I missed her name or if she never said it. "Is it just you and your husband here?" I asked.

"Oh no, we have three kids too. We had four, but one sadly died last year. We're still trying to deal with that."

I was stunned by the amount of sensitive information I was just given by this stranger.

"Oh my. I am so sorry to hear that," I said. My body went cold with sadness and the awkwardness of the conversation. I wasn't good at dealing with these situations and often struggled to find comforting words when confronted with them.

"Yes, thank you, dear. At least we still have these three around, though it took them a while to deal with the loss too." One dog was sticking his huge nose in the crack of the door trying to open it up while the others were jockeying for lead position.

It dawned on me that she might be talking about her dog dying. I couldn't believe it. I could understand that dogs can be part of the family, but telling a person you just met that your kid just died when you mean your dog is not the same thing. I was so aggravated at that point I just wanted to leave to go make lunch.

The husband said to me, "You have dogs of your own?"

"No, just fish," I said with a polite smile.

"Well," he continued, "you got a gun at least?" He waved the remote at me as he spoke.

Now I really felt uncomfortable, and I didn't want to talk about our indoor safety while standing outside.

"Because when your husband is away at night, you'll need to

protect yourself," he continued. "I have a whole arsenal inside my house. I used to be a cop in these parts. I know what goes on. Pretty bad stuff too. A lousy rape whistle isn't going to do anything for you."

"We just had a security system installed. I'll be fine," I said cheerfully, trying to lighten the situation. "Plus, you're next door to us!"

He waved dismissively. "Yeah, those don't do anything. People around here know they have about two minutes before anyone shows up, if they show up at all. Has anyone told you about the collection we take up?" I shook my head now, wishing this conversation would end soon. "Every month we collect twenty dollars from the neighbors around here to give to the police patrols so they come down our street more often. I'll come by next month for your donation. It helps to have extra eyes on the neighborhood."

"Oh, okay. I guess I'll see you next month!" I took the opening and turned to leave, grabbing Nick's hand as I did.

"Great meeting you!" yelled Nick as we walked back.

Once we got inside, I locked the door and looked him straight in the eye. "What was that? Why did you tell those people you were going to be gone at night? We just met them! You shouldn't be telling strangers that! What's your problem? And their kid died? Except it's not their kid—it's their *dog*. Who says that? Oh, I feel really safe now. I'm glad the security system we just bought is a joke. I'm not getting a gun. And why do I have to pay cops to do their job that they're already getting paid to do?" I was furious.

"You're right, I messed up. Sorry. I was just introducing myself to them and started talking."

"You don't have to tell strangers everything when you meet people, Nick!" I tried to keep my voice low so our new neighbors wouldn't hear me yelling through all our windows. I turned angrily away and walked quickly with purpose to the kitchen, accidentally kicking a hammer that was lying on the floor. It spun around and hit the corner of the newly tiled fireplace in the front room, creating a crack in it. "Dammit!" I said and grabbed my toe.

"Shit. Are you hurt?" asked Nick while he went over to examine the cracked tile.

"I'm fine," I said, still angry, then I paused. "Sorry about that."

"It's okay, I can fix it. Let's move on. You want lunch?"

"I was going to make it before I was called to meet our super amazing neighbors. Are you really not going to be coming home at night? How come you didn't tell me this?"

Nick rolled his eyes. I hated when he did that. "It's a possibility with my job. I don't know for certain yet. Don't worry about that." He paused, trying to think of a way to explain it to my apparently feeble mind. "It won't happen right away. You know there are some people who are gone for months in the military and don't get to come home at night. It's a possibility you signed up for. Remember?"

"I was just unaware that this possibility was a part of this New Orleans job, and I hate finding out about it from a neighbor."

"Okay, can we drop this and move on now?"

"Fine. Beer?" I reached in the fridge and opened one for me and passed one to him. I knew it would be a symbolic gesture that ended a conversation and started a new one.

"Thanks!"

I walked over and peered into the bubbling buckets. "It'll be so nice to get our fish tank up and running again," I said, changing the subject.

"We've been working really hard on the house nonstop. How about if we take a night off tonight and go see some music?" Nick suggested.

"That sounds great," I said, feeling my blood pressure go back to normal again. I really didn't want to think about staying here in this big empty house by myself anymore.

New Orleans nightfall rolled around in its promiscuous way, a gentle warm breeze with only the slightest hint of light in the sky. Instead of going down Bourbon Street again, we opted for the local's pick and went to a place called Rock 'n' Bowl. It was a strange place that wasn't quite sure if it was a nightclub or a bowling alley. There was a live band playing and the whole place shook with people dancing. The alleys were warped, which made bowling quite challenging and silly. It suited the city. It seemed as if everything in this city was saying, "Don't take life so seriously." The music was so good that we were dancing and drinking more than bowling, as were most people there.

Nick left to go get us another round at the bar and I held on to our little corner of the dance floor. Watching him saunter away confidently, looking so incredibly handsome in his black t-shirt and favorite blue jeans that he liked to say made his package look big, I couldn't believe how lucky I was to have him. Then, as he was ordering, I saw him glance over at a very attractive woman sitting on the stool next to him at the bar.

I could see how Nick would notice her—she had beautiful olive skin, long dark curly hair, and big brown sultry eyes. He'd always been attracted to dark-skinned girls, and as far as I knew, I was the only one he'd dated that had fair skin. My short dirty blonde hair and light green eyes were in direct contrast to his typical girl.

She was dressed to be noticed in a tight sparkly dress. My thoughts went to warp speed. *Who dresses like that in a bowling alley? Did he just buy her a drink? Now they're laughing? Great, she's funny too.*

The bartender gave Nick his order, and after a farewell smile to the woman he was talking to, he came walking back to me.

"Why did you buy that woman a drink?" I asked him curiously but also self-consciously.

"What? Oh, Susie Star over there? She's actually tonight's head-liner! Maybe we'll be able to hear her sing if we're still around when she gets on stage. Plus," he paused, "for her this is *work*—I wanted her to have some fun. Not everyone can have as good of a night as we are having right now." He gave me a wink. "Don't be so jealous."

I didn't appreciate him buying another woman a drink, but I wanted to just drop it and have a fun night.

"Susie Star?" I said and shook my head at the ridiculous name.

"Yeah, she's coming on after this band and DJ," Nick responded.

Then, something magical happened—our wedding song played: "What a Wonderful World."

"Did you request this?" I asked Nick as he put our drinks down and held me close on the dance floor.

"Oh man, that would have been smooth. I wish I did, but no, I didn't."

We danced, holding each other, and ended with a dip and a kiss.

"You kids newlyweds?" asked a stranger next to us.

"No," I replied, "we've been married for three years."

"Wow, I wouldn't have expected that, congratulations. I can tell your love is something special. You should always hold on to that."

"Thank you," I said, feeling myself blush. I had never had a stranger say anything like that to me.

The next morning I called home, eager to talk to the only other person in the world who really knew me. I brought my coffee out back to the crappy picnic table that had come with the house.

"Hello?" answered my mama in a tired, slower than usual voice.

"Hi, Mama. Is there something wrong?" I asked, concerned.

"Oh, hello, Collette! No, honey, I was just thinking of you!" She perked up once she heard my voice.

"Well, that's why I called," I teased.

"How is everything going down there?" she asked.

"Really good. We're almost done fixing the inside of the house and will probably start on the landscaping next week. The movers will deliver our things today and Nick will start work tomorrow. I guess it'll be up to me to unpack." I paused, realizing everything I had just said. "It's going to suck."

"Just do as much as you can. I'm sure Nicholas will help out evenings after he gets home," Mama said reassuringly.

"Yes, I know, I know. I do have some good news though—I got a job lead today, at Charity Hospital!"

"Oh, how wonderful! What would you be doing?"

"It's a RN position in the intensive care unit. I have a phone interview on Wednesday."

"Well, good luck, honey—it sounds perfect. I'll be praying for you."

"I really miss home, Mama," I said, surprising myself and her at how straightforwardly I delivered that statement. "I'm enjoying it here and trying to make the best of it, but it's not the same," I said as a quick follow up.

"Collette, I miss you too. I know it must be hard being away, but you and Nicholas are making some great memories there.

You have a beautiful new house, and once you're all moved in and start a job you won't feel so lonely. Plus, your father and I will be coming to visit very soon."

"I can't wait to see you both and show you around." I started to get a lump in my throat, but held on to her words about visiting soon.

"It'll be wonderful, honey. I'm looking forward to it. Oh, hold on a minute, love." Mama put the phone down, but I could hear her yelling to my dad. "What? They're on the bench! Honey," she said, picking up the phone again, "your father can't find his socks. Let me let you go so I can help him. I tell you, that man can't find things right in front of his nose."

"Okay. Love you, Mama. Bye."

"Bye, honey, love you too. I'll see you soon!"

Mama and Dad's relationship was very much one that was built in the 1950s, though Mama did have her own paying job now after having been a full-time stay-at-home caretaker. She had always been the one to keep up with the chores of the house and make sure everyone was fed and dressed. She still laid out my dad's clothes on a daily basis. My dad, to his credit, was in charge of paying the bills, sometimes by working the day shift as well as nights. They both knew how to keep busy and were constantly moving.

"Do you know when the movers will be here?" I asked Nick, who had just peeked out the back door to see what I was doing.

"They said 9 a.m., but I probably have time to run out to get some coffee and beignets to go, if you'd like."

"Oh, that sounds great," I said, coming up the porch steps to head back inside, "but I'd hate to be here alone if they get here early."

We opted for juice in a bottle and cereal served in paper bowls. My thoughts were swirling in my head as I scrutinized the paper dishes and plasticware I had grown to despise. I was so ready to use real plates and not live like a college student. Oh, and to sleep in my bed once again was going to be amazing. I didn't even want to look at that air mattress for another three years!

Ding-dong! The sound of our doorbell echoed in the large empty house.

"Whoa!" I said. "It's only 8:30! They must not be from around these parts!" By now I knew that doing anything early wasn't commonly done down here: "Louisiana time," they called it.

In came the boxes, followed by even more boxes. My excitement to get my household things quickly turned into panic and stress. Before I knew it, our large house was filled with stacks of boxes in every room. Thankfully, we'd cleaned up all the loose tools the day before.

The move-in day was a blur, organizing what rooms to put boxes in and directing the movers as to where to place the furniture. These guys were very quick. The whole embarrassingly large truck was empty by two o'clock in the afternoon. We thanked them as they left and we looked at each other, now surrounded by boxes in every room. We had to weave ourselves around the large boxes of various sizes, furniture that wasn't quite in the right place, and the oddities of stuff that didn't have a place yet in shelving.

"Should we set up the fish tank first?" Nick wondered aloud.

"No, we'll let the fish live in buckets a little longer. They don't seem to mind. I need my kitchen unpacked."

I only had the rest of today with Nick before he started his job, and I wanted to try to get settled as soon as possible. I loved eating out, but I was feeling it was also too much of a good thing. Nick went to the fridge and grabbed two beers and handed me one. I knew he was about to make some progress unpacking.

I hadn't even considered that unpacking was going to be an emotional process, but it was as if I had unpacked a time capsule of our life in Ohio. Unwrapping each item and holding it in my hands told the story of when we got it or who gave it to us. The blue glass vase, given to us by my aunt, thankfully wasn't damaged by the move; the family pictures of happy times, my beautiful wedding dress, my cookbooks—I already had a spot reserved for them in the kitchen. I was so grateful for the forest of trees that were used as wrapping paper to preserve my valuables in the move. Some of the items even had a slight smell of our previous house. I was so happy to be surrounded by our things once again. The house slowly became our new home with each unpacked box.

Nick left me in the morning, all dressed up in his uniform and looking very handsome. I was happy and grateful to have had his help yesterday with the unpacking, though he mostly concentrated on unpacking his workboxes and uniforms. Not exactly the help I was hoping for, but at least some boxes were removed from the multitudes. I could tell he was a little nervous to start the next day so I was careful not to outwardly complain about anything, but I wasn't ready to be left alone.

It turned out, the sheer amount of work kept me busy from thinking too much. Even though I was doing the domestic thing of unpacking boxes and settling into our house, I had this strange satisfaction of doing things for myself by myself. I was achieving a goal with an end point. *O-H-I-O*, I chanted to myself, cheering on my independence.

Before I knew it, the day had melted away. I heard the chirp of the alarm warning me that the door was being opened. "Hello?" I called out.

"Hi, honey, I'm home!" Nick answered like a guy from an old sitcom. "What's for dinner?" he continued.

Oh, don't even start with me, my face said to him without speaking a word.

"Boxes," I said in a sarcastic tone. "Do you like what I've done with the place?"

He came over and gave me a big hug and kiss. "You worked very hard today. It looks great!"

"How was your first day of school?" I asked.

"It was fine. Met some people, got my desk and ID. Boring stuff. It's going to be a busy job though. I may have to travel for work."

"Ugh!" I said as I pulled away from his embrace. "Why do you have to stress me out on your first day?"

"Come on." He tried to lighten the mood. "What smells good? Did you make something?"

I was wondering when he'd notice. "I did pop a little something into the oven," I told him. "But only because it's your first day! Don't get too comfortable with this domesticated woman; I'm going to be a working woman again soon."

"I know," he said reassuringly. "It'll be great for you to start work again, and for the bank account."

I really was looking forward to starting work. I needed to feel productive and meet people so that I didn't feel so isolated.

The morning of my phone interview arrived, and I was tired but ready. I took a break from unpacking boxes and just laid on the couch for a minute. I must have dozed off. Suddenly, I was jolted awake by the phone, and I panicked. "Oh no!" I cried. "Hello, hello, hello," I repeated until I answered the phone, so as to will myself awake and not sound groggy. "Hello?" I answered in a too chipper voice.

"Hello, may I speak with Collette Delaney?" the calm, measured voice on the other end stated.

"Yes!" I answered, then realized what I said and clarified my answer. "This is she."

"This is Dr. Hasselin. Did I wake you?"

"Me? Oh no!" I replied and laughed nervously. "I was just unpacking boxes from our move. How are you?" I tried desperately to change the subject. The interview continued, asking about my experience and qualifications. It seemed that I'd recovered from the embarrassing start. Then he said something curious.

"Are you preparing for the hurricane?"

Now I was caught off guard.

"I haven't heard of a hurricane coming," I said, steadying myself and mentally taking a note to ask Nick about this immediately after the call. Stealing a quick glance out the kitchen window, the sky was beautifully blue without a cloud in sight. "Is it a big one?"

"Well, right now it's nearing the Gulf, but these things have a tendency to swing left or right. The last big one to hit New Orleans was in 1965. I wouldn't worry too much about it, but do have a plan to be safe." He paused, then continued. "I'd like to hire you on to join our team; I think you'll be a good fit. I'll be in touch in the next few weeks to iron out the details."

My confusion and fear gave way to excitement.

"Thank you so much, Dr. Hasselin! I'm looking forward to joining the team!" I hung up and called Nick immediately—doing my happy dance while dialing his work number.

"Nick! I got the job!" I said before he could even say hello.

"That's wonderful! Congratulations! When I get home we'll celebrate."

"Hey, Dr. Hasselin mentioned a hurricane coming. Do you know anything about that?"

"Yeah, there's one we've been monitoring here. It's too early to predict where it's going to hit. I didn't want to worry you."

"Shit. What are people saying?"

"Well, if it's bad we'll evacuate inland. People deal with these things down here all the time. We'll talk more when I get home. Don't worry."

I found our tiny fourteen-inch TV, complete with bunny ear antennas with tinfoil on the ends, and set it up on the counter.

Neither one of us was a big fan of watching television. We always seemed to be too busy to sit and watch a show. I was trying to find a station while playing with the large bunny ears for reception. Static finally gave way to a picture. I turned the knob until I found a news station and forced myself to sit and watch it for any information on a hurricane coming. It was torture. Not able to sit and watch any longer, I turned up the volume and continued to unpack, half listening for key words.

After about a half hour, I still hadn't heard anything about a storm. I turned off what we referred to as the "stupid box" and figured it really wasn't anything to get worked up about. I scanned the boxes still piled in the corner on top of each other waiting to be unpacked, and then glanced at the other corner overflowing with empty boxes and paper. "I'm going to need to make room," I mumbled to myself.

After about an hour of emptying boxes and reorganizing, I decided to take a break and do something fun for myself, like finding some plants to decorate the outside. "All right," I said out loud, "let's go exploring." With keys in hand and courage on my sleeve, I drove to one of the only two stores I knew how to get to by heart, the hardware store.

I came back feeling very accomplished. Not only had I gotten a great deal on four hanging ferns, but I'd also found a place that would take all our empty boxes. Of course, hanging the plants and loading the collapsed boxes into the car would have to wait until Nick came. I didn't want him to think I was completely self-sufficient.

When he came home, he saw the four large plants on the front porch. I saw him staring at them through the window. I bounced outside excited to show him my finds.

"What did you do?" Nick asked.

This wasn't exactly the tone I was expecting to hear from him. I stood there confused. I was about to speak when he continued.

"You went off on your own and bought these? You should have asked or at least waited until I came home. We should have done this together. You need to think about your actions, Collette. You can't just decide these things on your own."

"Shit, Nick—they're only ferns. I thought it would make the house look nicer than the construction zone it currently looks like. Why are you so upset?" I had never seen him get so upset so quickly about something so trivial. Taken aback by this, I thought it best not to continue questioning him.

"There is potentially a big hurricane coming this way. You should have bought plywood, not plants." He brushed past me into the house.

I turned sheepishly and walked into the house behind him, leaving the big, beautiful ferns on the porch.

By the middle of the week I finally started to overhear, mainly from passing conversation, news about the approaching storm. I now kept the TV station on low while I continued to unpack the remaining handful of boxes. It was hard to know how I should feel about this storm. Should I be nervous, prepared, or scared? Or should I adopt the nonchalant attitude that surrounded this city?

People I met at the post office, grocery stores, even in our neighborhood were acting as if there was nothing to worry about. We went to Finn's, now our local bar, to get the real pulse of what was going on. It was packed with people; apparently the local rugby team was gathered there all dirty and wearing their dried bloody war wounds proudly as a badge of honor. There on the television screens was Hurricane Katrina and her projected path, screaming right toward New Orleans. I was amazed at the sheer size of this storm and that no one in the bar was even paying attention to this ominous report. I asked the large man next to me in line, "What do you think about this hurricane that's coming?" I tried to keep the terror in my voice to a bare minimum.

He laughed and said, "Yeah, it's going to turn, they always do. Gonna probably hit Texas or Florida. We haven't had a major hurricane here since '65. That was Betsy." He paused as if remembering. "She was a real nasty bitch. Lots of people died in that storm. It was horrible."

I looked at him in confusion. He wasn't worried about this Category 5 storm heading straight toward us, but clearly remembered what a bad storm could do. I was really having a hard time wrapping my head around how calm people were. On the other hand, I did like this indifferent way of thinking and living—it seemed peaceful. Maybe I was getting all worked up for nothing.

"You new around here?" the man asked.

"Yes, we just moved here about a month ago," I said while sliding my hand into Nick's and thinking about all the things we had just unpacked. We'd worked so hard finishing up the inside of our place.

"Ah," he said, understanding now. "Don't worry about the storm. If it's really bad, the city will have to evacuate and if we do, think of it as a mandatory vacation! You'll be back three days later. It's not going to happen though."

I thanked him and looked around at the patrons in the bar laughing, drinking, talking in that loud bar voice that makes you hoarse the next day. *It's going to be okay*, I told myself. *Maybe.*

"No one seems to be worried," I said to Nick.

"I know. It's a little weird. Katrina is a powerful storm—we'll probably be evacuating if the projections stay this way. The Coast Guard is already setting up a command center in Alexandria."

My anxiety returned. "Where's that? Am I coming with you? When is this happening?"

"It's in the middle of the state, but I think they want families to evacuate to a different location," Nick stated calmly.

"What?" I couldn't believe what I was just hearing from him. "I'm coming with you. I don't care. I'll hide under your bed if I have to."

"It's too early yet to make plans. We'll know the storm's path a little better in a few days. Right now, just enjoy the calm before the storm."

I didn't know how he was doing this—I was a complete mess. I tried thinking of the storm turning. It was horrible to wish this on anyone, but please, Katrina, anyone but us!

I got a call from my mother the next morning. She spoke in a rushed and panicked voice. "Did you hear about this storm coming? Are you in harm's way? If you have to leave you should come home. Your father and I can buy your tickets." Her voice was full of anticipation, as she was clearly waiting for me to answer yes and get me on the very next train, plane, or bus.

"Mama, I don't know what's going to happen. No one seems to know around here. Nick's work just got a whole lot busier and I think he's taking out his stress on me in weird ways, and—"

"What do you mean?" she interrupted me.

"He's just very snippy. He's not his usual easy-going self. It'll all be fine though." I paused, trying to sound convincing. "I'm going to stay with him whatever this storm does." I was so torn. If this was just going to be a three-day vacation, I wanted to stay with Nick. The problem was that no one knew for certain what was going to happen. The city hadn't said anything yet about evacuation, so I had to think maybe it was going to be okay after all. My neighbors were all staying in their houses and buying provisions. They'd stated, completely calm and nonchalant, how they were planning on camping inside the house with a host of candles and flashlights and canned food. Nope, not for me, thank you. Mama was concerned about her airline tickets to visit us, which was in a week.

"Here's the thing, Mama, we just need to wait and see what's going to happen. You can always get a credit for the tickets if you don't come next week. Or I'll see you next week and we'll have a great time!" I tried to sound positive. Their visit, as much as I'd looked forward to it, was not really what I needed to be worrying about right now.

Everyone was searching for answers no one had.

CHAPTER FOUR

AUGUST 29, 2005

"It's Friday, August 26th," chirped the newscaster. I had our small TV set up on the counter in the kitchen while I was working to drag the huge ferns I'd bought inside the house—I knew I couldn't ask Nick to help with that. I assessed the stuff on the floor and started putting it up on the chairs, tables, and counters. I heard the door open with that little *beep beep* from the alarm. "Hi, honey—you're home early!" I said, relieved to get some help preparing the house.

"I can't stay. Just grabbing some work binders. I need to get back immediately. There's lots of planning to move the command center and preparing the port for closure from ship traffic that I'm doing right now. Don't wait up for me."

He was in and out in minutes, without a single glance my way. As he was walking out the door, work binders tucked under one arm and some sort of duffel under the other, he yelled back, "Oh, I forgot to mention you were cleared to come with me.

My commanding officer said it would be good for me to have you there. He's probably bringing his wife too, but let's keep this between us."

I was so relieved to hear he was planning on bringing me with him instead of sending me to the other location where families were going, but now I realized getting the house together and packing was going to be left entirely to me.

I was lost, not knowing what I was doing or how to prepare for a hurricane. Preparing for snowstorms back home was easy compared to this. I didn't see any neighbors look like they were boarding up their houses, still thinking that the storm would hit somewhere else. I hadn't yet set up our desktop computer to the dial-up modem, doubting that I'd get any useful information from my AOL account anyway. I walked down the hall to the bathroom, rolling my vacuum cleaner behind me and carrying the small fig tree we got as a welcome gift from Nick's coworker. I put both in the tub, as suggested by him as well. I packed the suitcase with three days' worth of clothing for Nick and me. Not able to bring the fish with us, I set up the small twenty-gallon fish tank with a filter, conditioned the water, and put the fish inside. I found the small automatic fish feeder and set it up for the next few days.

The big task was going to be boarding up all the windows in the house. Nick tried to get plywood, but the stores saw a money-making opportunity and were charging twenty dollars per board. We needed to board up twenty windows and four doors. I was regretting buying such a large house.

It was up to me to figure out what to do. Nick was already back at work and was fine with just boarding up the doors. I didn't think he could handle any more decision-making, since his job was getting more demanding and stressful now. I had my concerns about leaving the windows uncovered, so I started to consider my options. We just had a fence replaced in our backyard and the old wood fence was still scattered on the back lawn. I'd cursed the builders for leaving behind so much lumber, but now I was so thankful they didn't finish the removal job. I found the nails and hammer and started to piece together boards to cover the windows. Originally thinking I was being smart, I quickly found out how heavy and unruly my makeshift window treatment was.

I needed help, but with no family or friends to call, I went sheepishly over to my crazy neighbor. I hated asking for help, especially being the typical woman in need of a man's strength. I buried my pride and frustration and walked next door. I heard the small horses bark even before I knocked, but I didn't get an answer from either neighbor. I walked back to the house and looked for signs of life anywhere.

Luckily, by chance, I saw our neighbor across the street walk by his front window. He was home, but I was unsure if he was busy preparing for the storm himself. Having only met him a few times, I hesitated to just show up on his doorstep, but desperate times call for desperate measures. I knocked on his door and smiled at the camera posted on his front porch. He had cameras everywhere. The door opened slightly, and he poked only his head out, seeing me, but also taking a quick glance around to make sure no one else he didn't know (or see on his camera) was there as well.

"Hello, Collette, what can I do for you?"

"Hello, Sam. I'm sorry to bother you, but Nick is at work until late tonight and I'm having trouble boarding up the windows myself. Could you help me? I'd be happy to pay you for your trouble."

"Oh, no trouble at all. Let me change into some work clothes and I'll be right over."

"Thank you!" I said, feeling a little better about my situation.

I didn't mind paying for help, but was happy he didn't take me up on it. I realized I didn't have any cash at home anyway. In any case, I'd probably offer him the currency of New Orleans, beer.

Sam was over in a few minutes and quickly understood why I was having trouble. The wood I used, though freely available, was simply too heavy. The two of us grunted and strained to put the lumber on the windows. After only finishing one on the side of the house, I realized I was wearing Sam out. "Maybe I'll just do this side of the house?" I suggested, and he readily agreed.

"Are these the boards from your fence? Were they out of plywood at the store already?" he asked.

"Yes and no. The plywood was too expensive at the store, so I made these myself with the wood left over from our fence," I said, smiling and feeling really dumb.

Sam's silence said a lot. Then he stated, "I'll help you board up the back doors. You'll need to do the front door as you leave." A much easier task, but it was still so helpful to have his assistance.

We finished a few hours later, exhausted.

"Sam, you don't know how much I appreciate you. Thank you so much. Are you sure I can't pay you for your time?"

"No, Collette, don't be silly. Just pay it forward."

He turned down the offer of beer, surprisingly, though he did take me up on taking some extra batteries I'd found. I wished him luck packing for the storm. He told me he was staying to protect his property from looters if the storm hit.

Oh great, I thought, *I didn't even think of that scenario.*

"How are you going to ride out a hurricane?" I said, shocked at the calm, nonchalant attitude of my neighbor.

"If the forecasters are actually right for once and Katrina does pay us a visit—which I doubt she will—we'll be ready. We'll fill up the bathtubs with water in case the water goes out and we'll have plenty of candles and flashlights . . . oh, and an axe," he said surprisingly calmly. "There's a bunch of canned food and we're stocked up on beer," he added with a wink.

I had to ask for clarification. "Is the axe for protection?" I said hesitantly, curious as to what possible role an axe would have in a hurricane scenario.

He answered after bellowing with laughter. "No! Guns are for protection! Axes are for chopping through the roof if the water gets too high." I stood there staring at him in amazement and he continued, clearly thinking I was confused. "So that we can escape to the roof."

My heart was beating so fast after this new information that I had no response for him. I couldn't quite process the fact that people were choosing to stay with an impending Cat 5 storm focused on New Orleans.

I sat in the darker than usual house, thanks to the boarded-up windows, feeling a bit nervous and unsettled. Nick said he'd be home four hours ago and was short on the phone when I tried to talk to him. I couldn't take listening to all the talk about the storm, now plentiful on the radio and TV, so I decided to just go to sleep and be refreshed for my mini vacation the next day.

I wasn't actually sure when Nick came home that night, but I knew it was sometime after midnight. Even though he barely slept, he was up before me and still very much in his military mode from the night before.

"We need to leave here by zero nine hundred," he said briskly. "We're carpooling with some of my team."

"What about our car?" I said with morning breath, not quite as awake as he.

"I moved it last night to a parking garage in case the streets flood."

"Oh shit. Is that what they think is going to happen?" My heart raced and I was fully awake now. No need for coffee.

Nick just looked at me and said, "We're preparing for the worst-case scenario." The clock on our nightstand read 7:30 a.m.

"I'm getting up. We're all packed and ready to go."

I wasn't sure what to feel. With each passing minute, I wavered from nervous to panicked to numb. Every emotion got its chance to audition to see if it was the appropriate one for the situation.

Our ride showed up in a government vehicle. Apparently, it was just as important to make sure all the GVs were safely evacuated along with personnel. I did one last walk around the house just to make sure everything was unplugged and secure. In the bathroom, I took a moment to collect myself. As I sat on the toilet, I looked at the floor. In between the boards I could see straight through to the ground beneath me. I had a vision that water would be coming up through them. I pushed that thought aside. Why did I need to be so dramatic? This wasn't helping me calm down at all. I should have been more concerned about the wide variety of creepy crawlers coming up into the house!

Then I got ahold of myself and told my inner voice to shut up. I took a breath and grabbed a few bottles of wine from our new wine fridge and an engagement picture of us, as I breezed through the bedroom. I took a moment to assess the state of the house. I normally wouldn't leave without it being completely clean. I quickly ran to get a rag to wipe down the counter and straightened the hand towel on the hook. It was a random list of last-minute, unnecessary, nervous to-do's. My hands and feet kept moving until we were out the door. I helped Nick secure the wood to the front door before turning to the waiting car.

"Wow, Cole, you did a lot on the house. Thank you—it's great."

It was the kindest thing he'd said to me in a few days.

Nick and I piled into the truck, now making five of us total. The other three Coasties greeted me kindly, but I caught a few side eyes after they saw the amount of stuff I was bringing.

"We'll just put it in the back," Nick said and gave me a look. I hadn't intended to embarrass him in front of his coworkers. I had no idea we were traveling with three other people. Thinking I wasn't bringing that much, I'd packed for three days, also taking our bills, checkbooks, valuables in the safe, and two bottles of "company" wine, just in case. Considering the two cases of really good wine I left behind, I thought I'd made some responsible decisions.

"Ready to roll, sir?" the Coastie driver asked Nick, who was the most senior officer in the car.

"All set, Ensign. Let's get out of here!"

I looked at Nick and smiled, loving seeing him interact in his world. For a brief moment, the storm was gone from my mind.

But then it was back.

Even though many of our neighbors were staying behind, it seemed that the whole city was leaving last minute to go on a mandatory weekend trip. The roads were packed with cars. We had the radio on and could hear that some routes were turning into contra flow—meaning both sides of a divided highway were now going in the same direction, out of town. *Whoa*, I thought, *that's serious*. Then the music stopped and a newsman's voice interrupted. "Breaking news, the mayor just announced an evacuation of the city. We suggest everyone leave the city due to the approaching hurricane. This is a serious storm and people must leave to be safe. Those who cannot leave should get to dedicated shelters."

As we started to leave the residential area behind, I saw police vehicles with megaphones snaking through the streets repeating the same message. "This is a mandatory evacuation of the city. Those who can't leave will need to get to dedicated shelters." The blood drained from my face. I grabbed Nick's hand and looked at him, terrified.

"It's going to be fine," he whispered. "They have to tell people to leave in a case like this."

It was Saturday and the storm was supposed to hit on Monday. *Why didn't they tell people earlier?* I thought but didn't say anything. I was so confused about this whole situation—I was really depending on Nick to lead the way now. The cars were in a dead stop on the narrow street, each one just waiting for the car in front of them to move. It was going to take a while to get out of town.

"Hey, let's take the levee road," one person in the truck suggested. "We can, right? We're in a GV."

"I don't think anyone will stop us," another one piped up, and Nick gave the thumbs up.

The Ensign turned the truck and gunned it up the large hill. I didn't know there was a dirt path on top of the levee. We sped along the top with envious drivers and passengers staring at us from below. I was so glad to be moving again and not stopped in the miles-long parking lot that had formed by idling cars.

The music started up again in the car after the announcement was over. Nick put a reassuring hand on my leg. He leaned over to me and said quietly, "It's going to be fine. I'm taking you on a three-day vacation to Alexandria."

I patted his hand on my leg. "How thoughtful and spontaneous of you." Forcing myself to push aside the gravity of the situation, I became lost in the music and imagined returning to our house a few days later.

Finally, four hours later, we made it to the hotel in Alexandria, our creative driving out of NOLA having saved us from being stuck in traffic for too long. The parking lot swarmed with GVs and cars. We all got out of the truck and gathered our personal items. I took a moment to stretch my legs and take in my new surroundings. It was a beautifully warm day, not a cloud in the sky. I viewed the sea of blue uniforms walking into and out of the hotel to the building next to us and immediately felt I was in a place I shouldn't be. I stayed with the truck and Nick checked into the hotel. I tried not to make eye contact or be seen. I really didn't want to get into trouble for being there. Nick finally returned to the truck after what felt to me as if he was gone for hours.

"All right, I don't have a roommate, yet," he said.

I knew he was as uncomfortable with this situation as I was. "Great!" I tried to sound positive.

"Let's get moved in. I have an all-hands at seventeen hundred."

I was so nervous I had to count on my fingers, adding one after twelve for each hour—okay, a 5 p.m. meeting.

We went into the room and I didn't unpack any of my things, so that it didn't seem as if Nick was staying with a woman in his room. After getting organized, he left and said he'd return after his meeting and we could get dinner together.

With nothing else to do, I turned on the TV. I was immediately met with every newscaster speculating on damage and almost giddy to see what a Category 5 storm could do. I clicked off the TV and sighed. I grabbed my phone and called home.

"Collette? Oh, praise Jesus! I was so worried."

"Hi, Mama, I'm fine. We're here in Alexandria, all checked into the hotel."

"Why are you whispering?" she asked.

"I'm kind of a stowaway. I wasn't supposed to come here with Nick. This hotel is only for active duty, and I don't want to get caught."

"Why didn't you just come home?" Mama said with a little whine in her voice.

"I may end up doing that depending on what's going to happen here, but everyone still thinks that we'll be back by Tuesday."

"Really? The news is calling for some bad damage there."

"Mama," I said, my tone changing to reflect how I didn't want to hear that. "No one knows what is going to happen, Katrina may slow down or turn." I was even surprised I said that, though I didn't believe it. It was what everyone was saying, hoping.

Click. I heard the door unlock then the handle move. My heart raced, my hands immediately became cold and clammy. "Mama, I'll call you later," I said quickly and hung up the phone. I tried not to look like a trapped animal. In came a tall, shaved-head man in the blue uniform.

"Oh, excuse me!" he said, sounding surprised and embarrassed.

I felt horrible. He was about to close the door, but I stood and said, "You probably have the right room." He paused and sheepishly came in. We both knew this situation could get everyone in trouble. I had to explain myself quickly.

"I'm Lieutenant Nick Delaney's wife. I'm a stowaway," I said with a smile and extended my hand.

"Oh, hello. I'm Richard Smith," he said as he shook my hand. He didn't give his rank, but I could see by his uniform he was the same rank as Nick. "I'm going to see if maybe there's an extra room no one has claimed yet."

"I'm so sorry to have caused you any trouble. I didn't have anywhere else to go," I said apologetically. I immediately regretted my comment. "Richard, I should be the one leaving. I'll try to find other arrangements."

He smiled courteously and said, "I'll see what the front desk can do. We may have to be roommates." With that, he grabbed his large dark blue duffel bag and left.

I sat on the bed depressed, alone, confused, and regretful. I had no life skill to deal with this hurricane situation. The stress overcame me and I cried big ugly tears into my hands. Feeling only slightly better, I blew my nose and sat back on the corner of the bed staring at the wall not knowing what to do. I reached into my bag and pulled out a book I packed at the last minute, *One Flew Over the Cuckoo's Nest*. Ugh, I sighed. *I suck at this.* I put the book back into the bag. *Click.* I stood up and looked toward the door. Nick came in and I let out a sigh of relief. "Oh thank God it's you," I said.

"Cole, you're going to drive yourself crazy. Don't get so worked up."

Done and done, I thought. "I met your roommate," I told him.

"Richard?"

"How did you know his name? Did you see him too?" I asked.

"Kind of. I overheard this guy telling everyone he found a hot woman in his room."

At that, I almost passed out.

"Just kidding!" Nick said in between laughter. He hugged me and said, "Not about the hot woman part though."

In a stern voice, I answered, "What am I going to do?"

"Nothing, love—he was at the front desk getting a different room. I think we'll be fine. Everyone who is coming here should be checked in by now. Ready for dinner?"

"I just feel horrible."

"It's okay, really. I think there are probably other wives who came too. I'd stay in the room though, until we see how this all shakes out."

I felt like the dog staying with his owner, able to leave only with permission. I began to think it may have been a mistake to have left our car behind. I couldn't leave now even if I wanted to.

"What did they tell you in the meeting?" I asked.

"I pulled the short straw, unfortunately. There are going to be two shifts so that there will be people working constantly. I'm on the night shift."

"Crap. That's going to be rough. We'll never see each other."

"You can stay up with me!" Nick said, half joking and half serious.

"In the room? By myself?"

"If it's bad, the other wives will eventually come out of their rooms. If Katrina dodges New Orleans we'll be back home in a few days. Let's just see how it turns out."

Every cell in my body shook. I hated uncertainty.

The next day I unpacked my things and moved into the hotel room, confident that now it would just be us there. I found the stack of mail I threw in the bag before we left. *I guess I can go through the mail and make out bills.* Nick was still sleeping, since his night shift started tonight. I took my time going through them and writing the checks, feeling a bit smug thinking how smart I was to bring the mail and keep up with responsibilities.

I opened a letter from our insurance carrier next. I had to read it twice. "Effective Friday August 26th flood and wind insurance will be canceled." What was this? This was crazy! I had to wake Nick up to tell him.

I gave his shoulder a shake. "Nick, honey, sorry to wake you, but you have to read this letter. Like, right now. Our insurance for the house is canceled!"

Nick rubbed at his eyes and sat up. "No, there must be a mistake. Let me see the letter."

I handed it to him hoping he was right.

"You have to call them and sort this out. We prepaid when we bought the house. I think we have a letter stating that. Give them a call today and set them straight. It's probably just a misunderstanding."

I realized I'd found my new job—secretary. I hated doing this stuff. "It's Sunday. I don't think anyone will be there, but I'll try anyway."

"Well, definitely call tomorrow then," he said, and with that, he assigned this task to me.

With time on my hands, I went for a walk around the grounds to burn off some anxiety. The storm was scheduled to make landfall Monday morning. It was as if we were living in an alternate universe waiting for something horrible to happen while the rest of the country went about their business. It was a beautiful day; the sun was shining and there was only a little breeze in the air. My body, however, was all confused as to whether I should be sleeping or awake. I'd tried to stay up late the previous night so that I could be on Nick's new schedule. Realizing that his shift was going to start again at 6 p.m., I decided to head back, curl up next to him, and enjoy the peaceful bliss of ignorance.

A few hours later, we awoke to have dinner for breakfast, then Nick left for his twelve-hour shift.

"Will you come back before the storm hits?" I begged. "I don't want to watch this alone."

"I'll try. The storm isn't projected to hit until after the shift, so it may work out. Enjoy your day!" He kissed me goodbye and again I was left to my own devices.

I tried to pass the time by calling home, but I found it hard to have a regular conversation under the circumstances. The topic kept coming back to Katrina, which frankly I didn't want to talk about again.

After a few hours of watching movies, I needed to get out of the room. I figured I'd do a little exploring and see what all was going on. I walked out of the hotel to a dark night sky. All around me stars glowed brightly. It was beautiful, especially since it was midday for me. I looked at my watch. Eleven p.m. I had seven hours to burn before I got to see Nick again and before the storm came blowing in. Adjacent to the hotel was the large conference center, lights ablaze. I saw a side door and decided to see what was going on in there. A few uniformed people were coming out and I waited until they left.

Feet from the door, I suddenly felt ridiculous and a little terrified trying to get into a building I wasn't supposed to be in. I didn't know what to expect for security and really didn't want to get caught, or worse, get Nick into trouble.

I turned around and walked back to the hotel. We were in the middle of nowhere, surrounded by highway and parking lots I had little choice but to wander. I walked into the hotel lobby and was affronted by the unnatural lighting and cold dry air. The space was small, but off to the side was a sitting area with TVs and a small bar. I saw a few people talking together, but not exclusively. It had a streetcar-like feel to the conversation, where strangers were talking politely but didn't necessarily know each other. Gaining confidence and looking for company to pass the time, I walked to the bar and ordered a beer. The weathermen were already in place along the Gulf Coast reporting from Mississippi, Alabama, and New Orleans, ready to show how they could stand upright in strong winds.

"Ready for the big event?" asked a woman sitting near where I was standing. I didn't see any buzz cuts sitting around her, so I figured she wasn't associated with the military. She would be relatively safe for me to talk to and not give my circumstances away.

"Honestly, not really. It's my first hurricane. I just recently moved down here with my husband."

"Ah, you're with the Blue Man Group then?"

"Pardon?" I asked, confused.

"The Coast Guard, darling, they're all over this hotel."

Shoot, a direct question. I was trying to be vague, but I could feel myself cracking under the pressure of my answer.

"Yes." I answered like a child caught in a lie. "Are you?" I was hoping to have a coconspirator.

"Me?" She laughed and continued. "Oh no, but if you know of any single men . . ." she said with a wink. "I do like me some men in uniform."

I could tell this woman had a wild side to her. She seemed to be a free spirit. Maybe just the kind of person I needed right now.

"I didn't want to leave," she continued, "but I thought it would be shitty to have my dogs drown. I just got here this morning with the mutts. It's rough in New Orleans right now. I traveled mostly in rain and wind. The palm trees were bending horizontal to the ground." She paused, then after a thought continued. "Yeah, I didn't want to stick around any longer. I figured I'd hightail it out of there and pregame here and watch the show." She raised her glass of beer. "I'm Susie Star." She held out her hand to shake mine.

I almost choked on my drink.

"I think I may have seen you sing at Rock 'n' Bowl a few weeks ago." My heart tightened, hoping she'd say that it wasn't her, despite the obvious truth.

"Ahh! That's so cool! Yep, that's me, Susie Star." And she arched a movement with her arm like in the *Reading Rainbow* shooting star. "That was my last gig before leaving town. What's your name, babe?"

"Collette Delaney," I said. "Nice to meet you!" I shook her hand. I wasn't quite sure if I should mention Nick. She sensed my hesitancy and continued talking.

"I know what you're thinking."

I looked at her, wondering if she was psychic, on top of everything else. Susie continued, "Star isn't really my last name. It's actually Bocello, but I didn't think people would come out to see Susie Bocello, so my stage name is Star. Because I'm a star, baby!" She laughed and planted a small smack on my back. "Plus, if Tony Bennett can change his Italian name and still be a huge success, so can I!"

"It does sound kind of exciting to adopt a different personality, be someone different. I'm kind of wishing right now I was someone not worrying about the storm."

"Well, the first thing you need to know about hurricanes is that they stink, a real pain in the ass, but if you have the right provisions you can get through it."

"What are the right provisions?" I asked.

"Alcohol. Everything is a party in New Orleans, you'll see, if you haven't already. Just make the best of any situation. Hell, we even celebrate death with a party. Ever see a second line?"

"No, I'm new to the whole New Orleans experience."

"You'll learn. Second lines are a party to celebrate the life a person lived. People follow the casket with decorative umbrellas, playing horns, tubas, drums, singing and dancing. It's a proper send-off."

"I've never seen anything like that. How long have you lived in New Orleans?"

"About fifteen years now. I came to New Orleans when I was eighteen and never left, except for my regular visits over here," Susie said with a determined smile.

As much as I wanted to not like this woman, she was just what I needed right now: a friend.

The newscaster on the television interrupted our conversation; it seemed that the show had begun. There were people reporting from Mississippi and Alabama, with a split screen to show the force of the wind and rain, but the reporter from New Orleans was curiously missing.

"Why aren't they showing New Orleans?" I finally asked to no one in particular.

"Maybe he got blown away," someone dryly replied.

I was getting annoyed at the lack of coverage there. Finally, a grainy feed came in from a camera mounted outside the Superdome. The picture was horrific. The entire sky was pitch-black, with rain assaulting the camera in every direction. Suddenly the camera shook and the feed was lost. The newscaster explained that the camera had blown away and the conditions were too dangerous to have someone outside reporting. It was an ominous tale. The rest of the coverage bounced between the other two states getting affected. I sat quietly in a room full of people I didn't know, but all felt a connection to one another. This was happening to us all and none of us knew exactly how the storm was affecting our city; we just knew it was bad. It was now early morning and I was exhausted from staying up all night. I said goodbye to my new friend and headed back to my room.

Returning to the hotel room, I opened the door and was so happy to be greeted by Nick. "When did you get back?" I asked and gave him a hug.

"About ten minutes ago. A bunch of us stayed to watch the beginning of the coverage, but I wanted to get back to you."

"Have you heard anything about the city? The news coverage isn't very good in New Orleans apparently."

"No, though I think we'll know more by later today or tomorrow. Want a nightcap?" he said as he grabbed a bottle of not-so-good wine I grabbed last minute as I left the house.

The sight of it made me sad. "I should have grabbed the better bottles."

"I'm glad you thought to get this one!" Nick said. It was clear he was trying to cheer me up. I sat on the bed and found a different station covering the storm, hoping to hear about home.

With no wine pull or glasses in the room, Nick pushed the cork into the bottle and sat next to me on the bed. We took turns drinking from the bottle, sitting on the bed together in silence watching the unbelievable events unfold in front of us. The whole situation put a tangible weight on my bones.

CHAPTER FIVE

ONE-TWO PUNCH

I awoke hours later, kicking the empty bottle off the bed. The dull *thunk* it made hitting the carpet woke up Nick. "Morning, love. What time is it?" he garbled.

I looked at the hotel clock. "Three p.m.," I said. Shifting my circadian clock to this lifestyle was just adding to my confusion and depression. "I feel as if I haven't seen daylight in days. This sucks."

"It's hard," Nick agreed.

I put on the news again, but Nick shut it off.

"Don't you want to know what happened?" I asked.

"I do. Get dressed—we're going to the command center," he said confidently.

"But what about me not being seen?"

"If the city is blown away or underwater there'll be bigger issues to deal with."

I didn't like either option, but I knew the people at the command center would have a better pulse about what was going on. We got ready and made our way over there. The day crew was in full operation. Nick opened the door with authority, something that I'd been too timid to do myself last night. I strategically let him go in first, following behind him like an obedient dog off its leash. We turned into this immense room filled with computers, desks, and the buzz of hundreds of people walking around with a purpose. Nick made some introductions to the curious onlookers and I smiled and shook hands and almost immediately forgot their names.

"There are a ton of people here," I said to him in a low voice.

"All hands on deck for this one, Cole. Disaster Assistance Response Teams, Maritime Safety and Security Teams, Port Security Units, Coast Guard strike teams, everyone's here."

We sat at a bay of computers, all with multiple screens. Nick started typing and up popped our address. On the second screen I saw our fate, but didn't comprehend the picture. There was our house with the roof still on, thankfully. Nick zoomed in on the image and revealed what I dreaded—standing water everywhere.

Our house was flooded.

"There's water on the street," Nick spoke gently.

"How much? Is it in the house?" I whispered, so as not to call any more attention to me.

"I can't tell, but see that little island there?" Nick pointed out a curious blob on the screen to me and continued. "That's the roof of our neighbor's big truck. I'd say there's at least seven to eight feet of standing water outside the house. Maybe four to six feet of water inside the house. In our area." Nick scanned what remained of the rest of the city; whole swaths where once there were normal-looking residential areas now only showed the rooftops of houses in a sea of water like little floating islands. Neither one of us said a word.

I tried to imagine that amount of water over everything, just sitting there, getting soaked in by the furniture, absorbed by the walls. It felt surreal. I knew it was happening, but I was unable to and unwilling to process the full reality of the situation. I wasn't sure how Nick felt, but he seemed to process it as if it was happening to someone else.

He zoomed out and saw the whole city covered in blue. "It looks like eighty percent of the city is underwater. Right, now we know," he said abruptly, clicking off the site and standing up to indicate we were done. "I've got a few hours to spare before I have to come back for work. Let's get something to eat. It's going to be an intense shift."

⌒

At dinner, we sat mostly in stunned, numb silence. Nick pushed food around on his plate. I was so confused I had to ask a question I didn't want to: "Weren't the levees supposed to keep the water out?"

Nick shook his head. "It was such a big storm that some of the levees failed; others had water within inches of spilling over. New Orleans is a bowl, built below sea level. People think it'll take weeks before the damaged pumps are repaired from their flooding to be able to pump all the water out of the city."

Knowing the situation didn't reassure me anymore. I didn't want to call home, though I knew everyone would want to hear from me. *Not yet*, I told them in my mind. *I need to process this bad dream.*

After dinner, Nick went in to work, and I sat on the bed, glaring at the dark screen of the TV. No news was good news, especially right now. I stood up suddenly, not quite knowing what I was going to do.

Then, it came to me. I needed to try to find Susie.

I didn't know how I was going to find her. I walked sheepishly to the hotel bar where I'd first seen her. I was never comfortable going places alone, but really needed some company. It was as if the hurricane party the night before had been one night only. The bartender walked over, slinging a bar towel over his shoulder. "What can I get you, darling?" he asked. I looked at him, but hadn't thought of drinking anything until that moment. I'd been too focused on searching for Susie.

"I'll give you a few moments," he said with a smile and a nod.

"Actually, sir . . ." I made eye contact with him and he came over, now cleaning off a pint glass absentmindedly. He looked at me, raised his eyebrows, and waited for me to continue. "I was looking for a woman I met here last night." The minute I said that, I regretted sounding like a cheap date. I quickly and awkwardly continued, "She's a friend. She has curly dark hair, shoulder length, about my height."

He laughed. "You must mean Susie! She's the life of the party! Usually comes down here around 9:00, though I haven't seen her yet."

My watch read 8:15. *Shoot*, I thought, *might as well get a drink.* "Thanks, I'll get an Abita Amber." I turned around and leaned on the bar just in time to catch Susie racing down the hall toward the door. I hesitated to call out to her. Maybe she was on her way to something important. Before I could overthink my situation any more I shouted, "Susie!"

She stopped and looked my direction. A big smile came over her face. "Girl!" she said, drawing out the word. "What cha doing right now?" she said quickly.

"I . . . um, nothing."

At that she grabbed my hand and yelled to the bartender. "Bill, put her drink on my tab and make it to go!"

Bill put my beer in a plastic cup, slid it in our direction, and smiled. "Have fun, ladies!" He waved.

"Where are we going?" I asked, excited and a little worried, as she still had my hand and her forward motion didn't stop.

"The casino!" Susie replied. "I'm so glad you saw me," she continued. "I've been thinking of you. I'm parked right over there. We can catch up in the car, come on, we're late!"

"Late for what?" I asked. *This is so exciting*, I thought, *and completely unsafe*. Mama would not be happy about this. No one knew where I was, not even Nick. *I don't really know this woman and I'm getting into a car going to a casino—somewhere!* I got in the car, but for good measure I brought out my phone to text Nick. What was I going to say, exactly? "I'm going to a casino with the woman you bought a drink for a few weeks ago." I put the phone back in my pocket, telling myself I'd text once I got more information. Plus, he was working—it wasn't like he was wondering what I was doing.

"If you get to the casino before 9 p.m., it's buy-one-get-one-free at the dance club. We'll have to pray to the gods for green lights," Susie said. She threw the keys in the ignition and floored it.

"How far away are we going?" I asked as I buckled up, balancing the beer.

She said, "It's about forty-five minutes away, but don't worry— we'll get there in time."

I could honestly say that I wasn't worried about that.

"You're going to have to pound that beer or grab a straw and lid from the glove compartment. We have open container laws, but you need to stick a straw in it."

This is going to be one hell of a night, I thought as I fumbled for a lid that fit. She had quite the collection. I was staring blankly ahead, sipping my beer through a straw with so many thoughts in my head and not saying any of them.

"Hey, lady, why so quiet? Did I kidnap you on a bad night?" Susie asked, stifling a laugh.

"No, not at all! I was actually hoping to run into you tonight. I was just thinking of Katrina. Sorry, I don't mean to be a downer." I barely knew this lady, but I wanted desperately to be friends with her. I wanted to really open up, but I feared so much coming across as a desperate and lonely housewife, winning the "who's in worse shape award," and most of all, being stranded at this casino.

"Katrina, what a bitch. I guess I'm lucky and happen to live in a dry spot. Not that I care all that much about the place since I'm renting! How did you make out?"

My stomach twisted. "I'm not sure yet. There's really not much news coming back from my area."

"Yeah, waiting is the worst. Best not to worry yourself about it until you can see firsthand." Susie looked at me and squeezed my hand. "We're going to have a blast tonight!"

I smiled back at her, forcing myself to just live in the moment. I took another big sip of beer out of my straw and thought about this ridiculous situation. I made up my mind that the night was going to be a blast.

Susie's Thunderbird squealed into the parking lot and we jumped out. I felt like a teenager again. She grabbed my hand and we ran laughing to the front door. We arrived with ten minutes to spare. The rush of cold, oxygenated air hit me immediately. I was awake and ready for an adventure with Susie at the helm. She directed me through the maze of lights and cacophony of bells, dings, and cheers of the casino. We ran straight into a long line of people all waiting to get in. *Aw, shoot. This stinks*, I thought. All that effort to just get stuck in line. I felt defeated, but Susie gave me a wink and kept us walking straight up to the bouncers, passing all the other girls waiting in heels and barely anything else. She gave the first large guy a big bear hug.

"Hello, love, I was wondering where you were," the enormous bouncer said to Susie.

"I have a friend tonight," Susie told him. "I want to show her around." All eyes were on me. I must have looked like fresh meat. I gave the best smile I could, but still felt like a girl from Ohio.

"Hello?" the bouncer asked—it was a question, waiting for an answer.

I didn't know if I should shake hands or hug him, so I did neither and curtsied instead. "Collette," I stated.

"Ah, nice to meet you, Collette. I'm sure you'll have a great time with Susie here. Try to keep her out of trouble."

And with that, the doors opened and we walked in.

Susie smacked me on the back, laughing. "Sweet move! But they'll expect a little hug next time, FYI. They can be a bit touchy-feely, but think of it as free cover charge. To the bar!" Susie led the way through the maze of people to reach an open spot at the bar.

In contrast to the casino, the dance club was pitch black with only a strobe now and then lighting up the place. The music was so loud I could feel the bass vibrating my rib bones. It was exhilarating. "I got the first round!" I yelled. "What can I buy you?"

"Jack and Ginger," Susie replied immediately. "I'll get the next round. What would you like?"

I hadn't thought yet about what I was going to drink, but said lamely, "Rum and Coke."

We bellied up to the bar and made eye contact with the young woman working there. She looked like a model.

I ordered and overheard Susie ordering at the same time too. I gave her a curious look.

"We only have five minutes left for the buy-one-get-one. We'll be double fisting!"

I only heard a fraction of what she said, but I understood once

I gave Susie her two orders of Jack and Gingers and she passed me my two rum and Cokes. *What am I going to do with two drinks on the dance floor*, I thought.

The music was so amazing; all I wanted to do was dance. What a release it would be to dance and sweat, but I was stuck holding two rum and Cokes that were so clear I thought the bartender had forgotten the Coke part. Susie wanted to dance too. She pounded the first drink and was working on the second while she shook and shimmied this way and that. I did my best to keep up. I finished the first drink, feeling the warmth of it fill my body, but left most of the second at the cocktail table. I wanted to dance, not stand around and drink. Susie was already dancing, making a small void of space on the dance floor. I ran up to join her. Before the second song started, I noticed beads of sweat forming on my brow and chest along with the encroachment of men, some of whom started to circle around us waiting for their opportunity to grind. I was out of practice with dancing pickups. Dancing and getting attention for it reminded me of when I was in college, before Nick.

I continued to dance without making eye contact so as not to send mixed signals, yet the attention was exciting. I spotted Susie shaking and strutting in our small, two-girls-only circle. She smiled a devilish smile to me and I laughed. This release was just what I needed. Sweating, laughing, and getting spilled on a little—mostly from Susie's drinks—we continued like this for hours.

We slowly walked back to the car in the light of the new day, our eardrums still pulsating, our bodies soaked in sweat and smelling like alcohol. The cool breeze was so refreshing.

"That was an amazing night! Thank you!" I screamed to Susie.

"You're so welcome! I can't hear a thing!" she said, laughing. "That place is crazy. And, girl, you're a great dancer!"

"I haven't danced like that in years! It was so much fun. A bit of a meat market though."

"Yeah, makes you feel good though, right? Ha! No one takes those dudes seriously." We got in the car and just sat there for a minute sinking into the leather seats. "Damn, it feels good to sit down!" Susie said as she started the car.

We arrived back at the hotel just as the change of shifts was taking place. I wanted to avoid seeing anyone I knew, but also really wanted to go to my room.

"I feel like this is a walk of shame," I said to Susie as we entered the lobby.

"Why? You've been out with me! It's a walk of pride, girl." She stopped and gave me a hug before heading off in the direction of her room. "Now get in there and take a shower!" she said, laughing.

"Thanks again for a great night. Maybe I'll see you at the hotel bar again?" I didn't want to sound as if I was picking her up, but I'd forgotten how making friends actually worked.

"Yes! See you tonight. I think there's going to be hotel bingo— I saw a sign announcing it in the elevator. What a hoot!"

I was so tired, hungry, and yet somehow still excited that I almost forgot I wasn't here on vacation. I quietly entered the room to find that Nick hadn't made it back yet. I dashed into the bathroom, tore off my clothes, and slid into the shower. *I have to see about a laundry around here*, I thought.

The hot water dripping down from my hair onto my body caused me to relax every muscle. I closed my eyes and for a second I felt stress lift away. Then I remembered that I had to call the insurance company again to speak with someone, anyone, who could help reinstate our insurance plan. Having dealt with insurance companies at the clinic for work, I knew it was going to be a daunting task. Let alone with one that had flat out denied us our pre-purchased and *existing* wind and flood coverage for our brand-new and expensive house. What was I going to plan on saying? If I couldn't convince them to reinstate us, what would we do? A knot gripped my stomach and I was back in purgatory.

I heard the door to the room click open. "Nick?" I called out from the shower, to which there was no answer. "Hello?" I said again, turning off the water and grabbing the towel. I stayed behind the locked bathroom door until I heard the room door shut again. Great. Now what was I going to do? Either someone was in my room waiting for me to get out, or no one was in the room and I could stop hiding behind the door with only a damp towel around me.

"Hello?" I said again.

No one answered.

I grabbed my pink razor, secured the towel around me, and quickly opened the door and jumped out, wielding the razor in front of me. I quickly scanned the room, but no one was there. My heart slowed its rapid adrenaline pounding to nervous pounding. The door clicked open again. I was frozen in my stance, not sure if I was going to fight or run.

But it was only Nick after all. "Jesus, Cole! It's just me. Are you okay?" he said as he saw me clutching my towel and razor.

I relaxed again, dropping the razor and sitting on the bed. "I heard someone come into the room when I was in the shower and I didn't know if anyone was still here. Then you came in and scared the crap out of me."

"Oh, love, come here. It was probably the cleaning person." Nick came over to me and embraced me in his big strong arms and starchy uniform.

Once my breathing steadied, he sat me on the bed and looked into my eyes. "I have some news you're probably not going to like."

I stared at him, not knowing what emotion was going to win this time.

"I'm going to head back to New Orleans to help open up the port. Only military is allowed back in right now and they need eyes on the ground to relay information as to what is happening there. No one knows."

I let this sink in. "So you're saying I'm stranded," I finally said. "This is just great. No car, no home, no job, and now no husband."

Before I could launch into a tirade of swearing, he added one more gem.

"Well, I thought you could head back north to be with family until the city reopens. You'll be better there around loved ones. Plus, there's another hurricane coming this way and you'll have to evacuate the hotel anyway."

"Are you fucking serious?" I couldn't believe what I was hearing.

"It's not confirmed yet, but this new one, Rita, is on a similar path."

"You know what? I'm done with all of this. This sucks. Who lives like this? I can't deal with all this stress and uncertainty. What are you going to do? You can't be ordered to stay there, can you?"

"No, I'll probably evacuate to Florida for a few days then go back in."

I could feel my cheeks flush, and then, without warning, unstoppable tears started streaming down my face. I cried for what felt like a whole day. I had such a tension headache by the end of my cry that I couldn't hear what Nick was trying to say to me. I held my head in my hands. He handed me my pajamas and he got into his boxers. We both crawled into bed and fell asleep, tightly holding each other as if to keep the cruel outside world from hurting us more.

The next day I saw Susie again at the bar talking to a man I assumed was a Coastie—he had short hair, muscular arms, was young and polite, and was dressed in a collared shirt. I took the chair on the other side of her and ordered my drink from the bartender.

Susie heard my voice and turned around. "Cole! It's you! Girl, where you been? I had to lose at bingo all by myself. Well, almost all by myself," she said in a leading way, smiling at the man next to her. "I thought I was going to see you too."

"Hi, Susie. I didn't feel much like bingo last night. Sorry. I hope I'm not interrupting," I said with a forced smile.

"Not at all, I was getting to know Richard a little better." She swiveled so we could see each other. "Richard, this is Cole. Cole, Richard."

"Hello," I said politely, quickly glancing at him and looking away. I was not in the mood to meet new people. Thoughts were swirling in my head as to what I was going to do about this new hurricane coming.

"Hello, ma'am, we actually already met. We were almost roommates."

"Oh, yes, that's right," I said. "I'm so sorry—I'm not myself today." I felt embarrassed that I hadn't taken the time to really look at him.

"Not a problem," he said cheerfully. "There's a lot going on."

"Yeah, that's an understatement." I turned to Susie. "I'm going to be leaving tomorrow to drive back north. Nick has orders to go back to New Orleans and there's yet another damn hurricane coming."

"Well," Susie said, "I hope you reconsider and come with me to Texas instead. I have some New Orleans friends hiding out there until they open the city up. I know a lot of cool dance clubs we could shake our booties at!"

"Thanks, but I don't feel much like dancing," I said. "I hope we can stay in touch, though."

"Of course! The offer still stands in case you change your mind."

"Thanks, Susie, I appreciate it. I hope I get to see you again when we're all back in the city."

I wasn't in the mood for small talk. Watching the other patrons at the bar, who were all laughing and having a good time, with apparently not a care in the world, made me feel isolated as I thought about the uncertain state my life was currently in.

I got my beer to go—something I would miss about New Orleans' culture—and walked slowly and deliberately toward the hallway, back toward the jail cell of my room. I opened up the door to our room and walked to the phone, feeling dread at what I had to do, rather than wanted to. I picked up the phone, but the dial tone was loud and offensive. I placed the receiver back down, stopping the obnoxious sound. I rummaged through my belongings and found my atlas. Opening up the large book, I spread it on the bed. I found my location and then viewed the swath of states leading back to Ohio. Not knowing anyone in between, I knew I had to either drive seventeen hours straight or stop somewhere alone, without Nick. Neither sounded like a great option. "Oh, crap," I said out loud to no one. I realized I was without a car. I flopped back on the bed. *This is going from bad to ridiculous*, I thought. I leaned on an elbow and grabbed the phone. I started calling any and all major airlines I could think of to try to figure out how I could fly out of here. Flights were still grounded out of most of Louisiana. I would need to get a ride to the next northern state or Texas, since the neighboring states to the east were all damaged by the storm. All options still required a car. A bus wasn't much of an option either, since there wasn't one around here and I really didn't want any more adventures in my life right now. *All right then, life: I see your challenge and I'll raise you.* I grabbed the phone and called Susie. It went to voicemail, which I expected. "I need a favor," I said. "Can I borrow your car tomorrow? I'm going to buy one so I can get the hell out of dodge." I hung up, feeling renewed in my willpower. I now had a plan: I was going to get a car and drive north. I'd found my big-girl pants, and I wasn't going to take them off.

CHAPTER SIX

BIG-GIRL PANTS

The next day started as almost all the previous ones had recently. Nick wasn't back yet from his shift and I was just waking from a fitful night, still not knowing which part of the day I belonged to. But this day I had a new determination in my step, feeling as if it was me alone against the world.

The hours were ticking away until Nick would leave me to go back to New Orleans, and I was not about to be stranded in this hotel. I found Susie's car keys slid under my door with a note of good luck. I didn't bother finding her, in case her night had led to more exciting events than mine. I grabbed the keys, thanking my lucky stars that I'd made a friend here, and walked down the dank hallway into the open air.

Most of the car dealerships opened in an hour, but I needed to just get out and start looking at what was available in the car lots. I'd never bought a car by myself before and didn't want to come across as the damsel in distress. I drove to the main street that had row after row of dealerships stocked with cars, thankfully.

It didn't take me long to rule out the ones I didn't want to be driving. It actually felt empowering to say no to a car salesman and see his face squish in disbelief. Giddy, I entered my borrowed car and drove to the next lot, repeating the process until I found one I could see myself driving away in. I couldn't decide on one I'd actually like and one that would be appropriate for my situation. I decided to work both angles. I sat down with one salesman, who was playing the typical part.

"So is your husband or dad meeting you here or are you shopping alone?" he asked.

"Can you believe it? I'm all by myself and aiming to buy a car today," I said, already a little aggravated.

"Oh, good. Do you have a favorite color you'd like to see?" he followed up.

My face reddened immediately and unintentionally. "Actually, I have a set price and would be willing to forgo my favorite color for affordability," I answered in a measured tone. I hated being treated as a dumb girl. He sat me down in his office filled with glass awards for Best Salesman of the Year. I knew what I wanted to spend on a car, and we went around and around on the price. He left me to sit alone for some time while he "spoke with his manager." I looked at my watch, realizing I had been dealing with this guy now for hours.

I knew what he was doing—waiting me out so that I'd crack and agree to his price, with the hopes of me leaving sooner rather than later. Though growing increasingly frustrated sitting in adult time out, I had the resolve to wait it out. What else did I have to do with my time anyway?

The salesman came back all smiles to tell me that he'd love to sell me the car at my price but could not. My body was sweating aggravation toward this man. Almost as if planned, my phone rang. It was Susie. I answered it right in front of him.

"Hello? Oh, yes, I am actually still very interested in the car! Really? That's great! I'm at another dealership, yes, looking at another car. I'll be right over though. Thank you for working with me." I hung up without giving Susie a chance to have any fun with my situation. "Oh, excuse me," I said to the salesman, whose blood was rushing from his face. "That was another dealership that accepted my offer."

"You're working with another dealership?" His eyes widened. "I thought you were interested in this car." His tone was full of agitation.

"Yes, I like this car better, but this other car is a better price and it doesn't have as many miles on it like this one does. Like I told you, I'm buying a car today," I said calmly. "You have my price and I'm already here. You can close the sale now with me or if you're not willing to meet my price, I'll go elsewhere," I said, cold and deadpan to his face.

"Wait here," he said as he left to find his manager. He returned with the signing papers. "If you agree to close the deal right now I can meet your price. Just sign here."

My heart leapt out of my chest with excitement. I didn't want to give too much away and forced myself to take a pause. I sighed. "Okay, you have a deal."

I signed all the required paperwork and made arrangements to pick the car up the following morning. I requested to have the car detailed before I picked it up, but didn't think it would happen considering our cordial but tense exchange. *Hell, I'm on a roll*, I thought. I left after nearly an entire twelve-hour day looking at cars with keys to my new-to-me car in hand. When I got back to the hotel parking lot I jumped out of Susie's car and ran, skipped, floated to greet her.

"I bought a car today!" I cried out.

Susie squealed and gave me a big bear hug. "I knew you could do it, girl! Nice play on the phone by the way!"

"It was perfect timing that you called! The deal was almost dead."

She grabbed my hand and we ran with her leading me to the bar. "I want to hear every detail!"

It was the happiest I'd felt in weeks.

After a beer, I wanted to share my excitement with Nick. I left Susie with the promise I'd meet up later that evening to catch up more. I opened the door to our room and saw Nick milling about. I ran toward him, my heart pounding with excitement. I was about to jump into his arms to tell him my good news when I saw his suitcase opened on the bed and fully packed. I stopped in front of him, feet glued to the floor and my arms weak as I looked up at him, trying to will him not to leave.

"You're leaving?" I asked, hoping to hear another reason for his packed bags.

"My orders came in today. I wanted to tell you but you weren't here. Where were you?"

I now felt foolish. "I bought a car today," I said, my elation seeping away. I felt empty.

"Oh! Really? What kind? Did you go with someone?"

"No. I went alone," I told him, saying it bitterly instead of with the joy and pride I had originally intended. I was beside myself with emotion. Seeing his suitcase all packed up made reality come slamming on my chest again.

"You went alone? You could have told me."

"I was trying to take care of myself in this situation. How else was I going to leave this hotel? Our car is in New Orleans." To which Nick didn't say anything. We looked at each other in silence.

I then slowly began to speak in a softer tone, realizing that we were both about to leave here and go our separate ways. I had no way of knowing when we'd be reunited. "I went by myself. Got a good deal. I'm picking the car up tomorrow. When are you leaving?"

"In just a few hours—I'm so glad I found you."

I threw my arms around him and started to sob.

"Cole, that's great about the car—I'm so proud of you. Are you going back up north?" He knew me so well—I felt simple and predictable.

"Yes, I don't know where else to go. When will I see you again?" I asked, negative thoughts seeping into my brain. Nick, the man who had taken me out of my comfort zone and dragged me south, was now leaving me because his job required him to do so. What kind of life had I signed up for?

"I don't know if I can make the trip by myself," I said. "I want you to be with me."

"Oh, Cole, I want to be with you too, but you know I have to go back to New Orleans. I have orders." My heart broke. He looked me right in my eyes and held my arms with his large hands. "Where is that Collette who just bought a car all by herself? Where is that person? You can do this. It's just temporary. Once they open up the city, I'll come up and get you, and we can be together again. It'll be okay." He squeezed me close to him.

"I'll miss you," I said desperately. We kissed passionately. He wiped the tears from my eyes and laid me down on the bed.

We made love and held each other tightly. We were calm and sweaty when he got up to leave. He dressed slowly and quietly. When he was done, I willed myself up as if I was having an out of body experience and walked with him to the door, clutching the bed sheet around me. He gave me one last kiss, said he loved me, and left. The door made the familiar empty dull thud as it closed.

I turned back toward the empty room and stared at the ugly beige walls. I stood there, sweat still dripping from me, beside myself as to what just happened and what I was supposed to do. It felt as if time had stopped. I moved to shake off reality. In the few weeks I'd spent there, New Orleans had taught me that reality was only a point of view. I forced myself to step out of the shell that was my body into my new self—confident, my survivor self.

◦

The next day I needed to pick up my car and make plans. I washed away any traces of the old Collette, the one that had stood terrified in the shower that night, and I emerged into my new self. I picked up the phone and called my one friend.

"Hello?" a groggy voice answered. It was 9:30 a.m.

"Girl! It's me!" I paused, being as persuasive as I could be with my next breath. "Time to pick up my getaway car!" I let the last word linger to sound more exciting. "Maybe it'll drive me to Texas."

"Oooh, don't you go teasing me now, Collette!" Susie's voice sounded much more awake now.

"I don't mean to bother you, but I need you to come with me to get Amelia."

"What?" Susie said incredulously and giggled. "Amelia? Is that the name of your car? I love it! I don't get it, but I love it! I'll be in the lobby in ten minutes."

I heard a male voice in the background and Susie hushing him up. A smile came across my face. I loved this woman—she truly had a knack for attacking life. I wanted to learn how to do that. I needed to learn in order to survive this situation.

I met Susie in the lobby, exchanged knowing smirks and a hug, and walked to her car.

"Okay, what's up with the name?" Susie asked directly.

"Well," I said, "Amelia Earhart had her plane to make an epic journey and I have this car. I'm channeling her for strength."

"You're so awesome!" Susie squealed, laughed, and continued. "Collette, how do you know a conversation with a pilot is half over?"

I looked at Susie wide eyed. "*The* pilot, Susie? Oh my God!" I giggled like a little girl now knowing who she was referring to.

"He stops talking about himself and starts talking about his plane!" Susie laughed so hard a snort came out of her and she hit me on my back. We both had tears in our eyes from laughing. Susie caught her breath. "Good for you, girl! I can't wait to meet Amelia!"

"We're going to have lots of adventures together," I remarked.

"Well, you'll need a soundtrack for your journey," Susie suggested.

"You're right. After I pick her up I'll go to the music store," I said with determination. As we drove out of the parking lot I thought about how lucky I was to have met her. "I'm so thankful you're helping me out," I said as I touched Susie's hand.

"Stop it, you're my friend, Cole. I'm happy I can help you," Susie responded, staring at me instead of the road, which made my heart skip a beat out of fear for crashing into something.

And there she was, just waiting for me to get in and start her up. Not detailed, as I'd requested, but I wasn't going to put up a stink about that. I let the salesman have that win. I just wanted to leave and start my new journey.

Susie and I hugged and wished each other luck as we parted ways. I drove off in my new-to-me car surrounded by its faint plastic car smell. Amelia took me to the nearest music shop. I got out and entered this utopia of songs that would signify my journey to come. I was in search of songs that were full of love, broken souls, and determination. I had no idea what I was about to do, but I needed encouragement. I bought Jim Morrison, Janis Joplin, Prince, and The Meters for good measure. I had my soundtrack for my trip to nowhere. I checked out and headed back to the hotel, determined to pack up and leave Louisiana. I was beside myself with confidence. My fuck-it attitude was emerging and I was not to be fucked with.

Gliding past the bar, I waved to Bill and headed to my room. I suppressed that familiar feeling of depression, packed it up and put it into the far corners of my heart and mind. I threw the rest of my stuff into a bag, did a quick check around the room, and left. I had been in that hotel room for days, but it felt much, much longer.

While packing, I found a check that my parents had sent me. It was from a collection that had been taken up in our names by my church back home. Mama had mentioned to the priest that we had lost everything we owned in Katrina. I held one thousand dollars in my hand in one flimsy piece of paper. I just stared at it. I didn't call to thank her for doing this for us; I was preoccupied by everything that had happened. But I knew that wasn't an excuse for my lack of communication. I packed up the car and drove to the nearest bank to deposit the check. I thought of Nick while I was driving. I hoped that he was doing okay. I wanted desperately to know what it was like back in New Orleans after the storm. My cell phone service was shaky, so my phone call to him would have to wait until I was on the road.

CHAPTER SEVEN

HOMEWARD BOUND

I sat in the car, hands on the wheel. I knew I had to drive and make a decision. Did I want the reality of going back home to stay with my parents, or did I want to take Susie up on her offer to drive to Texas with her?

I did miss home and my parents. I felt like a fish out of water in Louisiana, but something in me was slowly changing. I shook it off, opened the atlas again, and planned my trip.

With Nick gone, what else could I do? My security blanket was the north, and it was the only thing I knew and could count on. The hotel parking lot was now mostly empty, from families leaving to evacuate before the next hurricane blew toward us, but also from Coasties going to NOLA to report back on the current state of affairs there. There was a dearth of knowledge concerning the aftermath of this storm. I searched for my new Janis Joplin CD and slid it into the slot above the radio.

I needed something loud to drown out the screaming thoughts in my head. I started driving, singing and screaming with Janis down the road. It was very cathartic. The entire CD finished in what seemed like no time at all. I recognized a bank where I could deposit the check and spotted a coffee shop next door. *Yes*, I thought. I pulled in to get a coffee and stretch for the long drive ahead.

Just as I walked back outside with my cup o' joe, my phone rang. I couldn't believe it worked! I must have been in range now to receive calls. I grabbed it, hoping to see Nick's number, but it was Mama.

"Hi, Mama," I answered, feeling guilty for wishing it was Nick instead.

"Oh, honey, it's been so long since we talked!"

"My cell phone hasn't worked well since the storm."

"How are you?" she asked, sounding concerned at my tone. "Are you getting out of there? Why don't you come home?" It was a flurry of one-way conversation that was heavy with stress, emotion, and conviction.

"I am, Mama. I'm on my way now." I was about to continue but was cut off by her sudden screech.

"Oh, praise Jesus! I was hoping you'd come home! Where are you now? Is Nicholas with you?"

"It's complicated. I was going to call and tell you once I was in cell phone range again. There is no coverage here. Maybe the towers blew down? I don't know. I'm only an hour out of town, and I have a long drive ahead of me, but I'll stay in touch."

"Where's Nicholas?" Mama sounded concerned, and I scrambled for the right words to put her at ease.

"He was ordered to return to NOLA and report back, since no one has any real details about what is going on there."

"You're driving by yourself?" she said in disbelief. Mama herself was not a confident driver, ever since a car accident she'd had when she was younger.

"How else am I supposed to get home? I guess I can pick some-one up along the way . . ." I trailed off as if I was really thinking about doing this, and knew it would have the desired effect.

"No! Don't you dare! Oh, Collette, be safe while you're driving. Please don't make me worry."

Too late, I thought. "I'll be fine. I figure it'll take me a few days with stopping, so I'll be in touch." I wanted to get off the phone, but then remembered the check I just deposited. "Oh, and Mama, thank you for collecting and sending that money. I just deposited the check. It was a very kind and loving gesture. And very generous too," I added.

"We had to do something. The church had an extra collection for you. I'm so glad you're coming. Drive safely. I love you."

"Love you too." I hung up and felt as if the little confidence I had was gone now. *I can do this; it's just driving for God's sake.* I repeated the mantra to myself. *I can do this.*

Back in the car, I put Janis on replay and continued my jour-ney. After a while of driving out of town the scenery drastically changed. There was nothing for miles, just road and dirt. Huge metal poles stuck up from the ground every few miles. *What was that?* I wondered and tried to make sense of it. *There's another, and another. Where the hell am I?* I began to wonder and fear now. There were no distinguishing features to this landscape at all. Then finally a mysterious pole had the remaining attached advertised highway sign dangling by one corner and swaying slowly. *Holy shit*, I murmured to no one. Then more destruc-tion became visible. On the left side of the road was a roof that belonged to a gas station on the ground, as if it had been flat-tened by the weight of a giant's shoe. I saw my gas gauge and panicked a little, half full. Okay, no problem, at the next gas station I'd stop and fill up.

Miles passed with nothing but dusty visible grounds. Trees were scattered everywhere haphazardly with nothing else around. Where was everything? It was a wasteland for miles around. Another gas station came into view and my heart beat a little faster. As I drove closer, though, a surreal sight came into view: windows were blown out of what was left of the building, and gas lines and glass were strewn everywhere. I'd never seen such destruction. It dawned on me that I must be in Mississippi or possibly Alabama, but where? *Oh dear God, I'm lost already.* Both Mississippi and Alabama had been ravaged by Katrina along the coast. I meant to take a northern route, but I must have read a road wrong on my atlas. I must be going east, inadvertently taking a tour of Katrina's destruction firsthand. The whole area looked like a desert, with nothing for miles looking the way it should. My breathing became quick and my hands started to get cold and clammy even though it was ninety degrees outside. My gas gauge now read a little less than one-third of a tank. Ahead of me I began to see cars pulled off to the side of the road in a line. This was the first sign of life I'd seen in hours. There it was: a gas sign, like a mirage in a desolate place. "Yes!" I shouted to myself, so excited to catch a break. *I have all the time in the world,* I thought. *I'll wait in line for gas!* I was ecstatic. As I pulled off to get in line, I saw some people out of their cars milling about talking. I rolled down my window to eavesdrop.

"I'm not sure," said one guy.

"That's what I heard," said another.

"How is this possible?" a third said.

Now I needed to know what was going on. These were the first people I'd seen in hours and I needed to talk to them. Normally I'd avoid speaking to a group of older men at a gas station, but I felt that these extreme circumstances brought humanity together to help each other out.

"Hi," I said, smiling at them as I got out of my car and approached them. "What's going on here?"

"They're out of gas, hun," said the tall one wearing a baseball cap, with the brim creased down the middle.

I stood there in shock, eyes wide, my heart pumping. "No!" I said as if that could make the situation any different from what it was. "What am I going to do?"

"How much you got?" said the middle-aged man.

"Only a quarter tank," I said.

The third man, with dirty blue jeans, spoke up now with anger in his voice. "People are only supposed to fill up half their tank at a time during emergencies like this, so that everyone can get some gas. You get these assholes—pardon me, little lady—who fill up their whole truck and don't leave any for the rest of us."

"You may have enough to make it to the next station, but you're not getting any here," said the one wearing the baseball cap.

I turned in disbelief, stunned. My feet felt heavy as I willed them to walk back to the car. There was no emergency automotive assistance out there like there was back home to bring gas to you or give a tow. What was I going to do?

I got back in the car and tried to drive slow and coast when I could. On a mostly flat road, though, it didn't happen too often. I needed to do something to stretch out the remainder of gas I had. I was now praying out loud to find a gas station. I looked at the battery life on my phone and it read thirty percent. *Oh dear Jesus.*

I'd never been in this situation before. I couldn't draw on any past life experiences to help me. I was alone in the middle of nowhere with no food, water, gas, or phone charge.

For the next hour, I was on the verge of dry heaving. There was no music I could stand to listen to during this time. I drove in silence, scanning the road. I hadn't passed anything or anyone for miles. What were those people going to do back there?

I started to see a few abandoned cars along the side of the road. I needed a plan, but what was a good plan in this situation? I didn't seem to have many options. I could walk back to where those people were and maybe get help there. I'd have to leave my car—with all my luggage in it—behind just like the other cars I passed abandoned on the side of the road. *Maybe I should wait until the sun goes down so that I don't die in the heat without water*, I thought. Dire plan number two.

I looked at my melted ice swirling around in the brown water of what was left of my iced coffee. So dumb of me. Why hadn't I bought extra water or food when I had the chance? Why had I driven into Fucking Katrina-Town? My car's gas tank now read Empty. *How far can I go on "E"?* I wondered. *I guess I'm going to find out.*

I continued driving, scanning ahead of me for another station. Then I saw it. It was the most beautiful thing I'd seen all day, a working gas station. Though I wasn't sure if it was actually in use or damaged from Katrina. As I slowly coasted closer it seemed that it was in service. "Oh, thank you, Jesus," I said and started to cry, purging the pent-up emotions under pressure. I got out and through the intercom told the attendant what I thought my gas tank could hold. "Thirteen gallons, please." I flipped on the pump and beautiful gas started pumping into my car.

I got to the halfway point of the tank and remembered what the men had been discussing at the last gas station. I put my head down and truly felt guilt and shame as I squeezed the handle harder and filled my car all the way. *I don't know when the next time I'm going to be able to fill up will be*, I thought to myself, *and I'm lost, alone, and a woman.* I needed to look out for me right now. Thank God I had cash on me to pay for gas. Some last words of advice uttered from Nick instructed me to have lots of cash on me, since credit cards and ATMs weren't working anywhere in the destroyed areas. He should have warned me about bringing supplies too! I was such an idiot. I couldn't believe that this place was open and that I'd almost died. Walking into the small store to pay, I saw the few bottled waters remaining and grabbed two and a candy bar. There wasn't much else on the shelves. I thanked my lucky stars and the man working there.

"I'm just happy I still have gas left. Ya know, many stations are all out," he said.

"I'm wondering if you can help me out, sir," I said, trying not to sound too desperate. "I haven't seen any road signs, so my atlas isn't much help. I need to drive north and get to a more populated area. Can you direct me?"

"Sure thing, sweetie. You all alone?" His questioning brown eyes fixed on mine, waiting for my response. The words coming out of his mouth hung in the air like a possible threat.

Trying to figure out my next move, I looked to see how far away the door was. An icy sensation filled my arms, and the fear must have shown on my face, because the attendant noticed.

"I'm sorry, darling—wasn't my intention to make you nervous. Just follow this road until you see Cypress Street. Oh, hold on, that's right, the signage has all gone and blown away. Um, let me see here, there should be a big tree . . ."

Of course all the signs had blown away. *Could I just push reset on this video game now?* I wanted everything to be normal again. I was never going to be able to follow these directions.

I stopped listening once he started describing foliage I'd never even heard of before. I thanked him and left quickly, still not entirely sure of my safety. I got in the car, locked the doors, and drove off. Once down the road a bit I pulled over and looked at my map. I figured out where I'd taken the wrong turn a while ago and estimated where I was now. I tried to think of other clues to gain in my situation. I hadn't passed any cars in a long time, so trying to look at license plates for clues wasn't an option. There were few if any cars on the road. Even if I did spot one, how would I know if it was a local car or not? I looked at my gas receipt for a clue. The address header said Mobile, Alabama, yet another state that had gotten leveled from that bitch Katrina. I was too far in this state to just turn around. Interstate 65 should get me out of here. It was a main interstate, and I hoped that even if the signs were gone, the road would be more recognizable than some big tree I was supposed to turn by. That big tree might not even be standing at this point anyway.

With my car filled up and me sipping on the precious water I now had, I tried to head north yet again. In my long-term memory, I stored this life-saving bit of information: if I was to take any big solo trips in the future, I'd need to pack a blanket, phone charger, water, snacks, a flashlight, and, most importantly, avoid natural disaster areas.

I switched the radio back on and removed the screaming Janis for a new soundtrack, still loud and confident but not as manic. Prince and I bounced down the road and I imagined a little red Corvette. I had my new driving groove.

By some grace of God, I saw an overpass that looked like a highway, and entered what I was hoping was the on-ramp going north. I kept up the mantra *I can do this. I can do this.* I couldn't get to civilization fast enough.

I started seeing life around me: birds, people, cars, and intact signs. Relief rushed over me. I felt as if I was safe in America again and not the war-torn country I'd just come from. I pulled over at a real gas station, flush with people, lights, and advertisements, assured that there would be gas and a bounty of provisions. There were more cars here than I'd seen in hours, and all had Alabama plates. I entered the store with humility. I felt embarrassed to ask the clerk, but I needed to know. "Hello, ma'am, could you tell me what city this is?"

She paused and gave me a curious look as if I was a runaway or on drugs. "You're in Montgomery, Alabama, dear. Are you okay?" she asked, looking concerned.

"Oh, yes, thank you," I said, and quickly added, "I've evacuated from New Orleans and there was no signage on the roads anywhere."

"It's bad down on the coast. Glad you made it out safely! Have a good day now."

"Thank you," I said.

She nodded kindly and said "Next" to the customer behind me, though with no real hurry. I paid, smiled, and walked out the door. I got into the car with more snacks and opened up the atlas again: Montgomery was definitely heading north. Yes! I'm sure I looked like a crazy person. I was astonished at how just hours south people were struggling, dying, and suffering—such a stark difference from here. People were just going about their seemingly easy lives. I felt as if I'd just emerged from a different country and was now evaluating my own with fresh, critical eyes. I thought a lot about humanity on my continued long drive north.

CHAPTER EIGHT

FLOODED

In the early morning hours I turned into my parents' familiar neighborhood in Akron, Ohio. Rounding the corner, I saw the circle driveway to our house and pulled in. Mama and Dad greeted me at the steps with open arms. Mama hugged me first. For a small woman, her hugs were intense and strong.

"Okay, *okay*! I'm happy to see you too, Mama." I pulled away and gave her a kiss. Dad gave me a hug.

"How are you doing? You're okay." It was more of a statement than a question.

"Yes, Dad, I'm fine." That was the extent of our talk. He wasn't much into long emotional conversations—that was Mama's department.

I was so relieved that I'd been able to complete the long drive solo. My mind raced with events and scenarios that had kept me busy. I reminded myself that I still needed to call the insurance people, a task too difficult to accomplish when my days were my nights. While at the hotel, I'd even set my alarm to wake up at one in the afternoon to make my calls, only to be bombarded with busy signals and endless looping phone trees for hours. I was sure everyone was calling about their own claims. I could try to get my life in order now that I was back in the functional, non-flooded world up north.

I got my things from the car and brought them into the house. After removing my shoes, of course, I turned to head upstairs to my once familiar little girl's room. Standing there scanning the stuff that I'd grown up with I felt like a failed adult, back home with my parents. Downstairs Mama had the kettle on getting ready for the typically informative "talk" we were about to have. I used to love our talks when my life was simple and stable, but now I didn't even know where to begin or what to say. Mama was a bit of a worrier and always needed constant reassurance. In my current state, though, I was barely able to comfort myself, let alone others. I walked downstairs and Mama set two cups of tea out on the table and sat smiling with anticipating, loving eyes, inviting me to join her.

"Do you care if I make some calls first? I need to call the insurance company."

"Oh, sure honey," she said. "Can I stay?"

"Yeah." I didn't care how much personal information I said out loud. It wasn't lost on me that this was her intention in remaining at the table. There I sat, back at the same kitchen table with my mama doing my homework as if I was a little girl again and life was easy.

After a few failed attempts at getting a human being on the phone, I eventually was transferred to a person, then another, and another. Relieved, I finally got someone who I could explain my letter to.

"We have pictures of a workman's pole in front of your house indicating the house is still under construction and doesn't qualify for insurance assistance," she told me.

Anger and fear filled my body. "That's a mistake. We've been living in the house for two months. The pole was removed after we bought the house, and I set up the utilities myself. I even have receipts from the first payment," I said, so thankful that I'd brought the bills and paperwork with me in my last-minute rush out of our house.

Thinking I'd cleared up the little misunderstanding, I waited for the apology and reinstatement from the other end of the phone. Instead, the woman flatly stated there was no way of confirming my statement in order to overrule the decision. The insurance would not be reinstated. "Is there anything else I can do for you today?" she asked.

Shocked, I asked to speak to someone else, anyone else. My request was denied, and she hung up. I froze, listening to the harsh dial tone, defeated, confused, and angry. I looked at my mother, tears welling up in my eyes. "Life isn't going well for me right now," I told her. I tried to hold back the flood of emotion but couldn't. I put my head down in my arms and cried, still holding onto the cordless phone. Mama gently took the phone out of my hands and hung it up. Our long talk was now derailed. Without knowing words to say, Mama just rubbed my back, letting me release tears.

A week went by, with me mostly spending it in the quiet solitude of my mind. I kept texting Nick, waiting for him to reply. I wanted to tell him about the insurance and was worried about him in New Orleans. The news never had anything of value to me. It was all people struggling to survive in flooded streets. I wanted to hear if there were basic utilities back online, what the current state of our street was, and whether my house was safe. Was it still standing? I ached to hear Nick's voice. I took up knitting in order to look busy and feign content so that my hands could be doing something while my mind was busy replaying all the what-if scenarios. My parents were desperately trying to fill the days with normalcy: watching TV together, eating together, cleaning together—any activity where there was an uneasy sense of quiet purpose. As with most sensitive topics, not bringing it up was a way of making it go away.

⌒

I had just put down my knitting to make room for Pork Chop, our little Shih Tzu, to jump on my lap, when I thought of the joke Nick told me.

"What's the difference between a good zoo and a Shih Tzu? A good zoo serves beer. A Shih Tzu doesn't," to which he'd follow up with, "NOLA's zoo is a good zoo."

Pork Chop jumped off my lap and ran into the laundry room, emerging with one sock a few minutes later, tail wagging and hair flowing. I watched her happily prance by, probably off to find a good hiding place for it and knowing it would cause my mama frustration later when trying to find the match to the sock. Mama came into the room.

"You know who I ran into at the church Sunday? Of course you don't—if you'd come with me you would know," Mama said, answering her own question in a not-quite-teasing way.

"Jesus," I responded in the same tone.

She shook her head and waved her hands to dismiss my comment. Ignoring my sarcasm, she continued, "Peter and his mama! Everyone is so concerned about you and what you're going through. Peter is doing quite well for himself these days, you know. He got a promotion at his firm. Maybe you can talk to him about the insurance problem? He gave me his number for you."

"I don't know, Mama. Seems a bit odd for me to call him. We haven't spoken since I got married."

"Well, I don't see the harm in it. You both were so close."

"Not just close. We *dated*."

"Yes, I know that, but I don't think that should stop you from calling up an old friend. He might be able to give you some free advice too."

"I'll think about it."

It was a very appealing suggestion. I really needed to speak to someone to get real advice. Plus, it would be nice to catch up again, platonically of course. After dinner and helping Mama out with dishes, I decided to give Peter a call. I picked up the cordless phone and went upstairs to my bedroom. I felt silly, as if I were transported back to being that teenage girl again calling my boyfriend. Except this time, instead of being tethered to a wall and stretching the cord out to reach a semiprivate place to talk, I was lying on my bed staring at the phone's number pad in my hand.

I took a breath and dialed his number.

"Hello?" The sound of Peter's voice made me smile and I felt a small, guilty flutter in my chest.

"Hi, Peter. It's Collette."

"Collette! Hey! So happy that you called. How are you? It's been a while."

"Yes, I know. I hope you don't mind me giving you a call out of the blue. I heard from my mama you ran into her."

"Yes, at church. I give my mom a ride there on Sundays and then we go out for brunch. It's our way of seeing each other every week. My work can get a bit hectic and I tend to get smothered in to-do's."

The conversation had an awkward, nervous tension from us both.

"Congratulations on your promotion," I said.

"Ugh, it's so embarrassing when she does that. But thank you. I hear that New Orleans is a bit rough right now . . . your mom told me how you had to drive back home alone and mentioned your horrible insurance problem. I'm sorry that you're having to deal with so much. If I can be of any help, please let me know."

"I guess it's a silver lining of the hurricane that we get to talk again."

"Collette, once you got married, I didn't think it would be appropriate for me to be calling you."

"You're right, I completely understand. We have a lot to catch up on."

I started to explain what it was like preparing for the storm and then watching helplessly as it hit. I didn't want to get too much into my relationship troubles, but did want him to realize life wasn't going great right now for me, hoping that this would open the door for him to continue to talk to me. Of course, I had to tell him all about Susie too. Glancing at the clock on the wall, I couldn't believe we'd been talking together for over two hours. I heard all about his busy, wonderfully boring life as well. It sounded so normal. I yearned for life to be simple again.

"I hope that we can talk more while I'm at home," I told him.

"I'd really like that," he said.

Hanging up with Peter, I sat on the bed, flush with happiness. I was finally able to breathe and relax in a way that I hadn't felt in a long time.

Almost on cue, the phone rang shortly after I hung up.

"Hello?" I said in a silly, happy voice, thinking Peter may have forgotten to tell me something.

"Cole! Hey, babe, you sound great. How are you?"

Guilt and surprise flushed my cheeks. "Nick! Oh my gosh, hi, love. It's been so long since we've talked. I was just talking to Mama." I cringed. I didn't want to think how it would go over if he discovered I'd been talking to my old boyfriend, but I was so happy to finally hear his voice again.

"Aw. Tell her I said hello. I'm glad being there is good for you. But I do miss you."

"Same here. Where are you? What's going on?"

"I've been working like crazy down here. We've been pulling twelve-, sometimes fourteen-hour workdays every day. It's been pretty amazing though—the Coast Guard has really empowered people to make decisions so that tasks can get done quickly. Normally, things need to go all the way up the chain for approval. I'm actually getting to call some of the shots myself—it's so awesome. The sheer amount of work that needs to be done is so overwhelming. It's amazing to be so trusted in all of this." He paused, as if thinking about this statement he'd just made.

I muffled my urge for an outward *ugh*, and had to remind myself that I was supposed to be supporting him, cheering him on. I forced myself to step back away from my frustration about being separated from him. I was really thankful for all the Coast Guard was doing to get New Orleans on its feet again and grateful that I had Nick telling me about the progress that so many people had no idea about. I wished that the news outlets would make all the Coast Guard efforts more visible to the public so that everyone could know about what they were doing. Still, I was aware that my current situation involved Nick helping the people and the city of New Orleans out, and I was sitting there waiting for something to happen with my life.

"That's really great," I said, realizing I hadn't responded yet to his very long story.

He continued, apparently not noticing. "Do you know that the

Coast Guard put our team in charge of opening the port back up? It's a huge task."

"I think you told me, but I still don't understand what that means. I'm happy for you, though," I said, still trying to get interested in the conversation.

"It means that all the important US commerce, like food being harvested, needs to get to NOLA so that it can be distributed to the rest of the country. That's where they load up huge barge boats that travel down the Mississippi River. But guess what?"

He didn't wait for my rhetorical *what.*

"It's not that easy, because there's like a thousand ships that sank in the navigable waterways! Combine that mess with the fact that there's massive impacts to the surrounding environment that have to be remediated as well. There's a lot of oil in the water from the storms. Some reports have projected that there's like over a million gallons of petroleum that was either discharged into the water or leaked from storage tanks that just up and floated off their foundation into the river!"

"Oh my God." Knowing the magnitude of the situation was overwhelming. How would one even begin to fix this crazy situation? I felt conflicted. I was proud of him, that he got to be part of this insurmountable task; after all, if he did well at his job it would benefit the both of us, but having purpose and success in my own life was put on hold until New Orleans was fixed. "I'm proud of you," I said, kicking my ball of knitting yarn as I walked over and sat on the chair in my room.

"Thanks, Cole. I really appreciate that."

Thinking about the list of tasks Nick had just rattled off to me, I asked, "Are there even enough people there to do all that work? Where is everyone staying?"

"Good questions!" Nick was clearly very happy to talk more

about this exciting time. "Get this—they brought in a cruise ship for first responders, so that people have somewhere to stay while working here! Isn't that wild?"

"Are you on the ship?" I asked.

"No, there's also a hotel. But get this—I found a rental house in the dry part of town to stay in! It's really cool inside, lots of artwork. Glad you asked that."

He was clearly working up to tell me something.

"I know I've been babbling for a while, I'm just excited to fill you in on all the work I've been doing. But I didn't call just to brag about your amazing husband, I called because I have great news!"

"What is it? I love great news!" I sat up straighter on the chair with anticipation. I was a bit guarded, seriously wondering what could be so great when everything about our lives sucked at this point. Maybe we were getting re-stationed somewhere else? That *would* be amazing and wonderful.

"They opened the city back up! You can come home!"

I stopped breathing for a second. My heart began to race—all of a sudden I felt like a trapped animal. Nick was brimming with excitement, and I just wanted to scream at my misfortune. *Go home to what?* I wanted to ask.

Nick continued over my silence, speaking rapidly. "I was cleared to take a few days of leave since I've been working nonstop for weeks," he said. "I'll fly up there and we can drive back together. Again!" He threw that last part in to be funny, but it wasn't to me. How many times was I going to drive to NOLA?

"Cole? Honey, are you there? Why aren't you saying anything? This is great news!"

"I don't want to go back," I managed to say without showing my true emotions.

"Cole, look: I'm here for three years—we can't live apart that long, nor do I want to. Come back with me and we'll start over. Work hard, play hard, remember?"

"Go back to what, a flooded house? The whole city is broken."

"We'll fix our house together. Everything will be okay. We'll be together again! The house will be better than before. I already put in my leave chit and I'm flying up tomorrow."

"I . . ." I started to say something and then stopped. I was still in shock at the immediate turn of events. "I'm still processing everything you just told me."

"What is it? Don't you want to see me?"

"Of course I do. I just didn't realize it would be so soon."

"It's great, right? I love surprising you!" he continued, either oblivious to my hesitation or ignoring it. "And I found out that the Coast Guard is bringing in some support here for the service men and women and their families, like Jags and medical."

"Jags are lawyers, right?"

"Yes."

"Oh my God, that would be so great to have a military lawyer help us out. I'll be first in line to tell them about our canceled insurance. I've been trying to text you about it. I called the insurance company and they are not reinstating our insurance. How are we going to fix up that flooded house without money?"

"The Jags will make this right. They should be able to put pressure on the insurance company to reinstate us. What a bogus letter. Insurance companies are trying to not go broke with all the people filing total loss claims at once."

"I sure hope you're right about that, because if you're wrong we're screwed."

"I'll go with you to talk to them—let's see what they can do. Make sure you bring that letter with you."

"I definitely will. Why will medical be there?"

"Oh, the medical . . . The military wants everyone to get Hep B shots as a precaution before going back to New Orleans. The floodwaters are unsafe to touch."

I couldn't breathe. There was so much new information to wrap my head around. I was glad to hear from Nick, but felt as if I was being forced back to a life I didn't want. Apparently, I didn't have any other choice—unless I wanted to stay here and keep knitting.

My eyes widened and I inhaled a silent gasp. "Okay," I breathed out. "It'll be good to see you again. See you tomorrow then."

I hung up the phone. Numbness, anger, fear: the familiar trio of emotions I kept trying to push away relentlessly kept returning. I walked back downstairs into the silent room where only the TV was talking. My mama, now confused at my expression, demanded to know what happened. She thought I'd had a bad call with Peter.

"No, I heard from Nick. He's coming tomorrow to take me back to New Orleans."

"Oh, why do you have to go so soon," she whined. "I've loved having you here this past month. Plus the holidays are almost here. Stay with us until things get better," she implored. "You can move back into your old room. We could do things together again like we used to do. Maybe you can even get your old job back, just temporarily. Nicholas can concentrate on his job and deal with the house. You could visit him and then eventually move back down there—once the city is better, of course."

What horrible and conflicting advice. I couldn't believe she'd suggest that—how was I supposed to be a good supportive wife from a thousand miles away? Didn't I need to be with him during this crappy time? Wasn't she supposed to be urging me to stay with him, not saying to me everything I was thinking and feeling? Now I had to be the strong one and pretend this was what I wanted.

"What happened to 'keep your husband happy' and 'you have to be a good wife'?" I said. "I have to go back, you know that." It wasn't reassuring—to her or to me—or by any means a good argument, but it was the best I could do at that moment.

Later that night, I lay on my bed hugging my pillow surrounded by my old stuffed animals and awards I received in high school. I knew I couldn't just stay here, a married woman living with my parents. How embarrassing for the family and for me. If I was going to be a good military wife, I needed to support Nick and do everything I could to make this work out. At least we'd be together, like he'd said. *Keep it together, Collette,* I reminded myself. It wasn't lost on me, the sacrifices that families and couples had to make living the military service life. There were countless other women separated from their husbands while they went off fighting wars away from their families—instead we were lucky enough to be fighting to survive together.

The next day I packed up my few belongings, said goodbye again, and stoically went to the airport to pick up Nick in my getaway car.

"Hello, love!" Nick gave me a big smile and embraced me. "God, I missed seeing you."

"I missed seeing you too," I said. "I hated being away from you, but I . . . I just really don't want to go back."

"I know you're hesitant, love, but we'll do this together," he insisted. "It's an adventure! I'm just so happy that we're back together—nothing else matters."

I wanted to kick him in the shins. How could he be so positive?

"Remember how we wanted to get rid of some of our stuff before the next move?" A twinkle came to his eye as he gave me a kiss.

"Right." I grabbed his hand and looked him in the eyes. "It was only supposed to be your stuff!" I replied and kissed him back. "I just don't even know where we're going to start or if we'll have money to fix up the house."

"I put us on the list to talk to the Jags. Let's let them figure it out, I know they will. The letter was bullshit. As for the rest, we'll make everything right one step at a time."

On the long car ride back down to NOLA, we talked the whole way. It was so refreshing yet embarrassing to speak so freely and openly to him about my fears—fears I couldn't begin to share with Mama. She would have been unable to or unwilling to accept the current realities that I was experiencing due to her unrelenting worry. I needed someone more stable, even if Nick was acting like a Pollyanna. I needed to keep up the guise for Mama that everything was fine and that I was handling it well. This was of course the furthest thing from the truth. Nick and I both knew that we were embarking on a very challenging, yet shared, part of history. Only he and I and all the people on the Gulf Coast who had an intimate knowledge of the situation could understand.

"You can't even imagine what it was like there in the beginning," Nick began.

Nothing surprises me anymore about NOLA, I thought. "Well, I had heard a few things," I said. "The news is saying that it's crazy there, everyone for themselves, people guarding their houses from looters with guns?"

"Not quite everywhere, but that is happening. I'm glad you boarded up our house. It was like the Wild West there in the beginning when I went back, right after Katrina. I'd only hear gunshots at night instead of music. There were even rumors that some of the rescue helicopters were shot at! Unbelievable. Most missions were during the day so the rescue teams could see people on their roofs or a hand poking out of an attic window. Oh, and there were a lot of random fires just blazing, smoke was everywhere."

"Sounds apocalyptic," I said, imagining some of the worst movie scenes I could recall.

"There's a lot of police presence, but I don't necessarily feel safer with them around. Everyone is spread really thin."

I sat there just listening to him describe scenes and stories of New Orleans I hadn't seen or heard before.

He went on. "I walked down Bourbon Street the one night and it was completely empty, quiet, and dark. The only bar open was Lafitte's." Nick's smile widened and he laughed a bit. "The bar looked the same after the storm as it did before—candles were flickering on every windowsill and table, not a lit light bulb anywhere."

"Please refrain from telling me about strippers who bravely stayed behind to keep spirits and other things high," I said. "Or fun fables of you buying more lonely girls drinks."

Nick looked at me in a calm, parental way. "Cole, you're crazy. No one was around. Only the day workers, the brazen people who stayed, and the military were in the city."

Not exactly the reassurance I wanted to hear, but it was something.

"There was one guy I saw," Nick continued, "obviously very drunk, minding his own business, when a group of kids came around the corner and saw him. I thought they were going to help him get home or something, but instead they just beat the shit out of him. I was hoping an MP would show up to handle the situation, but there was no one in sight and I sure as hell wasn't going to insert myself in a losing situation."

"Remind me why you think bringing me back is a good idea?" I asked. My mind flashed to our neighbors' house with all the guns in it, and I now wished I had some protection of my own.

Nick continued, "When we first arrived, we were driving around in a military jeep to see what downtown looked like. We were driving over lots of glass from the blown-out windows of the tall buildings, lots of debris, and of course standing water. As we drove over the bridge approaching the Superdome . . ." He paused, unsure if he should continue. "You know that all of the cell phone towers blew away, right? There was not much information coming out of NOLA about the city or the people in those early days right after the storm."

"I know; that's why we were only able to text each other." I motioned for him to continue with his story.

"Driving in and seeing the city for the first time was shocking. It was like the city had been reborn as a swamp again. Any oaks still standing poked out of the water around the flooded houses. The whole city was dark. There was no electricity, no air conditioning, it was insanely hot. When we came over the top of the interstate there were rows of dead bodies, covered and lined up on the side of the road. Who knows what happened when they were trying to escape. The people who evacuated to the Superdome suffered too. There weren't enough supplies. Not enough food, baby formula, just everything. Toilets backed up too—it was a mess. They're going to need to rebuild that whole thing." He was lost in thought for a minute, then looked at me and said, "I've been down our street too. There was still standing water on it, too high for regular cars to get through, but easy with an MV."

I was sitting in silence, trying to comprehend the gravity of everything he was describing to me. I hung on every word—especially once he started describing our street, which he hadn't done before. It was the first time he'd mentioned it. My heart pounded with the reality that I too was going to be immersed in this now.

I had so many questions to ask, but I wasn't sure I wanted the answers anymore.

"Remember the building on the corner of our street?" Nick said.

"Yeah," I said slowly.

"The entire metal roof blew off and landed all over the streets. It even hit some houses. Our house is okay though."

"It is?" I asked. "You mean from the roof or—"

He quickly clarified. "I mean, it's totally flooded, you can see the black water line on the exterior wood, but it's still boarded up and standing. Nothing appeared to have hit it though." This was supposed to make me feel better.

I sank back down into my seat. "What do you mean, 'water line'?"

"The whole city has dirty black water lines: the buildings, trees, anything that's still standing. It shows how deep the water got before it started to drain out. It took about six weeks, because the huge pumps that are supposed to move standing water out of the city flooded too, so the disgusting water filled with oil, sewage, household and industrial chemicals, gas, paint, mud . . . it just sat and soaked into everything. Wait until you see the cars!"

I let out a little groan. Nick continued over it.

"There are cars abandoned everywhere—they were parked under bridges and in parking lots when people evacuated. They're all flooded over their roofs and some floated away. I saw a huge boat that ended up on one of the major streets and had to drive around it."

The magnitude of disaster cleanup was making me dizzy. I glanced out my window as we rolled into NOLA proper. I spotted a large cardboard sign that read *Yankees Go Home*. I couldn't agree more.

CHAPTER NINE

ABANDONED

We moved into a rental apartment on the dry side of town with only a few of our belongings—luckily, the house was fully furnished with everything we needed. It was a year-long rental agreement, but I really hoped we wouldn't be living there for that long. Rentals were in high demand for the few souls determined enough or crazy enough to come back and start rebuilding their lives and homes again. The houses that were on high ground stood as trophies throughout the city. The lucky ones who had unknowingly bought in an area that didn't get destroyed. I fought back feelings of jealousy and anger. Why couldn't we have been the lucky few? I could just imagine the joy of coming back to the city, dusting off our furniture from weeks of neglect, and having only one concern: wondering when we could get a new refrigerator delivered.

Looking around the city I'd known only briefly, I now only saw damage in every direction. There was despair and garbage everywhere. The city's new skyline consisted of five-story-tall piles of trash: some for damaged, water-soaked wood and others for damaged, water-soaked personal items that told intimate stories of the lives everyone had had before August 29th. There stood the relics of happier days, destroyed and discarded from the homes they had inhabited just a short time ago. Children's toys and stuffed animals, once loved, were now covered in wet dirt and oil. They performed a balancing act on the garbage piles with broken chairs, tables, beds, books, and wet family pictures.

The whole city had blocks of abandoned houses with the tell-tale X on the door or on the wood siding that marked when someone had entered to search for those who had decided to stay behind and suffered the ultimate consequence. A number on the bottom of the X indicated how many dead bodies had been found inside.

Now I saw firsthand what Nick had described. The entire city had a dirty black line wrapping around everything. Trees, houses, cars—any and every erect structure—showed the height of the chemical- and sewage-filled water. Abandoned cars that had been parked under highways for safety were now fully drained of brackish water and were strewn about in dirty, haphazard piles. Boats were found on streets and on top of trees and houses, where the water had forced them to their new locations.

The areas not affected by Katrina were few, and the unaffected houses flaunted themselves proudly on the high ground they stood upon. The city was eerily quiet and still, grieving for the joyful, carefree New Orleans it had been.

As people started to slowly trickle back into town, the next items in line to decorate the streets were refrigerators duct-taped shut with the handles removed. People were advised to not open the doors for fear of the smell and mold that would come spilling out of the abandoned warm food coffins. They were considered a health hazard.

It was all too much to take in. Everywhere I looked there was movement, houses were being emptied of their contents and years of memories, the signs of daily life like appliances, furniture, decorations—the list was never ending. People were left with a shell of their broken houses and the broken souls who had once lived in them. Insurance companies were requiring a list of items damaged. It was a cruel task to ask of people to write down everything they'd used to make a life, along with the structure itself.

There was no one to help with this incredible task of removing items and rebuilding houses. No one to hire as day workers, since the only people allowed back into the city were the residents and military. All the manual labor to deal with the destruction was supplied by the homeowners and renters themselves.

Nick drove me to our house after a few days, once I was settled in the rental and he had some time off work. He tried to brace me for what I was about to see inside. Parking our car, I looked out the window and saw for the first time our broken home.

"I'm really glad you're here with me now. It's been really depressing for me to see so much destruction everywhere I go, including seeing our house. I never had the time to tell you about the house with work being unrelenting, but I also didn't know what to say to you, especially by text. I know we'll be stronger tackling this together," Nick said. "I want you to prepare yourself. It's going to be a shock. I've been back inside a few times and I'm not going to lie, the first time, it was really hard for me to look around. There's black mold everywhere and the place is a wreck. If we're doing it together, though, I think it'll be a lot easier on the both of us."

I held his hand and looked into his eyes. I knew this was something we had to do, but I didn't want to face it. I knew Nick had been through a lot recently—and that he trusted me enough to lean on me now in his time of need. I hated to remember how selfish I'd been to have wanted to avoid returning to our house.

"We can do this together," I said and gave him a kiss on the lips.

Cautiously, we went to face the house together, armed to the nines with the Tyvek suits Nick had obtained from work, along with face ventilators, booties, and gloves. I felt ridiculous gearing up on the street just to enter our house, but the inside wasn't safe with six weeks of black mold growing in it. It didn't help that the heat and humidity were the same inside the house as outside.

As I was getting ready, I could see everything was dead surrounding the house. The grass, trees, flowers. The neighborhood houses themselves had lost their life—their colors were drab, and all wore the black watermark of humiliation. I paused to fix my mask, the world around us completely still and quiet. No birds were singing, no voices were talking, no dogs were barking, no cars were moving, no wind was blowing. The only loud, piercing sound in the silence was the zipping up of our suits and the car doors shutting with a louder-than-normal thud.

Entering our house in full protective garb, I now saw firsthand what was left of our home. I stood in complete shock and dismay looking at the overturned tables, broken chairs, books with pages stuck to the floor, and the fish from our temporary tanks stuck to the walls—a cruel testament to their futile escape. The house told a story of what had happened in the darkness while we were gone. I imagined the house filling slowly with water, soaking everything we owned and moving it around the house as the water rose higher and then finally, six weeks later, lazily exited like a house guest that just wouldn't get the hint to leave. There was the sense of slow, deliberate movement created by the rising and falling of water instead of movements of people. Loved items had socialized, floating to other rooms. Fish had swum and died in the turbid toxic water; the refrigerator had floated up like a buoy and fallen back, splashing stagnant water on the walls and ceilings. Now it was settled like a noxious coffin on the wet floors.

Scum covered everything. Ceiling fan blades sagged from the excessive heat and humidity. Our ferns had grown to an excessive size, apparently loving this new environment. I walked slowly to the back of the house in a daze as Nick brushed by me, numb to the familiar destruction after everything he'd already seen. Before the storm we'd thoughtlessly gone shopping, filling the refrigerator with fresh vegetables, meat, fish, and beer. Clothes, some still hanging, were now streaked with black lines. Other objects were solidly stuck to the walls and furniture in a haphazard fashion. The pictures were the worst—once happy reminders of loved ones and experiences were now glued together by the brackish water and heat, and strewn randomly throughout the house, reduced to wet clumps of glossy paper.

Nick tried to snap me out of my walking coma by directing me to start collecting things that we could possibly clean and not throw out in the mound of trash he'd started outside on the lawn. I drifted back toward the kitchen and glanced into our bedroom, stopping at the entrance. I noticed the large flat box between the bed and the dresser with heavy wet pillows on top of it. I knelt and cautiously removed them, hoping that what I was about to find wasn't what I feared it was. Removing the pillows, I saw the warped, peeled corrugated cardboard box that held my wedding dress. Peering through the once clear window of the box, now covered with a murky film, I saw a deep-black-and-brown-stained satin dress.

My hands shook as I traced the outline of the black-stained lace bodice. Droplets of my own salted tears hit the warped cardboard, making soft dull thuds. I was as still as the stale air around me. Sadness and regret quietly stood on each side of me. My chest tightened as I tried to control my emotions, and I rose up, willed by something other than myself, and walked into the kitchen. In complete numbness, I started collecting our silverware, glasses, and pots—all brand new a few months ago, they now looked as if we'd found them in a dumpster. With only the rhythmic sound of my breath through the ventilator mask, I began to make a "clean" pile for keeping, while Nick continued to haul everything we owned to the curb.

"Cole? Can you help me with this couch?" he yelled through his mask.

I met him in the other room and grabbed the opposite arm of our once proudly purchased piece of newlywed furniture—we'd bought the loveseat a few months before our move, but now water-logged and mold-covered, it looked like a petri dish. Taking tiny steps under its weight, we finally heaved it out the door and down the broken steps. Stopping to regain my strength and breath, we made eye contact with each other and lifted each side again to finally place it on the street next to all our other trash. I took my mask off to breathe in the still, humid, moldy air.

Sweating through my plastic suit, I viewed the reminders of our past life, items that were now ruined and staged on the lawn. I saw our once gorgeous loveseat that I hadn't dared to even eat on a few months earlier. Defiantly, now standing on top of it, I let the springs move me up and down. The booties I wore to cover my shoes left black footprints on top of the cushions, which were themselves a gross brown color.

Nick watched me for a minute and then walked back inside. I couldn't tell what he was thinking or feeling with his ventilator on. I stepped down from the couch and slowly walked back up our broken steps and continued to work in our personal hell. It was starting to get dark outside, making it even darker inside. Hungry, dirty, and emotionally exhausted, we finally decided to take a break.

There was no electricity in our part of civilization, Mid-City. As night fell, the shadows masked the damage that was strikingly clear during the day. The neighborhood seemed more abandoned now that it was lacking light as well. We left the darkness and slowly saw streetlights coming on in the dry section of the city. We drove back to our rental in silence, too many thoughts and feelings whirling around in our heads. Nick parked the car on the street and we entered the dry, well-lit house—an alternate version of our lives. This one seemed made up, not chosen by us but by someone and something else. Living in NOLA had been a choice of realities, and those realities were changing with each new day.

Coming home from work, Nick opened the door of the rental house dramatically and bounded in to find me sitting on the couch staring at one of the paintings hanging on the wall.

"Collette! You'll never believe it! This is going to make your day!"

Startled from his entrance, I sat up. "Well, what is it?"

"The Jags were able to get our insurance reinstated! They're sending the check for the full amount of the house!"

I jumped off the couch and almost out of my skin with excitement. "Nick!" I yelled. "That's awesome!" I bounced up and down holding his hands like a kid. I suddenly stopped at a realization that popped in my mind. "Do you think we could sell our place and just buy another house? Maybe start over?"

"We could certainly look to see what's on the market. I'm sure any place still standing is asking top dollar, but it's worth checking out. I'll make some calls," Nick answered. I was giddy with the thought of running away from the destroyed house and hitting reset. An uncommon feeling of joy started to fill me up.

Within a few days Nick had found a realtor and a list of places in the dry zone, which was mainly Uptown. On Nick's day off we went looking at the houses that were not quite in our price range, but still hopeful. We looked at place after place, at houses that were like an oasis: clean, no water lines, but still with NOLA-style oddities about them. One had no grass whatsoever—it was all cement-paved where the lawn would have been. Another had the washer and dryer next to the stove in the kitchen. One we loved, but at the last minute the owner pulled it off the market; a change of heart, we were told.

"I do have one more you might be interested in," the realtor said. "It didn't sustain flood damage, but does have wind damage."

This was now the new bar to judge houses in NOLA; wind damage was better than water damage. We pulled up to the house on the Irish Channel side of town. It was small, but we didn't need anything large, especially not anymore. It looked perfect.

Surprisingly, it was lower in asking price than the other houses we saw that day. It all seemed too good to be true. I crossed all my fingers as we opened the door. Entering the first room, we didn't see anything wrong.

"Looks good so far," I said and glanced at Nick with hopefulness.

"There aren't any offers on this one?" Nick asked incredulously.

"Not yet," replied the realtor. We began to make our way through the single shotgun house and walked through the hallway to the kitchen. The sight before us took our breath away.

"Oh my God!" I shrieked. There was a gigantic tree poking through the roof like a lance.

The realtor smiled and said, "The tree comes free with the house." Not feeling the humor in the situation, I turned and walked out. On the ride home Nick spoke to me about possibilities. "We could just repair the roof and have a functional house, as opposed to fixing up an entire house."

"So we could own two destroyed houses?" I asked. "Let's just continue with our big crappy house." I paused and took a breath, feeling angry and duped. "We can fix it up. Maybe if we just get one room and a bathroom finished, we can move back in and save rental money."

"Right," Nick said. He was just as frustrated as I was. Our bubble of hope popped. We were back to only one option. With a new sense of determination, he grabbed my hand and said, "Sounds like a plan." We drove back to the rental with fresh optimism, ready to fix up our place and start living again.

CHAPTER TEN

A NEW VERNACULAR

Paying a mortgage on a destroyed house and rent on a livable one every month was our new reality. I needed to find purpose in my life other than awaiting Nick to return from work daily. The incredible task of rebuilding our house by ourselves nightly was becoming rote. I walked downtown and searched for Charity Hospital, the one that Dr. Hasselin had originally called me to work in before the storm came. I realized my life was beginning to be compartmentalized into "before the storm" and "after the storm." Walking around I immediately saw a bunch of chain-linked fences surrounding the beautiful old building with warning signs to stay out. I stood there in amazement, wondering why the hospital was boarded up when it seemed that now it would be needed more than ever.

"It's a shame, ain't it?" said a man as he walked up to me, seeing me looking at the building through the metal fence.

"I don't understand why it's barricaded? I'd think people would need emergency services, especially now," I said.

"You're exactly right. Don't make no sense. This hospital has been around for decades helping out the people of this here city."

I stood there waiting for him to go on, too embarrassed and ashamed thinking how I was supposed to be working there but never had the chance due to my evacuation from Katrina. I realized that there must be other means for me to be helping people, maybe other hospitals or temporary units.

"Once the city began to fill with water she flooded. All the electricity failed, no lights, no services, no help. Where was the government?" The man's face became intense and his voice rose in frustration. "People were hand-ventilating patients for hours at a time. Staff were making signs for help and hanging them out the window for anyone to see. People died. People were forgotten. Only a few lucky ones were transferred to Tulane Hospital."

He fell silent.

"I'm so sorry," I said, again lost for words and filled with sadness. "Are the hospital staff operating somewhere else? Maybe at another hospital?"

"There's a tent offering some basic services a few blocks over. This is all part of the big plan though. The city ain't gonna rebuild Charity. They've been wanting to knock it down for years and now they finally have a reason. It's just a damn shame."

The man looked at me. "You have a blessed day now," he said and walked on, shaking his head, leaving me to stare at the abandoned hospital in front of me.

I stood there wondering what my next move would be. What should I do? I wanted to help—it was my vocation, after all—but I didn't feel whole. My life. My job. My home. I was living in the space between what had been and what was now. I started to meander through the streets, thinking of taking pictures of the destruction so that I could someday look at the "before" shots and fill them in with happy "after" ones, only I couldn't get myself to do that either. Who wanted to remember this? Not me. Instead I meandered around, allowing the images of destruction to burn their memories into the soft tissue of my brain.

Walking around I noticed the only businesses that were open and thriving were restaurants. These became a daily necessity for everyone, since people were relying on going out to eat for every single meal. It was impossible to have a functioning kitchen; refrigerators were on back order for months and most houses were uninhabitable. Grocery stores were either still being rebuilt or closed for good. Opened functional stores were few and far between. I had gone to one I'd heard was open for business close to our neighborhood, excited to stop the endless cycle of hamburgers or hotdogs for every meal that Nick and I had gotten into. I quickly realized that though the store was open, the shelves were mostly empty. Lots of dismayed people were wandering around looking for food that wasn't there.

I couldn't believe something like this could happen in America. My eyes welled up with tears. I had never experienced this feeling of sadness and frustration as I walked out of the store with empty hands.

At one of our usual restaurants, I sat beside Nick outside in the heat—the inside was still getting remodeled. A huge Hummer rolled down the street with armed military members hanging from the sides. I watched in horror.

"Are we being invaded?" I asked Nick, who barely noticed.

"They're just here keeping peace," he said dismissively, while scanning the menu for something different from our usual order.

Restaurants were working on limited offerings too, and food delivery trucks were a rare sight in the city.

As I looked around, I noticed a few tables away were more military, all suited up with their M16s resting next to their chairs.

Slowly my hunger started to fade away.

I wanted to work, needed to work, to do something productive to get my mind off everything. I didn't have formal training working in a kitchen, but also didn't want to waitress. There was no way I could be a jovial service provider right now. *This could be my rare opportunity to work in the back of the house*, I thought. It was the first idea that cheered me up in weeks.

At each restaurant we ate at, I scanned the slowly emerging but still limited menu items to see if I could envision myself as part of that team. Nick was always very confused at each one I turned down as a potential source of employment.

"What's wrong with this one?" he asked while we were eating at a small place with only a few chairs and tables. "Though to be honest, I can't even understand why you'd want to go into cooking right now," he said in between chewing.

I needed something creative in my life, a diversion from reality. "I like it," I said. "This is my opportunity to learn some real cooking; and," I continued as I examined the menu, "every place is hiring help." I paused in thought. "They're serving crap with cream cheese here and frozen burgers," I stated dismissively in my newly adopted role as restaurant critic.

The next day, I took a walk around the corner from our rental while Nick was at work and found a restaurant in a beautiful two-story brick building with large, inviting open windows in front.

The sign was advertising food items I couldn't even pronounce. *Yes! This is the place!* I thought.

I entered the white-tableclothed dining room and was greeted by a hostess.

"Table for one?" she asked. I saw that the reservation book was open and unsurprisingly quite full.

"I was actually hoping to apply for a job," I said meekly.

"Oh, great! I'll get you an application. Were you looking for a waitress or hostess position?"

"I thought," I paused, then gained the confidence to continue. "Is there a cooking position open?" I replied, not exactly sure if I was speaking to someone with hiring capabilities.

"Oh, yes, of course! I'll get the chef!" she said, and headed off to the kitchen.

Shit. I wasn't ready to interview already! I had to get my game on fast. Out came the chef all in white, with a blue bandana around his head. He was a tall, skinny older man with long gray hair pulled back in a ponytail. By the look on his face, it seemed like he was dismissing me already.

I was well aware that normally a person without prior training and internships in cooking couldn't just walk up to a restaurant and get a job, especially in NOLA, the mecca of Creole cuisine. However, nothing was normal anymore. So maybe I had a chance.

"So you want to cook?" He got right to it. We sat outside at a nice bistro table, and he had an application in one hand and a lit cigarette in the other.

"I'd love to work here," I said, trying to sound confident but not annoying.

Letting the smoke come out of his mouth right before the words did, he asked, "Do you have any prior cooking experience?"

"I do not. But I'm a nurse. Or I was, until recently. I can follow directions, I'm responsible, and I often had to make up medicines for patients, which requires attention to detail and care."

He seemed intrigued. After another drag on his cigarette he said, "I'm still waiting for my usual crew to come back to the city. At the very least, I guess having someone around who knows how to handle burns and cuts would be good. Here, fill out this paperwork and start tomorrow morning at eight. Bring knives. You'll get minimum wage," he said with a smile.

I was shocked at how fast that happened. "Thank you, Chef!" I said sincerely. I'd gotten a job! As a cook! In New Orleans! I couldn't believe it.

"My name is James," he said as he rose from his seat, indicating the meeting was over.

"Thank you, Chef James," I said, to which he just rolled his eyes and gave a snicker.

I floated back to the rental house filled with excitement and joy. I searched the house looking for my best chef knives and thanking my lucky stars that my in-laws had ponied up for the good Henckels. They were some of the kitchen items I'd managed to salvage from our flooded house, the good pile. I found four, gathering up all that we had: an eight-inch chef knife, a six-inch utility knife, a bread knife, and a paring knife. I didn't have anything to carry them in, so I found some paper towels and wrapped each knife in it like a bandage and put everything in a plastic bag—a few hundred dollars' worth of knives being carried around like garbage I was taking to the curb.

∽

Walking to work the next day, I quickly realized I'd need a better system. My brand-new knives were poking through the bag and cutting into my leg. Ugh, I couldn't arrive my first day bleeding already! I opted to hold the suspicious bag in my arms. I came to the kitchen entrance, which was around back in the building, at 8 a.m. sharp. I reached for the heavily worn wooden door and pulled it open. Immediately I was bombarded by a loud alarm going off all around me. *Oh my God*, I thought, fear filling my body as I panicked. I quickly shut the door, hoping the alarm would stop. How had I set it off on my first day?

With blazing sirens as cop cars approached, I tried to calm myself down by repeating over and over to myself, *You did nothing wrong*. I took a seat on the stoop and prayed the tills were all straight from the night before. I saw the cop cars round the corner and stop in front of where I was sitting. One of the officers approached, immediately asking me for my name and personal details. After moving away and talking to whoever was on the other end of the phone, presumably the restaurant owner, the cop came back over and looked at me.

"According to the owner there's no Collette Delaney on the roster."

"It's my first day," I explained. "That's why no one knows who I am. Chef James is expecting me today." Thankfully, I remembered his name. I was cleared, the ear-piercing alarms gratefully stopped, and I saw Chef James saunter toward the restaurant, grinning.

"Making a statement on the first day," he greeted me. "I don't know why the door wasn't locked. Night crew," he scoffed.

It was a dizzying day getting familiar with the multitude of foods I had never heard of before, along with how to put the individual ingredients together at warp speed. I was in charge of the garde manger station—basically, three-quarters of the menu options came from my station, which I was solely responsible for making. I quickly learned this position was no joke. Appetizers, salads, and desserts, as well as arranging all the orders by table number together in the pass—a window to put completed dishes in for servers to pick up. It all fell to me. I looked longingly at the hot side, which was only responsible for the main meal.

All day long, tickets kept on coming back to me like boomerangs. I picked up on the back of the house lingo pretty quickly. "Fire!," "hat," "all day," "eighty-six," and of course "in the weeds" became part of my repertoire. The only communication I found difficult was the Creole vernacular exchanged in rapid fire. The local inmates doing soft time were given day passes and allowed to work at the restaurant to earn some money before they were permanently released. They peeled twenty pounds of shrimp daily, washed dishes, cleaned and mopped, and helped out doing various small tasks. One lucky guy was trained on the grill. I knew they were all talking about me, but I couldn't understand anything. "Got a marks-a-lot?" sounded like it was all one word, which quickly became just "Marks-a-lot!" repeated again with more frustration.

"I'm sorry, can you point to what you need?" I said, desperately trying my hardest to figure it out.

One of the guys, who introduced himself as Mike, pointed with exasperation to my Sharpie.

"Oh! Here!" I said with a smile.

Chef James had to explain that I wasn't from around these parts and I wasn't trying to be rude.

"She don't understand English?" one said. I got that one.

After a few weeks I did pick up the banter and, like a proud foreign exchange student, I could easily understand phrases like "sho-do" (for "shut the door") or "Where y'at?" ("Where are you at?"), and of course the popular phrase said by everyone during football season, "Who dat' say gonna beat dem' Saints?" I also realized that a pecan ("pee-can") is something you pee in, but a pecan ("pah-con") is what you eat. One day it just clicked, and I understood the colorful stories some were telling to get under the skin of one of the workers. I smiled discreetly, and Mike picked up on that. "Oh shit! She gets it!"

I smiled and said, "Oh yeah, it's on now." Which was followed by a bunch of laughter, shouts, and muffled "oh no's!" It was a big day for me in the kitchen—I finally fit in.

The day crew and night crew had their differences in the back of the house. I knew that the night crew were actually trained as legitimate cooks and that working night shift came with its glory. It also included perks of bellying up to the bar after shift and drinking for free. The night crew liked me in general, because I wasn't a threat and I covered for them, sometimes working double shifts due to a sudden illness (which I could diagnose almost every time as alcohol poisoning). The nights were exhilarating, working in fits of busy times and lows. A good Saturday night flew by.

When dinner rush ended the kitchen went into overdrive, frantically cleaning and wrapping up any food worth keeping for the next day. Plastic wrap would fly, making criss-cross wrappings of every kind of kitchen pan: nines, quarters, halves, sheets. Once the familiar "Soul Kitchen" song came on by The Doors, we knew the front of the house was closed and the shift drinks began flowing.

Working days kept me honest at night. It was far too easy to slip into drinking a lot in NOLA. There was bountiful alcohol in the city at any hour. Even the drive-through daiquiri shops—which I'd learned were exactly what they sounded like—made a comeback after a short time.

Nick came home one night ecstatic. "I have some great news," he began. I was beginning to figure out that statement usually meant the opposite, and could feel myself bracing for impact.

He smiled proudly. "I've been given the opportunity to travel to Texas to inspect some offshore facilities there with Brad."

"When?" was all I could utter. I thought we finally had found our groove in life. Both of us working by day and fixing up our house together at night. It was exhausting and almost normal. Now a new wrench had been thrown into our situation. The universe seemed determined to make life difficult for us.

"We leave Wednesday and I'll be back Tuesday. A short six days, and a great opportunity for my career," he went on.

I wasn't thrilled to be left alone in our big, work-in-progress house that we had only recently moved back into. I was glad that we'd been able to move back in before the lease needed to be extended on the rental house—a happy goal we both celebrated. All the hard work had paid off. We had completely finished gutting the house and we'd paid for the necessary mold remediation spray. Nick had worked very hard rewiring everything, saving us thousands of dollars, and the sheetrock was almost all up. The few contracting crews that were beginning to come into the city could easily do the work and charged anything they wanted. They usually got it too. It was a city filled with insurance money.

"I guess I can pick up extra shifts," I responded to Nick, thinking out loud as to how I could manage with him being gone. I was still getting used to the drive from our house in Mid-City to the restaurant in the Garden District and really enjoyed coming home to him there.

"Yeah! That would be great," Nick said in his happy excited voice. Just another notch in the good wife belt for me, I guessed.

Thankfully, the days Nick was gone flew by, partly due to the extra shifts at the restaurant and partly because I lost track of time. I clocked out and realized it had been three days since Nick left. *Halfway there*, I thought as I drove home, my shift meal on the passenger's seat and my belly rumbling. I couldn't wait to kick off my shoes, engulf my food, and crash on the bed. In that order. My phone started buzzing in my pocket as I got out of my car and walked up our steps. Juggling my keys, food, and my knives, which were now in proper sheaths and a leather holder, I answered.

"What's up, bitch!" came a female voice on the other line. I paused, trying to place the familiar voice.

"Susie?" I asked.

"Yo! Back in New Orleans, girl! Where y'at?"

"Susie! You always call at the perfect time. I'm just getting off work." I giggled with excitement to be talking with her again.

"Ooh! Hitting that big nursing gig again, huh?"

"Ha! Not yet—I'm going for plan B right now and cooking."

"Girl, no way! Super cool! We have to hang out to catch up! I'm going to hear Kermit Ruffins play at Tipitina's later tonight—want to go and keep a lonely girl company? You can even have that sexy husband of yours tag along with a super cute friend or any friend!"

"Well—he's out of town at the moment, but I can keep you company." I suddenly had gotten my second wind somehow.

"Niiice! I'm heading over to Ms. Mae's first. See you in a few?"

"Okay, lady, getting changed and heading over." *What the hell,* I thought. It wasn't like Nick was going to call me anyway; our short exchanges only happened during the day. Considering that I had the next day off, there was no need to act responsible.

I scrubbed off the food smell, changed into acceptable clothing, and hopped in the car, thrilled I was about to see Susie again.

I walked into Ms. Mae's, a local dive bar on Magazine Street. Upon entering the low-lit place, I snaked through the crowd to the bar. I knew Susie would probably be on a bar stool somewhere. Reaching the bar, I leaned on it and looked down both sides, trying to find her face.

"Looking for someone or a drink?" the bartender asked. The tattooed woman scanned the crowds of people waiting to order then looked back at me.

"Hi, I'm trying to find my friend Susie, but I'll take an Amber. Thanks."

"Got it." She turned back to me. "Susie Star?"

How does this girl know so many people? I thought in amazement. "Yes! Have you seen her?"

"She's the one at the end surrounded by all those people. I'll send your drink down there."

"Awesome, thanks!" I bee-lined toward the swath of people surrounding Ms. Star. "Excuse me, can I have your autograph?" I said as I wiggled in between people not too willing to make room for me. Susie saw me and a huge grin came over her face.

"For my number one fan! Of course! Come here, darling." She gave me a big hug and kiss on the cheek.

"I hope I'm not interrupting you," I said as the crowd dispersed a bit.

"Horsefeathers!"

"What?" I said, laughing, not completely understanding her.

"Don't be silly—I was just drumming up business and keeping the crowds remembering my name."

"The bartender knew who you were! You must be famous."

"Not yet, love, but maybe someday. I landed a gig here next week."

The bartender put my pint on the bar near Susie. "Want another usual?" she asked her.

Susie nodded and passed me the drink. "It's so awesome to see you again! I need a drinking buddy."

"Same here, friend! Nick's gone for another three days, so I'm all yours tonight. Congrats on the gig!" I held up my pint to cheers with what was left of hers. "If I have the night off I'll totally be here listening to your set!" Susie gave me a silly smile.

The night was loud, filled with brass-forward music, fun, and drinks, a typical Susie night on the town—enough to make me slow to rise and start my day the next morning.

I saw Susie often over the remaining days Nick was gone, making it challenging getting up in time for the early morning shift, but it was worth it. I was proud of myself keeping it all together between second shifts and nights out. Susie took me to see so many good bands: Trombone Shorty, a Meters cover band, Dumpstaphunk, Big Sam's Funky Nation. I couldn't believe the intense, spirit-filling sound coming from this place that was going through its own struggles. Everyone we met had their own Katrina story and the heavy baggage that came with that. So many people going through their own personal hell. Music and alcohol helped glue the broken people and their spirits back together, if only temporarily.

Nick came back bearing gifts and looking rejuvenated.

"How was your trip?" I asked, giving him a long welcome kiss and wrapping my arms around him. "Did you learn a lot?"

"Hi, babe, so good to see you! Yeah, it was great! Learned a lot and had a great time. The area we stayed in was beautiful and I got you something." He held out a box.

I opened it to find shiny silver dangling earrings shaped like fishhooks. I had never worn large dangling earrings before, not to mention ones that looked like fishing gear.

"Oh, they're pretty," I said, confused as to why he would choose these.

"You like them? They were made by a local artist."

"I hope you didn't pay too much for them," I said.

"Don't worry about it." He paused, looking at me as if considering what to say, and then said, "So, I was asked back next week."

I stared directly into his eyes. "You just got home! What about our house? I don't want to live in a half-finished house for our whole time here." I wasn't even sure his bags had touched the floor yet. I couldn't believe he was leaving again so soon.

"It'll get fixed, don't worry. How was your week?" he asked half-heartedly, clearly trying to change the subject.

"It was fine. I worked a lot. Reconnected with Susie. She's back in the city at her old place. I guess it fared well."

"That's great to hear! I'm glad you had a good time."

Something was off with him, but I couldn't figure it out—it almost seemed like he was relieved I had Susie to hang out with. Maybe that's all it was.

Nick continued to fly off to Texas for a week at a time over the next two months, coming back with gifts each time, though I asked him to stop. With him being gone so much and my unwillingness to use power tools by myself, I found myself walking over piles of wood throughout the house yet to be measured and cut. There were some jobs that clearly were Nick's to finish. I was willing to paint and help, but major construction was never my forte. I really wanted to believe him that the house would get done before our time here was up, but progress had slowed down considerably.

Then it happened. I found the last puzzle piece.

One afternoon on my day off, I was attempting to clean up the house as best I could to separate the piles of power tools, paint, and new wood flooring from the more delicate items like laundry and household plants. It was a constant struggle living in a half-finished house and accepting this way of living as the new normal.

Separating out the lights from the darks of dirty laundry, I saw the still unpacked luggage flung in the corner of our bedroom. I reached in to remove Nick's belongings and froze in place. I held in between my thumb and forefinger a thin piece of fabric—a thong. It sure as hell wasn't mine. Discreetly buried in one of the folds of his luggage. I looked at it in disgust and rage. My heart raced, and anger filled my body. I didn't know what to do with it.

Nick was at the office. I called Susie.

"Ring a ding, ding!" she answered.

"Susie, I—" I was at a loss for words, trying to identify an emotion out of the many taking turns flashing through me.

"Hey, Cole, what is it? Are you okay?"

"I need to get out of here. Can I come over?"

"Yes, of course! Door's unlocked and I'll have something cold for you."

"Perfect." I hung up and got in Amelia to once again flee my situation.

Driving through the streets, my heart was beating as fast as my foot was pressing the pedal. My hands were hot and sweaty. Not looking anywhere but straight ahead, I heard the cop's voice over the megaphone.

"Pull the car over, now."

Shit. Shit. Shit. I immediately slowed and pulled over to a stop. Throwing my head back against the head rest, I couldn't believe I could be so careless. How long had the cop been behind me? I must have looked like I was trying to outrun him. *I'm so stupid!* I thought.

He slowly approached the car. I made sure my hands were on the wheel and sat still so as not to look like a criminal fleeing a crime scene.

"What's the hurry, lady? You realize how fast you were going?"

"No, officer, I'm so sorry. I was distracted. It won't happen again."

"You were going almost fifty in a school zone."

"A school zone?" I said, shocked. "Where's the school?" I looked outside at my surroundings for the first time.

"Right next to you. License and registration."

I passed my paperwork to the policeman and saw the boarded-up building he'd pointed to. Trying to be calm, I asked in a very measured tone, "Officer, are you referring to the school there? The building isn't even in working order!"

"Laws are still to be followed," he replied, and he left to write up the ticket.

Knowing my fate was sealed, I swore to myself as he smugly went back to his car. "I fucking hate this place!" I didn't even care if he heard me.

He returned, handing me my documents and the five-hundred-dollar ticket, then walked back to his car and proceeded to wait there until I drove fifteen miles an hour down the street, past the abandoned school and all the other boarded-up houses quietly waiting to be occupied again.

Susie was sitting on the railing of her front porch waiting with two Abitas in her hands. I managed to get out of the car and crumpled in a heap of tears.

"Collette! Oh, girl." At the sight of me Susie put the beers on the ground and ran over, throwing her arms around me and letting me sob uncontrollably. I eventually stopped sobbing and graciously accepted Susie's help up the porch along with the box of tissues obviously placed there awaiting my arrival. "You don't have to tell me if you don't want to, but if you want to talk, I'm here for you."

I couldn't look at her through my puffy eyes. I crumpled the ticket in my hand and I stared at the stiff weedy grass. I said out loud, for the first time in my life, something I never thought I would have to say. "Nick cheated on me."

Susie's eyes narrowed and she said, "What an asshole. Shit. How did you find out?"

"I was washing his fucking dirty laundry like a good wife and I found a dirty thong." I started crying uncontrollably again. All the hurt and pain of New Orleans was pouring out of me, creating my own personal Category 5 flood of tears. My phone rang as if on cue. We both knew who it was and I silenced it. "I don't know what to do."

"You can stay here with me!" Susie suggested. "Tonight, in fact! Don't go home."

I was filled with gratitude that I had Susie in my life. Just then, I couldn't think of anyone else I could turn to or trust.

CHAPTER ELEVEN

WOUNDED

I did eventually go home the next day; I had to. I was getting multiple annoying phone calls from Nick wondering where I was. Plus, I was scheduled to work.

Cautiously, I pulled up to the house, not seeing any signs that he was there. I opened the door and listened after the little beeps stopped. The house was silent. *All clear.* I sighed with relief, took a super quick shower, changed into my work clothes, grabbed my knives, and got out of there. I didn't want to see him or talk to him at this point.

Wrapping my apron around my waist, I realized there was no way I could run forever from this. Nick eventually found me in classic cook tradition—at work. Before I could spot him and stop him, he had entered my sanctuary of the kitchen.

"You can't be back here," I said through the pass window.

"Cole! I'm so glad you're okay! I was worried about you!"

"I'll talk to you at home," I said, as I was putting remoulade sauce on fried shrimp finished with chives, cut on a bias, and sprinkled brunoised red bell peppers to finish the dish. I was embarrassed he was bringing our personal life into my work life. I didn't barge into his stupid unit and start babbling.

Nick got the hint and left, looking confused and concerned. I watched as he turned away, the back of his dark blue uniform showing those huge white letters, USCG. I rolled my eyes and continued making the orders on the slips hanging on my ticket holder.

"Problems in paradise?" Chef James wryly asked, but my silence was enough for him to drop the uncomfortable subject. Chef himself, along with all the rest of the restaurant sect, had failed marriages for one reason or another, and I guessed that he'd probably identified the issue immediately. "Fire table 14!" I shouted, as I placed another two apps and a salad on the pass.

Nick was still up waiting for me when I got home from my double. Stinking like a kitchen, sweaty and exhausted, and with a strong shift drink in me, I wanted to take a hot shower and crash in bed—alone.

"Busy night?" he asked.

I looked at him, seething.

"What's wrong with you?" he asked.

I couldn't remain calm or pretend that nothing was wrong anymore.

"How could you? How dare you? Coming home, pretending every day that everything is fine. I've been nothing but supportive of you in all you do. I even came back to this shithole for you, and you treat me like dirt. And now this!" It was a bombardment of questions and raw feelings without pauses.

Nick, now more cautious, was quiet. I could see him planning his next carefully asked question like a verbal game of chess.

"I don't understand," he said. "Did I do something wrong? I'm confused."

I couldn't believe he was lying to my face.

"I can't believe you right now." I needed to be blunt. "I found the thong in your luggage. It's not mine, in case you're still *confused*."

"Why are you going through my luggage?"

"Are you kidding me right now? I was doing your damn laundry!"

"You shouldn't be going through my things."

"Are you having an affair?"

"No!"

The word just hung there in the stagnant air between us. "Then why is there a fucking thong in your luggage?"

"I think Brad was trying to be funny, I don't know. Nothing happened, Cole."

"Why would Brad do something like that? Do you think it's funny?"

"No! I'm telling you the truth. I don't know how that got there. I'm sorry you found it."

"You're sorry you got caught."

"Listen, you need to trust me that nothing happened. That's the truth."

I wanted to believe him, I really did. My heart was broken and confused. Why the hell would a coworker do that? And where had he gotten it from? Something wasn't adding up, but I ached for our relationship to be normal. I ached for our life to be normal.

Nick came over and gave me a hug. "I love you," he said. "I don't know why or how that got in there. I'm sorry you got so upset. Trust me."

I did. I desperately wanted to believe that shitty story. I wanted to place blame on someone, anyone else. I wanted to believe nothing happened. I blocked out any doubting thoughts. What if Brad was being a jerk and had planted it there? What if I was wrong? I didn't want to push Nick away, not now. I fell into his arms and hugged him tightly. "I want to believe you, Nick. I love you too." I couldn't think of anything else to say. I just started to sob again thinking of the possibility I was wrong.

As the weeks went by, I slowly felt the doubt I had about him and our relationship fading away. I must have overreacted. I requested only day shifts at work, so that I could be home more at night with Nick. We started to go out again at night, listening to live music, drinking, meeting other people. That part was great, but the wound of sorrow and hurt was still present within my soul. I tried to create a scab over that emotional cut so that we could move on as a couple. I didn't want to bring up the thong incident again and opted to bury it in the back of my mind and heart. We got back on track with our lives as partners, even making enough progress on the house to start expanding our living space and moving back into our original back bedroom. With most of the kitchen redesigned and completed, along with a working second bathroom, the house was starting to shape up nicely. We started to slowly purchase some replacement furniture, starting with the bedroom, so that we didn't have to sleep on an air mattress again. The dining room contained a makeshift table constructed from work horses and plywood, and our chairs were beach chairs, but at least the kitchen was in working order. Work hard, play hard—our original mantra—seemed to be ringing true. Though it was more work hard and less play hard lately.

I came home one Saturday afternoon after an especially long work week for the both of us, and stated, "Tomorrow's the first time in a while I don't have to work brunch. I'm getting burnt out from working on the house every night. Can we do something different tonight?" I longed for those early days when we'd spent our nights going to bars and listening to music. "Let's be tourists in New Orleans again. It's been weeks since we've gone out together."

"Okay, sure," Nick said. "Though I'd like to finish hanging the shelves in the laundry room. I guess that can wait until tomorrow. You're right—we both need a break. Let's walk over to Finn's and see what they've done to the new place."

Walking through our neighborhood, small signs of progress were evident. The streets were a mix in terms of states of living: some homes were powered by generators, there were a few functional lit houses, like ours, and some were still dark and vacant. There were also houses that were occupied by squatters and not the actual owners. Streetlights were now on, lighting our path through the uneven sidewalks. Entering the bar for the first time since the storm, everything looked different. The inside had been completely gutted and redone. The shiny new brass bar lights and new flooring were nice touches. The back room had been expanded to feature bar games like shuffleboard and darts.

"Wow, it looks completely different!" I said, amazed and filled with hope that one day we'd be done with our own *little* project as well.

"I'm going to get us a drink. Want to play darts?" Nick asked.

"Sure," I said. I wasn't very good, but I wasn't going to let that stop me from having a fun evening.

Nick smiled and walked over to get the drinks, returning with bar-issued darts and the beers.

"I was instructed to not hit any patrons," he said.

After a few warm-up shots, our game began. I somehow hit a double bullseye on my second throw.

"You've been holding out on me!" Nick said.

"Haha. I get better the more you drink too," I said, teasing him.

"Hey, you two want to have a game?" A girl approached us. She was wearing ripped jeans and an old AC/DC shirt that was fraying around the arm cuffs. She held in her hand a little leather case. "My friends here and I play darts on Tuesdays and the other team hasn't showed yet," she said, motioning to the other two guys with her, both wearing similar vintage garb.

"Well, we don't play competitively," I said, realizing as she unzipped the leather case she was holding that she had her own set of darts complete with special flights.

Nick said, "We're up for a game, sure! This is Cole—she's our secret weapon."

"Nice to meet you all. I'm Jamie, and this is Dave and Felix."

"Do you all live in Mid-City?" I asked, wondering if we'd just met some cool new neighbors.

They all looked at each other for a few seconds, and then Jamie spoke up again.

"Close enough, more like Bayou St. John, but we love Finn's."

"Did you all flood?" Nick asked—the requisite question of most conversations.

"We were one of the lucky ones. Only had a few feet of water on Esplanade, none in the house," said Jamie. "Still got that government cash though to pay for these nice darts!" The rest of her group laughed.

"We own a house in the same area—but it's raised, so we didn't get badly flooded. A couple shingles flew off but not bad," Dave added.

"What about you?" Felix asked.

"We're just around the corner from here, so we got smacked up pretty bad," Nick said. "Hoping to have a great finished house like this place here soon though!" I hated feeling like we'd somehow "won" at the "who had the worst damage" game, but Nick, as always, sounded optimistic.

"How about that game? I don't want to get too cool over here. I was just scaring Nick with all my good shots." I gave him a coy smile.

Jamie laughed. "I see you got game there. How about the one who gets the first double bullseye has the other team buy them a drink of their choice," she suggested.

"Sounds fun!" I accepted the challenge along with the rest of the group.

As the night rolled on, our group became rowdier and the tall bar table next to us filled up with empty glasses. Occasionally one of us yelled in excitement over the music when a double bullseye was struck. The bartender had the anticipated drinks ready the whole time.

We played surprisingly close games for hours. I realized that it was the most fun I'd had with Nick since the storm.

"It was really great meeting you all," I said when it was finally time to head home. We all heard "last call" ring out from the bartender.

"Same here," Jamie and Dave chorused.

"Same time same place next week?" Felix suggested.

"Yeah, that would be great!" Nick agreed.

After a few weeks of keeping our standing weekly dart game at Finn's with our new friends—a welcome distraction from work and the house—Nick told me he had to go back to Texas again. I felt sick. Despite my hesitation and pleading, he packed his bags again. We were really clicking like we used to. I didn't want to have any more distractions, just wanted to concentrate on us and this house. Orders are orders and there was apparently no negotiation.

"I can't say no," he flatly explained.

Without him around I felt myself falling into a depression. I kept thinking of all the horrible possibilities that could happen there. Brad once again was accompanying him. I hated Brad, and I hadn't even met him.

Trying to fill my time with something other than work and drinking alone in our house, I looked around, deciding on what I could possibly accomplish by myself. I walked in and out of rooms, noticing everything that still had to be done: hammering in the baseboards, putting a second coat of paint on that one, fixing the tape on the new drywall section, replacing the warped ceiling fan blades, painting the ceilings. I opted for the lowest hanging fruit on the to-do list. I went around replacing the open outlets with new outlet covers. I couldn't believe we'd been working on this house for over a year and a half already—a year and a half since Katrina. It was the project that never ended, and I was so done with all of this nonsense. While moving from a corner of the room to another putting the covers on, I accidentally kicked the painters' tarp and dried paint flecks floated up in a plume above it.

The quiet time alone after work wasn't good for my mental state. I kept thinking of Nick in Texas. Unwilling to work on anything else in the house by myself, I called the kitchen and picked up a few extra shifts here and there to make the days go faster. The night crew especially liked it when I could work the day after a holiday, or Sunday brunch. For a group whose days didn't start until one or two in the afternoon, waking up at eight in the morning wasn't an ideal situation. The word "brunch" was synonymous with a swear word.

Late one night, after my shift, I pulled up to our driveway and paused to take in the house. The house looked dark but lived in. The neighborhood was slowly starting to become repopulated. Utilities were slow to be brought back online, making progress at the typical slow pace for the city. Signs of life were returning to Mid-City. The sight of squirrels displaced sightings of rats. Birds began to fill the air with sound, competing over the noisy generators. The city issued new huge garbage bins for people to use—the kind that trucks could lift themselves—but there still wasn't any recycling available, making it obvious on garbage day which homes had the most empty bottles and cans from their libations.

On some lawns there was the telltale sign of a destroyed house: a FEMA trailer. After almost a year of waiting for their turn to get one, Frank and Jenny, the neighbors next to Sam, were thrilled to finally have their number come up to receive the prized trailer. We still hadn't seen our other neighbors with the huge dogs since we'd left for the storm. Their house was becoming increasingly moldy by the week. I wasn't sure if they were ever planning on returning.

"Do you like what we did to the place?" Frank asked. The lower part of his belly showed under his too-small blue t-shirt. I didn't see anything different about his house, but didn't want to discourage him at all.

"Yes, your place is coming along! Baby steps, am I right?"

"No, no, we put a satellite dish on the trailer! Got a bunch of channels now," he proclaimed proudly as he pointed to the dish.

"Oh, congrats," I said and gave a little smile, not wanting to be rude.

Progress on rebuilding their house was noticeably a little slower after the satellite dish was installed—but I couldn't blame them. It was easy to burn out fixing a broken house when it was just easier to live in a clean trailer.

I walked up the steps to our house and overheard Sam yelling at the electric company in a feeble attempt to try to get his house back on the grid so that he didn't have to keep using a generator. Trying to make small advances of progress was increasingly difficult with all the confusing rules. I was thankful that Nick had rewired the house and we were able to get an inspector out to clear us for city electric while in the early stages of rebuilding. Flipping on a switch for lights seemed like a luxury now.

Nick returned from Texas midday on a Wednesday, and I made arrangements to get off from work early so I could meet him at home. I was excited to finally have him back in our vast house once again. I bought flowers, wine, and the necessary ingredients for my planned meal of seared duck, andouille sausage, sauteed duck fat potatoes, and a pea shoot garnish. I'd learned to make the dish at the restaurant and was getting quite good at French and Creole cooking. I couldn't wait to show off my newfound skills to Nick.

"Hey, honey!" Nick said as he came walking into the kitchen. He looked happy to see me.

"Welcome home!" I said from over by the stove.

He came over and hugged me from behind. I put down my kitchen tongs and turned around.

"The house looks great! The flowers are a nice touch too." He gave me a big kiss.

I was so happy to have him back. "I'm making us a new meal I learned at the restaurant this week," I said.

"Yum! Can't wait. Let me put these in the bedroom and I'll pour the wine." He motioned to the two bags sitting in the middle of the kitchen.

"I'll let you unpack them," I said, a weak attempt at a joke.

He gave me a smirk. "You can watch me," he said in a challenging voice.

"Okay, let's just drop it," I said, eager to put that behind us.

"Agreed, I want this to be a great night. I brought you something."

The acid in my stomach churned. I immediately felt that I was being bought off again. A few nights ago, while talking with Susie, she'd jokingly mentioned me selling her all the jewelry I wasn't wearing from Nick. I started thinking about the gifts and my mind went into overdrive connecting all the what-if's during his times away.

Nick must have sensed my hesitation. "Come on—you'll like this," he said. We sat outside on our back steps, which were still stained and weathered from the storm. I opened up the small box, and inside was a beautiful amber and silver ring. "Oh, so pretty! Is this from the same artist you got the other things from? You must be his best customer," I said, thinking of all the past jewelry Nick had given me.

"He gives me good deals. He knows me now."

"Well, I hope your Texas travel is over. We still have more to work on with the house."

"I can put a pause on it," Nick said. It was the best thing he'd said to me in a while.

"Thank you!" I reached over and gave him a huge hug and kiss. "Let's open that bottle," I said while getting up and heading back into the house so that I could start prepping the duck.

"Sounds great!" Nick followed me in. "I'd like to take a shower to get this airplane stink off me before we eat."

"Yes please!" I agreed, and winked at him.

I heard the shower go on. I seasoned the duck lightly with salt and pepper, made shallow cuts on the skin side, and seared it in the hot pan. I flipped it over when the skin was perfectly crispy, basting the flesh with the rendered fat. I added herbed sliced fingerling potatoes and the sausage. Reaching to open my oven I'd personally picked out, I put the whole pan in to finish slowly. I had some time now. I grabbed my wine glass and headed into the bathroom. I opened the flimsy plastic shower curtain and said, "Peek-a-boo!"

"Ah!" Nick said, in a high-pitched lady's voice, playing along. I made no attempt to avert my eyes. "I'm looking forward to dinner," he said as he washed the shampoo out of his hair. He turned around to get the soap out of his eyes and I saw his back. There were unmistakable fingernail scratches from his shoulder blade to his waist. My glass fell out of my hand and broke on the hard floor below.

Nick turned around quickly. "Cole, be careful! Shit, can you clean that up? I don't want to step on glass."

My heart, which had been so light and happy moments before, turned ice cold. I heard my voice become low and steady—as if I was having an out of body experience, and it felt that way. "Of course. I wouldn't want *you* to get hurt," I said, bending down and starting to pick up the large shards of glass. I paused, looking at them in my hand. Slowly, I walked over to the garbage and threw them away. My mind was racing. The shower turned off.

Nick reached for the towel and stood there waiting until all the glass was removed from the floor before stepping out. "It's okay—I don't want that to ruin our great night," he said.

"You thought you could get away with it, didn't you," I said in a calm cold voice.

He looked at me, dripping wet and clearly trying to figure out what he was going to say next.

"You almost did," I said. "Except for those scratches all over your fucking back."

I felt sick. Everything felt surreal. It wasn't me anymore saying these words. This wasn't the Nick I knew standing in front of me.

This wasn't us.

Everything felt disconnected. I went into the bedroom in a daze and started packing a few things, unconcerned about the duck I'd put in the oven. This time, I was going to leave prepared. My feet were guiding my fogged mind. I had no idea what my plan was.

"Shit," I heard Nick say from the other room. He wrapped the towel around his still dripping body, leaving puddles with each step he walked. Normally I would have cared about the wet floor, but I didn't feel anything now. I grabbed handfuls of underwear, not counting out how many or caring. I continued mindlessly grabbing clothes without knowing whether they matched or not. I also grabbed all my work white t-shirts and checkered pants.

Nick started talking quickly. "Cole, listen to me, it's not my fault. Brad wanted to celebrate the success of our last trip there. It was a celebration for all the hard work and long hours we were putting in! It just got out of hand. I should have stopped drinking and taken a cab back to the hotel, but I stayed. He started talking to some girls at the bar—it was nothing. It didn't mean anything. I don't remember any of it! I didn't think anything had happened. It didn't mean anything. Let's talk about this. We can get through this."

I didn't even want to look at him. I was too mad to cry or say anything.

"Where are you going?" Nick said, still dripping and wrapped in his towel. I walked out the door, quickly threw my stuff on the passenger side of the car, got in, and started driving.

I should just run home to Ohio, I thought—but knew I couldn't leave now for such a long road trip, not that late in the evening. Instead, on autopilot, I headed to Susie's. My thoughts were all over the place as I drove through the streets.

CHAPTER TWELVE

THE VISITORS

Susie's place was becoming a go-to safehouse, I thought, annoyed at my situation as I walked up to her door. I knocked, but she wasn't home. Frustrated, I got back in the car, closing the door behind me and locking it. I sat there thinking, staring at nothing but my imagination in front of me. I thought about what had just happened. Give him a second chance, he'd said! I'd already given him a second chance; had he forgotten that morsel already? Wanting to lay the blame somewhere other than on us, I figured it must be this place, this abnormal state of being we were being forced to live in. NOLA was all about second, third, fourth chances—no big deal, *laissez les bons temps rouler*. I had gradually been led to believe this sort of thing was expected, that everyone went through it at some point. My mind flashed back to a conversation I'd overheard between two servers talking in the kitchen where one of them was complaining about her boyfriend cheating again. I'd foolishly thought, *That will never happen to me.*

This wasn't how I wanted to live. It certainly wasn't how I expected to live when I said "I do." It had been about trust. Trust that had been severely eroded, leaving a huge chasm in our relationship. I wanted to throw all that stupid jewelry into it.

I had been led to believe a lie. No one ever warned me that marriage was fragile. I thought naïvely that it was a solid unbreakable bond between two people. I never had thought of divorce as an option, but maybe it would be now. I felt like a failure. I should have never left Ohio, my home, my safety net.

I didn't have anyone else. I was second guessing everything and I hated this feeling. I didn't know this person I married anymore, the one I thought I knew so well. I didn't know myself anymore either. I looked at my hands gripping the steering wheel as I sat parked in front of Susie's house. I reversed out of her driveway and started driving again without a particular destination. Turning around to find a familiar direction, streets that I recognized, I drove back to Uptown toward the restaurant and bar scene. I was starving. The duck I'd made for Nick was probably a shriveled, burnt piece of meat by now, or maybe the smoking overcooked meal set off the fire alarms after I left. Either way, I hoped he didn't get to eat it. Ahead of me, I saw the sign in bright lights on the corner shining at me like a brilliant idea—Juan's! Yes! It was like a mirage.

I parked on a dimly lit street, numb and naïvely unafraid of anything, and walked into Juan's Flying Burrito. The Mexican dive place was just starting to get busy with the after-work crowd. I ordered a large margarita on the rocks and a large wet burrito. I started digging into the chips and salsa when I heard my name being called.

"Yo! Collette Cat!" It was Jamie at a booth diagonal from me with Dave and Felix, and some other friends I didn't recognize. "Come join us! You alone?"

I was thrilled to see her. Her friends seemed welcoming, and honestly, I was happy for the distraction. I got up and walked over to her.

"Jamie! So good to see you! What are you doing on this side of town?" I asked and simultaneously answered her question. "Yes, Nick's in Texas again," I lied.

"Nice! We have you to ourselves tonight!" She smiled. "Yeah, we don't only hang out at Finn's—we like to mix it up a bit," she jokingly answered my question. "We just ordered—come join us. There's a dart board over there you can practice on after we eat."

"Ha. I'll gladly join, but we all know you may need the practice after our last game!" I scooted into the bench, so relieved to see familiar faces. My phone vibrated in my pocket, and I discreetly turned it off. "What are we doing tonight?" I asked, eager to step into whatever adventure the group was planning.

"Getting some grub first, then heading over to the Maple Leaf to watch a few sets—there's a Meters cover band and Dumpstaphunk is eventually playing. You know how it is," Jamie said.

"Oh, fun!" I replied, up for basically anything they'd offer. I knew the music scene advertised a 10 p.m. start, but bands didn't start playing until 1 a.m. "Could I crash at your place afterward? I hate going home to an empty house." I tried to sound natural. Jamie had a mouthful of chips and held out her pointer finger, signaling to me to give her a minute to reply while she swallowed. I immediately regretted asking. I hadn't intended to be so forward.

"Hey, I'm leaving in two days for a little R&R—you can stay at my place as long as you help Felix take care of my cats. He sucks at it," Dave said, smiling at Felix, who gave him an amused look.

"Awesome, thanks!" I said, not letting on that I didn't like cats. I forced a smile in between bites of my burrito.

For as hard as it was to live in NOLA, sometimes life could

be easy. All six of us ate, drank, and attacked the night. We had a blast. I forgot my reality and embraced NOLA's alternative one.

⌒◡

The following morning, I woke up on a futon with a splitting headache and smelling like alcohol. I ran to the bathroom and threw up. *Fuck me*, I thought. I hated consequences. I heard movement in the kitchen.

"Sounds like Cole's up!" I heard someone say, followed by laughter. I peeled off the thick bar of soap that was stuck to the counter, washed my hands and face with it, and walked out to greet the others.

"The party animal arises!" Felix said.

"It's *alive!*" Dave joked.

"Oh my God, you guys, I feel like shit." I slumped down on the floor, propping myself against the couch. "Did we see Jimmy Buffett last night?" I had vague memories of walking into this hole in the wall bar and seeing him play. A roar of laughter rose up from the crew.

"Girl, you not only saw him, you bought him a drink and sang a duet!" Dave recalled to the group who were flung about the living room.

"It was epic!" I heard Jamie say.

"Please tell me no one filmed it," I said with my hands over my face.

"Naw, girl, but it did somehow get on Myspace," Dave said with a smirk.

"What the hell is Myspace?" I asked, suddenly feeling a little paranoid.

"It's like an online social group where you can share stuff

like pictures, videos, and stories," Dave explained. "Think of it like decorating your old high school locker, only it's online. No worries, girl, it's cool. Some chick named Susie commented 'That's my girl!' on the post. You're famous!" Dave proudly showed me his laptop with the post, and I ran to the bathroom again to dry heave.

After my bout with the toilet, I turned my phone back on only to see a bunch of texts from Susie—apparently wanting to party with me. I was so thankful I had today off. It was already ten in the morning. I'd asked for the day off in advance to spend time with the asshole who had only sent me one text since I'd left: "Are you coming home?"

I couldn't believe he could be so ignorant, asinine, and optimistic all within one comment. *Go call someone else, mister.*

There was a buzz of simultaneous conversation in the house as everyone planned the next adventure: what bands were playing when, where to get food versus who had the better ideas, various random commitments, who was and was not taking a break from the alcohol. The banter made my head pound. I wanted to remain in this fog that was pushing against the real world as long as I could. All I knew was that tomorrow I was on day shift again, so I had today and tonight to enjoy this ride. I called Susie.

She picked up on the second ring. "Well, hello, backup singer!"

"Shut up!" I said with a laugh. "I may have had a drink or two."

"That video was mad cool, girl! Where y'at?" Susie said, sounding very chipper.

"I'm at a friend's house and might be for a while. There's some shit going on," I said quietly into the phone.

"Tell me where you are, I'm coming for you!" Susie said. I could hear her falling over stuff probably trying to get dressed as she was talking. I loved that girl.

I told her Dave's address. I knew he wouldn't care; shit, he'd probably thank me for bringing over another girl. Forty-five minutes later there was a knock at the door, and Felix answered. "Did someone order a hot girl?" he hollered over her shoulder and opened the door.

"I'm here for Cole," Susie said with a wink. Hoots and hollers immediately followed.

"You continue to surprise me, Cat!" Dave said with a huge smile.

"Settle down, children," I said. "This is the one and only Susie Star." I introduced her and she gave me a big hug and kiss on the cheek.

She looked at me and laughed. "You need some breakfast."

I couldn't have agreed more. "Dave, I'll call you later—I'm taking that cat sitting job!" I hollered as I left. Susie gave me a side eye as we walked to her car.

Dave left me alone in his house. I found myself sitting on the torn, cat-scratched couch, surrounded by used tissues from all my allergic sneezing and wondering what exactly in the hell I was doing. Three days later, I decided I needed to go live back in my own place; I'd had enough of cat sitting, and I told Felix to take over for me. I'd have to return to face my normalcy at some point anyway. Sitting on the couch, I was having a staring contest with the cat, who was perched at the edge of the table, planning his opportunity to jump on my legs with his claws, when my phone loudly rang. The cat jumped backward suddenly, jolting him out of his surprise attack plans, and fell off the table, letting out a surprised meow. Unfazed, I answered the phone.

"Hello?"

"Hi, Collette!" my mother trilled. "Oh, honey, I'm so happy you picked up! I have an exciting plan to share with you."

Oh no, I thought.

"Your father and I were talking, and we think it's time we come for a visit! You've been living there for two and a half years already and we haven't even seen your house or the area you live in yet! Before you know it, it'll be time for you to move on to another location."

"Oh, Mama, that's a kind thought, but this really isn't a good time," I said, thinking of all the issues that would be front and center, obvious to any visitor, but especially Mama.

"It's never going to be a perfect time," she said cheerfully. "Listen, I can help you fix up the house and your father can help Nicholas build or fix whatever it is he's working on right now. You know how he loves woodworking anyway. While he's keeping busy with him, we can have some time together!"

"Really, Mama, it won't be a good trip if you come here right now."

"Why would you say that? We won't be a problem, I promise. It'll be fun! I've never been to the Big Easy before. What's your mantra you two say again? 'Work hard, play hard'? We'll do that together!"

"No, it's not that, Mama." *It's that I can't stand to be around Nick right now,* I thought but didn't say out loud. How would I even start to explain that to her?

"Well, our bags are already packed and we just bought the plane tickets for this weekend," she said with a little whine in her voice. "They were a good deal. Your father wanted to surprise you, but I thought you'd like to know ahead of time."

I wanted to scream. This meant I'd now have to put on the

guise that everything was just great. My house, this city, my husband . . . all great."

"Well then, great! I got to go, Mama. See you soon."

"Oh fun! Okay then, see you soon, honey."

I hung up the phone and just sat there staring at it.

Crap. I tried to breathe in and out control breaths. I needed to tell Nick. I wasn't good at pretending, and I knew my mother would see right through my act. Unless maybe I couldn't get off from work? That was the only solution I could think of to keep me away from this situation and at the restaurant for as many hours as humanly possible.

I drove home frustrated and angry with all my current situations. I walked up to the front door and hesitated, unsure of what I'd be walking into. My heart started racing as fast as my mind with having to speak with Nick again, but now I needed to talk to him.

I jammed my key into the lock with determination and anger and opened the door. I heard the familiar annoying beep of the security system that still wasn't hooked up to any monitoring. Hopefully, no one else around here knew that.

I entered my house and unpacked the few belongings I'd brought with me. Nick's existence in the house was evident everywhere. Dirty dishes left in the sink, cans of beer left on the counter, laundry piled next to the hamper—*not* in it. Each little out of place item pulled at me, daring me to react. Successfully ignoring every obvious assault to order, I changed into work clothes, grabbed my knives, and left a note, assuming Nick would return from work in a few hours to read it: "My parents are coming to visit this weekend. Please clean up your mess. I'll be home after my shift."

I stood there hovering the pen over the back of the envelope I'd found on the counter. I couldn't get myself to write more. I didn't know what else to say.

It was 1 a.m. when I returned home, tired and hoping he was already asleep. I quietly opened the door, but my arrival was announced. *Beep, beep, beep.* "Stupid alarm," I said quietly and shut the door behind me. I stood there wondering where I would now sleep. I should have put the air mattress out in the second bedroom before I left for work. I couldn't blow it up now and risk waking him up. I guessed I'd have to sleep on the new couch.

I awoke a few hours later to Nick making coffee in the kitchen. He walked over to me, knowing I'd probably wake up.

"I got your note." He paused. "Glad to see you home again."

"While my parents are here, we're going to have to pretend everything is fine with us. I don't want to display our issues for everyone to see."

"Yup," he said, and went to get ready for work.

As he walked away, I immediately felt the brokenness of our relationship growing.

I picked up my parents at the airport, forcing myself to put on a happy face. This was about to be a challenging five days for me.

"Collette!" Mama said, so excited and happy to see me. She was waving her hands to get my attention while Dad wheeled the luggage behind him, smiling.

"Hi, Mama! Hi, Dad!" I got out of the car and opened the trunk. Mama gave one of her boa constrictor hugs and a hard kiss on the cheek. Once released, I gave Dad a kiss on the cheek and loaded the car.

"Oh, honey, it's so good to see you! You look so skinny! Don't they feed you at the restaurant? And your hair has gotten longer." My mother paused when she looked at my drawn, worried face. "You look good," she said, now more gently.

"We're excited to see the city and your house," Dad said, apparently unfazed by my looks. "I can't wait to get my hands on some of those shiny new tools of yours!"

"It's nice to see you both. So, I asked Chef and I couldn't get all five days off from work on short notice, but did manage to get two off together. I thought I could spend the days with you and work nights." I fibbed a little bit.

"Maybe I should talk to your chef," Mama said in a teasing way. "No, but really Collette, that sounds great, love. I realize we didn't give you much notice." She gave my hand a squeeze. "What about Nicholas? Will he be home with you?"

"He'll have the weekend off but will need to work the weekdays, of course. It's still busy at work for him."

"Well, I was hoping we'd get more time with you both, but we'll make the best of the time we have. We're going to keep ourselves busy, so don't worry about entertaining us. We're looking forward to helping you out and rebuilding New Orleans in the process!"

"Thanks, guys, sounds like a plan," I said.

I drove us to our place, and seeing their shocked faces as they viewed our neighborhood with fresh eyes was a reminder of how much I had become numb to the situation around me, taking for granted that this area was still very much a work in progress. I glanced at them when I parked. Trying to sound positive, I stated, "This is actually a huge improvement from two years ago, guys." I was hoping to snap them out of their shock, but that only seemed to make it worse.

"Oh, honey," Mama said, trying to cover up her disbelief. "I thought everything would have been fixed up by now. You've made such progress."

"Lots of people still haven't returned yet. The inside of our house has a better view than the outside. Yard work is on our still long list of things to do. Let's go inside and I'll show you around."

"Okay, well, let's get moving." Dad's fresh determination was at odds with the tired surroundings.

I carried in their bags and showed them all the improvements, pointing to the cleaned tile and painted rooms. As we slowly walked through the house, I explained how we'd had to gut the house to the studs first and then have mold remediation work done before replacing the wiring, insulation, and walls. I continued the post-Katrina tour, pointing to the new appliances that had been on back order for so long because practically every house in the city needed new ones.

I opened the two French wooden and glass back doors, allowing the humid air to mix with our air conditioning. The view revealed wood and debris we hadn't had time to remove yet, along with a variety of tall weeds and an unexpected papaya tree growing in the corner of our lot.

"Well, I can certainly help out with that. Along with tightening up this here door," Dad said while taking a thoughtful look at the hinges.

"I'm sure you'll find lots to keep you busy, Dad."

Mama turned to me. "You've done so much here, Collette. No wonder you look so tired. You should be proud about all you and Nicholas have been able to accomplish in the past two years."

"Thanks." I wished that my marriage was in as great of shape as the newly fixed house. "It's a never-ending list of things to do," I said cheerfully.

"You'll finish it up before your next move. I'm sure of it."

I smiled at them. "It's nice to have you both here. It's like you brought a little bit of home with you. I was thinking we could go out for a typical New Orleans boil at a restaurant. You'll love it. We get to eat with our hands, just like I did as a kid," I said in a teasing way.

"That sounds fun, honey! When does Nicholas get off work?" Mama asked.

"Oh, I'm not sure, he usually works late. We can go without him," I said, trying to sound normal and not smooch my face up in disgust at the mention of his name. Mama gave me a worried look. I turned to walk back into the kitchen to avoid any more conversation about that. "Want a beer, Dad?" I said over my shoulder, changing the subject. "The Abitas are local."

The next few days went smoothly, considering the challenging circumstances. I visited with my parents during the day, showing them parts of the city that had recovered and those that were still renovating. I escaped to work at night, successfully avoiding extra time with both Nick and my parents. I was a bit worried what would happen at night when they were all together alone without me, but knowing my parents didn't stay up too late, I figured there wouldn't be much overlap. I had advised Nick ahead of time that though I'd be sharing the bed with him for the next few days, he was to keep all his parts on his side.

"Collette," Mama said one morning. "You've both been working so hard. Why don't we go out to dinner all together? You have tomorrow night off, and it's our last night here with you both."

"Thanks, Mama, you don't have to do that."

"We want to," Mama said, a bit too determined. "Plus, it'll give you and Nicholas some time to be together. You two barely see each other with him working days and you working nights. Why can't you work during the day as well?"

I thought this question might arise. "Please don't start with me about that, Mama. I'll ask Nick when he comes home later about dinner," I responded curtly. My patience with everyone was wearing thin.

"We already checked with him last night! He thought it was a great idea," Mama said, clearly proud of herself for devising this plan.

"I guess it's settled, then," I said, inwardly cringing at the arranged dinner engagement. "Did you all decide on the restaurant too?" I said, doubling down on my frustration.

"No, we thought you'd be better at deciding that," Dad piped in.

"There are a few well-known restaurants that have reopened we can try. Commander's Palace and Brennan's are back up and running. I can see if either of them has openings."

"We thought maybe it would be nice to eat at your restaurant," Mama suggested.

"No," I said a bit too quickly. "I'm there all the time. It'll be nice to see what our competitors are serving." I reminded myself to remain calm.

For the first time in a long time, Nick and I got dressed up to go out to dinner. Arriving at Brennan's, he kept trying to hold my hands, though I kept putting them in my pockets or holding onto my purse until he finally got the hint to stop trying. I tried to sit next to Mama, but she arranged herself to sit next to Dad, forcing Nick and me to eat next to each other. The meal that night was better than the company.

"Collette, I'm worried that something's not right between you and Nicholas," Mama said to me privately once we arrived back home while Nick and Dad were outside talking about the remaining plans for the backyard.

"No, of course not," I lied. "Nothing's wrong."

She stood there waiting for me to either go on or break into the truth.

"You can see everything we've done here. It's just a lot. We don't get time to go out to eat much." I smiled, hugging her close, realizing once again how short she was. "Thank you for dinner. It's been a nice visit with you and Dad. We appreciate all the work you both have done here as well," I said, speaking over her head.

Mama pulled away and looked at me, not entirely sure if she believed my account of the situation.

"I can sense that something isn't right. I hope you two figure it out. Stop working so much at the restaurant and start spending time with each other."

I gave my mother a kiss. I did love them, but I was relieved their visit was over tomorrow and I didn't have to pretend around them anymore. "Okay, Mama, I'll try."

CHAPTER THIRTEEN

GREENER GRASSES

My phone vibrated—it was a text from Nick while I was in between shifts, working a double again at the restaurant. Taking up extra shifts helped me to continue to ignore my situation at home and stay busy, and the extra money was a nice perk.

Four months had passed since that horrible night in the bathroom that sent our relationship spinning out of control. Reluctantly, I looked at my phone. It read: "Need to make plans for the next tour and need to know if you're coming with me or not."

I stared at that text for a while. It wasn't the words that bothered me, or the tone, if one can gauge tone from a text; it was what it didn't say. No mention of "I want you to come with me" or "I miss you" or even "I'm sorry." It was dry, matter of fact, and to the point.

I sat with those words all night. My motley crew back of the house family knew me well enough by now to know something was off, but questions had to wait until after the dinner rush, as the only banter in the kitchen revolved around what the next table to fire was and if we eighty-sixed anything.

Hours later my station was a disaster, with bits of food scattered on the counter and mostly empty small kitchen pans floating in the large half-sheet pans of water and ice. With sweat dripping down my shirt and physically exhausted, I grabbed my plastic quart storage container, wet with condensation from watered-down soda, and left my messy station. I sat outside on the steps, joining the contingent of other line cooks, who all lit up their dinner cigarettes in unison. We were all still in the happy afterglow of adrenaline rush from the busy night and welcomed silence before having to start cleaning up for the night. The Doors hadn't started playing yet, but the kitchen was thankfully closed.

"Hey, Cole, thanks for picking up the double shift on short notice tonight," said Chef, breaking the silence. "Why don't you grab a shift drink and clock out. The rest of the crew can clean up." It was a thoughtful and infrequent offer that was given to those who helped out on unexpected shifts.

"Thanks, Chef, I appreciate that, but I don't have anyone important to hurry home to."

Chef sat down next to me on the stoop outside, lit a cig, and took a big drag. "Ya know, Cole, this is a tough life. You're on your feet constantly, working insane hours, never getting thanks for the masterpieces that are created night after night. It takes a toll on the body and on loved ones, but I wouldn't trade it for the world. I love this fucking life." He paused. "I'm on my second marriage and possibly my second divorce too. Not many people can understand or put up with a cook's life. Passion is what keeps me going. Passion for the beautiful food I create night after night." He took another deep drag, slowly exhaled, and continued. "You're a great kid—talented, smart, reliable—but you need to ask yourself if this is your passion. I'm not sure what's happening in your personal life and I don't want to know, but I can tell that you're unhappy. This crew here, including myself, we're all fuckups. There are things I probably could have done differently, but I don't regret any choices I've made. Picture your life in ten years and make that life happen."

He smiled at me, flicked what was left of his cigarette into the street, and walked back inside the kitchen, where the rest of the crew was already rapidly cleaning up.

I sat there for a moment in the steamy heat of the night. Chef wasn't one to give pep talks or advice. I felt thankful. I walked back into the kitchen, gathered up my knives, and said, "Peace, losers," to the crew and clocked out, leaving the remaining staff to finish cleaning up. Laughter and muffled salutations were shouted back at me.

Chef's words were circling in my head. Memories of when Nick and I had danced at the Rock 'n' Bowl and how that stranger mentioned our special love poked at me. I needed to talk to Nick and figure out what my next ten years were going to be like. My keys rattled in the car door, and I started up the engine and drove to Mid-City, not knowing what sort of scene I'd walk into at home. Would he be there? Would he be there *alone*? I needed to stop making up scenarios and tormenting myself.

The streetlamps were still inconsistent, and despite it being almost three years since the storm, the block wasn't filled yet with occupied houses. A few houses still sat there growing increasingly moldy by the day, wounded and patiently waiting to be rescued by their owners. I still hadn't seen or heard from our neighbors who had the huge dogs. Our house was the best looking one on the street. Dust, dirt, and a steady flow of garbage rolled through the streets like Wild West tumbleweeds. It only took a slight breeze to send the discarded bottles, go-cups, and random bits of paper airborne, only to take up residence on a different property.

Our constant building and fixing post-Katrina, racing against a looming deadline, had created a beautiful end product. Some people, like Frank and Jenny, still remained in the FEMA-supplied trailers on their property. Not everyone had the willpower, help, or additional funds for undertaking the daunting task of rebuilding. Nick and I were under a military-induced timeline to get our house fixed before the next move. Besides the new interior, our roof and shutters had been fixed, a fresh coat of exterior paint made the house bright again, and a newly sodded lawn almost made it seem as if the house had been unaffected by the storm. The only punch list item now was much-needed landscaping.

I entered the house thinking I knew what I was going to say to him. Then confusion and doubt set in.

"Cole? Is that you?" Nick yelled from the living room.

I walked to the back of the house. "Hey," I said.

He was watching TV on the couch. He greeted me with a tentative hug. "I'm happy to see you! I waited up for you so we could talk." He paused and just stood there hugging me. I wrapped my arms weakly around his waist, feeling his warmth and smelling his familiar scent. It was our first time touching in a very long time. We stood in each other's embrace for an extended minute, just being present with one another.

I realized I had so much to say but nothing was coming out. An awkward moment of silence and staring at each other ended when I blurted out, "How's work going?"

Nick, seemingly relieved that I'd said something, responded by filling me in with the newest updates on boat traffic, port updates, and something called an oily-water separator. I began to drift off in my own thoughts, really looking at him for the first time in a long time: *What the hell is he talking about? His hair is touching his ears; he should really get it cut before he gets in trouble.*

"Cole? Did you hear what I said?" Nick interrupted my daydreaming. "I said I scheduled the PCS move date."

"Yes, I heard that," I weakly answered.

"I wanted to talk with you about that. I got orders to California—Santa Barbara, in fact—I thought you'd be really happy about that. I got my first choice! It's going to be great for us both. It's a really good position for me and you'll love Santa Barbara. I scheduled the entire house to move, not just my stuff. I'm hoping you'll come with me," he said and flashed a smile.

"That's presumptive of you," I said, annoyed that he assumed I'd just go along willingly like a dog, but also relieved because I wanted that option.

"I wanted to talk with you—to plan with you—but you haven't been around and you're not answering your phone. That's why I left you the text," said Nick.

"We'll need to talk before I just blindly follow you. Why didn't you put down Ohio? You made a decision about where we'd move next without talking to me about it. Not to mention that we still need to have a conversation about your actions. You hurt me, Nick, badly. You broke my trust, my love, my faith in our relationship."

Nick pulled away and sat back on the couch. "Cole, we don't have time for this. I needed to make decisions that are going to be good for my career and you continued to ignore me. Movers are scheduled, I needed to get things organized."

"And it looks like you did," I said. "All on your own."

"Are you saying you want to throw everything we've built together away? We've gone through this already," Nick said, now without the happy tone in his voice. "I thought we could move on. If that's not the case, you need to let me know, so that I have a chance to start again too. I'm in the prime of my life."

Darkness started to descend over the fragile conversation. We were at a crossroads, a horrible Choose Your Own Adventure book; only in this version I couldn't go back and choose a different path once the pages were read. This conversation wasn't going how I'd envisioned it would.

"It wasn't me who thought I could do anything I wanted without repercussions. Your actions were premeditated." My voice was getting louder and more passionate beyond my control.

"Whoa, Cole. First off, stop yelling at me. If you want to have a conversation, I'll have one with you, but I will not be yelled at."

I couldn't believe him at that moment—I resisted the urge to break something, the wall or his face. I was furious.

"You do not get to tell me how to act. You have no idea how you destroyed me, and you didn't even apologize! I'm hearing no remorse from you and you want me to calmly talk about relocating to the other side of the country!"

Nick took a measured breath and paused. "I never wanted to hurt you. What I did was wrong. I was drunk and not thinking. It won't happen again."

I forced myself to calm down and control this situation. I sat next to him and looked at my shaking hands. "I appreciate that, but you eroded my trust. How do I know it won't happen again? It already happened at least twice. It was never supposed to happen in the first place."

"I know you're still upset. I love you, Collette. You're my wife. Come with me to Santa Barbara, it'll be a new adventure for us. We'll start over. I'll show you I'm the man you married years ago."

I knew he was trying, but I couldn't allow myself to just say, "Sure, no worries about your infidelity! I'll just forget everything that happened and you can drag me to the other side of the country!" I still wondered where that horrible outburst of his came from. It didn't seem like him. I was beginning to wonder who he really was. So many of his behaviors and actions during our time in this place didn't seem to line up with the man I married. What if he didn't change? I was starting to go down that dark hallway of unhealthy thoughts.

I needed to think. I needed to figure out how to forgive him and myself and move on or move out.

"It's going to take time for me, Nick. I need to think. I don't know if I can allow myself to be treated so poorly again, and—"

"I already told you it's never going to happen again," Nick interrupted me. "How many times do you need to hear that from me?" His tone was impatient. "You may need time to think, but the movers are coming in two weeks. If you don't want your stuff moved, I can leave it here along with the house. We have to put this place up for sale or rent soon. You can stay here so you can think, I'll give you your space." Nick looked at me and put his hand on my shoulder, easing his tone. "I hope that you won't need more time than that. I need my road trip buddy."

I didn't like the corner I was being put into—I felt trapped. The military's timeline was forcing me into a decision my heart wanted to make, but my mind couldn't.

"I don't have an answer for you right now. I have to figure all this out. Take all the stuff. I have everything I need. Put the house up for sale or rent—I don't care. I realize I only have two weeks to think about the rest of my life, but it's something I've been trying to figure out daily." I knew I was contradicting myself, but I was full of opposing ideas. I wanted a hug, telling me everything was going to be okay, from the Nick I once knew, and simultaneously wanted to kick the present Nick in the balls.

"Not making a decision is a decision," a mentor of mine once said. I decided I wouldn't decide anything just yet.

I couldn't move back in the house. I needed time without Nick to see for myself if this was how I wanted to live. Nick called my cell the next day.

"Cole, have you made your decision yet about the house or moving with me?"

"Partly. Let's sell the house. Lots of people are returning back to the city now and we might be able to sell it for more than we put into it."

"Okay, I'll get it listed today. Are you coming back home?"

"No, I'm going to stay with Susie for now." I couldn't explain my thoughts more to him. Why did I have to? "Have you thought at all about our situation?"

"Yes, I think you're being really selfish. Come home and let's work together to sell the house and move."

"Oh, I see, you need help?"

"Of course I need help." He stopped and clarified. "No, I *want* you to help me. We should be doing this as a married couple."

Nick could only see the issues in front of him. The task of selling and moving. He couldn't see the more important task of rebuilding our relationship. "Well, I wouldn't want to act self-centered." I paused to let that sink in. "I'll stop by on my days off and help to clean up the house for the realtor."

A week later my phone vibrated. Luckily, it was a slow day at the restaurant, so I was only cutting herbs to remake some dressings. I picked it up to read, *Our first showing is tomorrow. The realtor is expecting a good turnout.* I "liked" the comment and put the phone back in my work pants. I continued chopping away, wondering what I was doing with my life.

The day finally arrived. It was moving day, only this time I wasn't there to be a part of it. I could imagine the flurry of activity again with everything packed up being loaded onto the truck. There were probably a lot fewer boxes this time around, thanks to Katrina. Then it was over and he was gone.

I drove by the house the next day. There stood the final product of three hard years of life, a beautifully rebuilt house. The house we'd rebuilt together. It was finally complete and stood looking as if nothing bad had happened there. It was good at keeping secrets. The evidence of the destruction between its bones had been cleaned and removed. Now it waited patiently for a new family to love it. A For Sale sign was posted on the newly sodded front lawn. My soul felt as empty as the house. I couldn't believe that only two weeks ago, Nick and I had been having a conversation about the moving date. I looked at my old texts to see the most recent one, sent yesterday by Nick on the day he left. It was only a California address in Santa Barbara with no additional words.

How had my life turned into this? What had happened to us? Sitting in my car across the street, I remembered being in this same spot with Nick, calling home to relay our excitement about finding this house. Memories came flowing back of our first time meeting at an Irish bar not far from where we would end up living together in Ohio. I'd spotted this tall, confident, handsome man making jokes, all while loving the attention he was drawing to himself. His clean-shaven face, short hair, and muscular body hinted at a military man. He'd caught me staring at him and instead of averting his eyes, he looked at me, smiled, and mouthed, "Can I buy you a drink?"

I'd never met someone like that. I was head over heels for him. I'd envisioned our new life together to be rich with excitement, family, and love, as all new young lovers imagine their futures to be. Now I snapped back to the harsh reality at hand—I was holding a phone with my husband's new address sent in a text message, and he was living on the other side of the country without me.

What did my future life look like? What was my ten-year plan? I had moved in with Susie and was still working at the restaurant, with less manic scheduled hours. I craved normalcy: working in my trained field as a nurse, coming home to a loving family, living a simple life, feeling and being rooted. I realized that I wanted to get out of this alternative life I'd built for myself. It wasn't sustainable. I also knew that Nick wouldn't wait for me forever. Our fate was a decision I wanted to be a part of making. I didn't want Nick to decide our relationship's fate the way he decided to live in California, by himself.

Was I willing to throw everything away and start over? Could I start over? I didn't want to live in NOLA, though I liked my friends here. I just didn't feel like myself anymore—I was a version of myself now, unfamiliar even to me. I seemed to transform along with this city, the people, and my old house. All were a new modification of what was, before Katrina came to visit.

NOLA had begun to evolve, with new and more restaurants popping up offering cuisine other than Creole and Cajun fare. There were now a few Mexican restaurants with authentic food that emerged mostly from the migrant workers coming to rebuild the city. There were more Texans around than before, bringing a Tex-Mex vibe. Opportunistic tours through some of the most destroyed neighborhoods, like the 9th Ward, were disgustingly popular with tourists. People seemed to like seeing other people's sadness and destruction, like slowing down to look at a car accident. I knew I couldn't continue to live like this. I needed to go back to my roots, get back to me again so that I could see which page in life's path I should turn to and live out. I drove back to Susie's house hoping she'd be there.

I walked up the steep steps to Susie's side of the double shotgun rental and opened the large exterior shutter door, then the wooden one. Susie liked the added shade and privacy it provided.

"Hey, are you here?" I yelled to an empty house. Damn. I needed to talk things through with her. I decided to call home—the next best option, as I needed someone to talk to right then and there. Mama picked up on the first ring.

"Hello?" Her voice was sad and measured.

"Hi, Mama, it's me. Is something wrong?"

She immediately perked up. "Oh, Collette! You remembered! I knew you wouldn't forget my birthday!"

I tried sounding as natural as possible.

"What? Not me!" A little nervous laugh fell from me. "Happy birthday. How's your day going?" I really wanted to talk, but now realized this wasn't the conversation to tell her that I was living without my husband.

"Oh, it's good. Your father is going to take me to a late lunch downtown and then we're having some cake with neighbors. How are things with you? I haven't heard from you in such a long time, I was getting worried."

"Things here are the same. We sold the house and Nick got orders to California." *Shit, I hope I didn't say too much.*

"You sold the house? That's wonderful! I didn't realize you were getting ready to move so soon. Time passes so quickly. I'm glad we were able to visit with you and Nicholas down there. Is he still there with you? Everything is okay, isn't it?"

I could sense the questions swirling around in her head, along with worst-case scenarios that probably weren't that far off from the truth. She had a knack for knowing what exactly was going on without asking for confirmation. I couldn't get into my situation on this phone call, especially not on her birthday, which I had happened to forget, being wrapped up in my mess of a life. "Yes, everything's fine. The house sold fast, after only eight days on the market. He's looking for a house in California for us. I couldn't get off work."

"Collette, when are you going to quit working as a cook and start nursing again? You need to stay with your husband, go with him on these journeys."

"Yes, Mama, I know. Well, I hope you have a great rest of your day. I'll call again soon. Love you."

"I hope everything is all right, honey. Love you too."

I hung up, realizing I hadn't eased her mind one little bit. I was going to need to fix this now, too. I was the one who needed to be lifted up and now I needed to pretend everything was normal. *Stay with your husband.* Those words were not the ones I wanted to hear. I sat on the couch and started counting the few remaining hours I had left before starting my shift at work.

Susie finally returned to find me eating a pint of Ben & Jerry's and mindlessly watching HGTV.

"Don't tell me you miss hammering nails and painting." Susie came in, suppressing a smile.

"I'm so glad you're home," I said. "I need to talk to someone and I feel as if I can't really talk to anyone. I'm not ready to speak to Nick, and my mama wouldn't be able to handle this situation. I can't be this open to anyone else."

"Okay, girl, hold on—let me get a spoon to help you with that ice cream," she said, running into the kitchen. "Lay it on me. I'm all ears," she said, and flopped on the couch next to me, digging into the pint.

I leaned over and gave her a hug. "Thank you for being so awesome."

"We've all been where you are now at some point in our lives. Needing someone to vent to and not knowing who could handle the shitstorm you're about to unload. Years ago, I was married." She paused and looked at my wide eyes. "Surprise! Haha, I bet you weren't expecting that one."

"No, I had no idea. What happened?" I asked.

"Oh, he told me he didn't love me anymore and then married a little bitch he worked with."

"Oh my gosh, Susie." Her matter-of-fact storytelling was impressive. "Did you know?"

"Nope, it was a complete shock. I didn't know he was having this relationship on the side. Apparently, it went on for a year. I felt pretty stupid. He always had a reason for why he was gone or didn't come home and I believed him. I was pretty ignorant and beat myself up over it for many months. Then I realized it wasn't my fault and I didn't bring this on myself." She paused, then continued with a little laugh. "Ha! Years' worth of therapy summed up in a few sentences." She grabbed another spoonful of ice cream.

"That's exactly how I'm feeling right now. Dumb, embarrassed, naïve, and that I did something to cause him to stray."

"Don't be ridiculous. You've been an amazing wife. People fuck up. Nick majorly fucked up, but he didn't have a secret relationship for a year. Has he said he doesn't love you anymore?"

"No, not yet," I replied. It didn't make me feel better, but a small flame of hope was lit again.

"Okay, so you need to talk to him in order to see where you

guys are in this relationship. Forgive yourself and see if you can begin to forgive him. Either way, you need to start living again."

A thoughtful pause passed between us.

"I was thinking of taking a trip somewhere to get out of NOLA for a bit to figure out where my head is," I said. "Would you like to come with me?"

"Oh, hell yes! I was just thinking the same thing. People need to leave this city from time to time. It's just too much, but they come back eventually. Where are we going? Want to go to my family's house in Texas?" Susie said excitedly.

"No, I don't think I can ever go to Texas now! I was thinking of heading north, maybe Kentucky?"

"Oh, right, right. Who do you know in Kentucky?"

"No one," I said. We both laughed and shoved more ice cream in our mouths.

"Well, we can't leave for another few weeks," Susie informed me. "You're not going to believe this, but I decided to try to start making a real go at this singing career and stop wasting my time with little gigs. I met a guy who's a booking agent for some big names in this town. I even went out and made a demo recording in a studio! Can you believe it? He said that he wouldn't be able to fit me into any larger audiences for a few weeks though. Something about on-boarding with the company and building out my image. Whatever that means!"

"Susie, oh my God, that's amazing! I'm so proud of you. I'm so glad that you're starting to take yourself seriously—you have an amazing voice. I can't wait to see *Susie Star* in big lights!" I gave her a big hug. "Do you still want to leave to go with me though? What if some opportunity comes up?"

"Fiddlesticks, Cole! I'm going with you."

"Fiddlesticks?" She always knew what would make me smile.

"Okay then, leaving in a few weeks gives me time to give notice at the restaurant and get my money together. I guess I need to search for a place to rent or a hotel as well." I was making a mental list of all the realistic planning I needed to do.

"Oh snap, I almost forgot, Cole! This is the first year Mid-City Krewe is rolling back through Mid-City since that bitch Katrina showed up. We have to stay to watch at least that part of Mardi Gras."

Susie always had good ideas and, really, what was my rush? Two weeks here or there didn't really matter in the big scheme of things. My life could be messy *and* fun, for a little longer.

Mid-City Krewe, though not as massively popular as Zulu or Rex, still drew impressive local crowds proud of their cultural contribution to Mardi Gras. This year especially Mid-City Krewe was eager to roll through the restored neighborhoods, showcasing New Orleans's character and strength to the people who'd come back to rebuild their lives and to tourists alike. Our house—our *former* house—was perfectly positioned only two short blocks off the parade route. That prime location was now for the new owners to enjoy, which meant they would now have the convenience of stumbling back to use a real bathroom throughout the day. I tried not to be jealous.

For a moment, I thought of how great it would have been for Nick and me to have had a Mardi Gras party at our house. It would have been wonderful. *That's not reality now*, I thought. I pushed that thought away—Susie had friends everywhere in this town and I didn't need the old house or him to enjoy the parade.

"Can we watch the parade from the balcony of your friend's place this year?" I asked, hopeful of the possibility of other prime locations.

"Cole, that would be awesome, but I had to break that off. That boy was getting a bit too clingy for my comfort," Susie said dismissively. "But don't you worry, we'll get a good spot—whether that's camping out or finding our way up to another balcony, we'll need to wear something cute," she said with a wink. "But first we have to start planning the fun grand opening of Mardi Gras!"

"What's that?" My brow furrowed trying to think what she was talking about.

"We're going to see Krewe du Vieux! They're a hoot—rowdy, fun, and naughty! They give a proper start to the Mardi Gras season."

Susie was right—it was fun and surprising. I finally got to do a little pretending myself and become a confident, carefree woman, if only for a night. I stretched on a tight crop top and donned a short skirt that showed off my long legs. I was ready, willing, and expecting a great night.

Watching the parade roll right in front of me, I saw all sorts of things I'd never seen before. "What are those people doing?" I yelled to Susie. "They look like they're dancing with fire!"

"Ha, they are! Those backpacks are filled with kerosene for the lanterns they're holding. They're little walking, dancing bombs!" She laughed and grabbed another beer out of her traveling cooler, passing one to me as well.

Reality once again took a back seat for a night, and I entered the NOLA dimension where anything goes and there's no repercussions for actions. One group was walking by the crowd passing out cards for free kisses. There were a lot of takers.

Planning for parades meant filling up on alcohol that was portable and didn't require an opener of some sort. As I was learning, you also needed a healthy stash of Gatorade and aspirins for the next morning, which usually wasn't as fun. Susie and I were sitting on her couch planning out the next few parades we wanted to attend when she came upon the krewe we'd been waiting to see.

She gave a squeal. "Ooh, Cole, look! Mid-City Krewe is rolling on Sunday!"

"Shoot, Sunday?" I said, smiling. Susie shot me a look. "I have to go to church." I barely got the sentence out before laughing at my statement.

"You're a goofball," she said and laughed with me. "You can pray on Ash Wednesday along with the rest of the city!"

Tape had appeared overnight like magic on the neutral grounds, marking claimed real estate for the patrons along the parade route. Strolling through the route, planning out where our little spot would be, I saw colorful, decorated ladders everywhere.

"What are these for?" I asked Susie as we strolled down the street. The ladders were fashioned with inverted wooden toolboxes to make seats on top. Large side wheels were fastened on either side of the toolbox so that the huge contraptions could be easily moved.

"They're for the kiddos to catch the throws and see the floats with unobstructed views! Family friendly, Cole," Susie explained while actively scanning for the best spot for us to watch the parade.

I was in awe of the amount of effort it must have taken to make the ladders. They were colorfully painted, decorated with beads, some with family names, and often included cup holders for parents and kids to share.

"It's just like claiming a spot at the pool or beach, except instead of placing a boring old towel down on a beach chair, you put a crazy bedazzled ladder there," said Susie, my personal tour guide.

The time arrived for the parade. Susie came home with bags and a big smile. "Are you ready, girl?" she asked.

"So ready!" I smiled, looking at Susie holding large bags in her hands. "What do you have in the bags?"

"Well, you do look great in your cute little getup, but this here's a serious party!" Susie said, looking at the outfit I'd chosen. "Here, put these on. I stopped off at the vintage store earlier." Out came a bright red one-piece jumpsuit with a matching red wig and red sunglasses. The other outfit was a short purple hooped dress decorated with feathers on the shoulders and around the hem, also with matching purple hair and jeweled sunglasses. "I thought you could be the lady in red, but I love them both, so you choose!"

"What fun! I can't believe you found these!" I grabbed the red one and tried it on, reinventing myself for yet another time.

"This one is just perfect!" I said and struck a pose.

Squeals of excitement came from both of us. "Oh, I almost forgot," Susie said and ran back to her bedroom to grab two matching boas. We threw the boas dramatically around our necks, laughing.

We looked at ourselves in the full-length mirror hanging near the door. Susie, all dressed in purple, was making glamour poses in the mirror while puckering her bright red lips and batting her long fake eyelashes. I stuffed a section of my hair, which had grown longer, back under the red wig. I was smiling at Susie, but in my reflection I saw that my eyes were still drawn from worry and sadness. The pounds I'd shed while working in the restaurant, where I was now accustomed to nibbling rather than eating meals, gave me a distinct little waistline. I put my red sunglasses over my eyes, with a mental note to keep them there. I adjusted my boa around my neck and dramatically proclaimed, "Let the parading begin!"

We laughed and strutted out the door side by side. Following Susie's lead, we walked to Canal Street. The crowds were already gathering at near capacity, spilling out over the sidewalks and into the street itself. "Let's try walking along the sidewalk and see if there's any available spots for two hotties. Everyone will have to step back to the curb to let the floats drive by anyway," Susie said.

We found a little patch of open pavement and decided to lay claim to our space. Susie was toting around a small over-the-shoulder cooler. She set it down and grabbed two beers for her and me. "Cheers, my friend!" she said.

"Susie, I don't know what I'd do without you."

She gave me a little hug. "Girl—you'd be miserable without me!" She laughed. "And I'd be miserable without you!"

Just then a group of young cops appeared to assess the crowd. One made eye contact with us and smiled. "Hey, Mr. November!" Susie said with a big flirtatious smile.

I looked at her and whispered, "I think he's a cop, not a fireman."

"No, girl, he's with the firemen—see them all over there?" She nodded her head to about six more men walking down the street. "The city gets everyone to come out for crowd control and to monitor the barricades. Plus, firemen are *way* cooler than the cops around here."

I still got a little uncomfortable seeing uniformed men. It had a way of reminding me of when I'd first seen Nick in his crisp blues.

To my surprise, one of the firemen left his side of the street and walked right by us and said hello. I felt a thrill at being noticed.

"Where you going so fast, Mr. November?" Susie called after him. "The fun is over here."

"Got a job to do, little lady," the fireman said with a smile. "You two stay out of trouble." With that he walked on, but looked back once to smile again.

"Oh, Cole, he's delicious," Susie teased. "When he comes by again, slip him your number."

"Um, technically, I'm still married," I said, the frustration and sadness in my voice surprising me.

"Okay, okay, I was just giving you first dibs. Let's save the serious conversations for later—we're here for fun today. Look! Here comes the marching band! It's starting!"

The bouncing music could be heard down the street, with a beat driven by brass horns and drums. It made everyone get up and start moving. Everyone was intertwined, swinging and dancing. The air was filled with tangible notes and beats replacing the stale humidity and smell of mold still present from the storm. I kept seeing Nick and me and our past relationship in everyone everywhere I looked, and I willed myself past this memory, knowing that I needed to be purposeful in making new happy memories, starting now. I saw Susie next to me, singing at the top of her lungs with the brass bands, and I floated along with the music and allowed myself to be swept up, forgetting my irritating thoughts and problems just for the day. The floats and bands kept coming, and you could only tell when one krewe ended and the next began by the introductory banner ahead of the new line of floats and the change in what the riders threw to the crowd. Float after endless colorful float came by tossing a continuous supply of beads, cups, and doubloons. Both Susie and I had ridiculous amounts of beads around our necks, weighing us down at times. We started opting instead for the stackable cups, yelling "Cup, cup, cup!" at the floats.

At the end of the parade, the streets and trees lining them were heavily festooned with multicolored beads, intact and broken strands alike. The trees looked as if they'd had as much fun collecting the throws as the crowds of people had.

"Susie," I slurred. "I'm starving." Though it didn't seem she heard me over the noise of the crowds.

I stumbled into a group of people laughing. "Oh, excuse me," I said in what I perceived to be absolutely fine English.

"The pleasure is all mine, beautiful!" said a man, all smiles. "That would be a stunning outfit for the Red Dress Run."

"Is that today?" I asked, confused and thinking it was yet another Mardi Gras festivity. "Ha! No, but soon. It's a wonderful time where you can get away with wearing the same red dress to more than one event!" he said with a big smile and continued. "There's a little running involved, or you can walk, and of course there's a little beer too."

Susie perked up at this explanation. "Oh, I've done that before! It's a blast! You're a hasher, right?"

"On-on! Sir Comes a Lot, at your service," he said, with a curtsy. At this point, the rest of the pack joined in with the introductions, all names more ridiculous than the next: "Little Oral Annie," "Re-Leash Me," "Pinch a Loaf," "Butt Floss," "Better Moans and Gardens," "Dental Dam-Zel," "Calvin Klimax," "Tighty Whitey."

Everyone politely shook our hands. We laughed at the way everyone said their name with complete seriousness. Some had on colorful t-shirts. Tighty Whitey's shirt read "Orgasm Donor," while Pinch a Loaf's shirt proudly displayed "Rehab Is for Quitters." "I never heard of this group before," I admitted and felt myself blushing.

"We're a drinking club with a running problem," a few said in unison.

"But if we're talking to cops, we're running for Jesus," said Pinch a Loaf, smirking. "That usually leaves us alone."

"Tell us when the next run is and maybe we'll join," Susie said eagerly. Sir Comes a Lot, who happened to have a Sharpie in hand, wrote the date, time, and place on one of the multiple cups we'd gathered as throws. "I'm the hare that day. Looking forward to you both being there!" he said. Seeing my quizzical face, he explained: "I'm setting a trail for everyone to follow. It's fun! Hope to see you both there!"

I took the cup and, arm in arm with Susie, said thank you and "Goodbye, Sir" with a laugh, at which they all departed, saying "On-on!" and singing some song that sounded like a dirty nursery rhyme.

"Those people are crazy!" I said to Susie, laughing. "Sounds fun, though."

"You have no idea," she said. "We'll need to go, but first food! I don't know about you, but I'm starving!" I laughed, thinking to myself, *Didn't I just say that?* We stumbled back to her place to eat, since finding food anywhere nearby with short lines during Mardi Gras was impossible.

CHAPTER FOURTEEN

REVELATION

Mardi Gras ended, and the city itself seemed as if it needed all forty days of Lent to recover. Susie couldn't ever seem to nail down a date to leave. Her agent was calling more often too. Between business meetings, a must-go-to party here, and a potential money-making opportunity there, I could see that she was trying to balance her new devotion to making it big with still having fun with me. I loved her and her free spirit. I was proud of her and really cared for her as a good friend. But I certainly didn't want to be in the way of her newfound personal goals. I wanted her to succeed, and at the same time I needed to move on myself. The city was growing and reinventing itself. I didn't want to stick around and watch everything change in front of me all over again. Strength and courage had started to show up for me. I began to seriously consider the next strategies for my life. I kept a notebook by my bed and wrote down any ideas of where and what I could do as the inspirations came quietly to me.

The city markets were open and busy again, selling every-thing from decorated voodoo dolls, New Orleans magnets, and chicory coffee to reclaimed wood and Katrina relics for travelers who wanted a piece of history. Live music events were popping up at public squares. Jazz Fest had been up and running, which gave the entire city new hope that everything was going to be all right. Even the thoroughbred horses were coming back to the Fair Grounds Race Course. All this growth and change came with increased prices. Po'boys weren't so po' anymore. Tent City, the extensive homeless population that lived under the car overpasses, was moved to another location to make the city more appealing to the much-needed tourists and their money. Similar to the city's rebranding, I needed to feel that hope and rebirth in myself. I decided that running to another city unknown to me was just irre-sponsible and didn't help me resolve anything. How could I heal and move on if I kept delaying that decision? I did the hardest thing I knew I had to do—I called home.

"Oh, I'm so happy to hear from you!" Mama said. "How are things? Where are you now? Is Nicholas there with you?"

Ah, the onslaught of questions. The firehose of worry and need of information had opened. I took control of the conversation in a calm and assertive voice.

"Hi, Mama. Hey, I have news you're going to like. I'm taking some time off and coming back to visit. It's been a while since I've been home and I wanted to see you and Dad again."

"Oh, honey, how wonderful!" I could practically hear the smile growing on her face. "When are you coming? Will Nicholas come with you?"

"I'll be there tomorrow. Nick can't get off of work, but I'm looking forward to our visit." I tried to stay on point and not give too much information. I'd spill the beans over the "talks with tea" that would certainly be coming.

"How wonderful! Chuck!" my mother yelled into the phone and to the rest of the house, not bothering to muffle the receiver. "Chuck! Collette's coming to visit tomorrow!" I heard a "That's great!" in the distance from Dad.

"Mama, I'm going to get going, but I'll call tomorrow with more details. I'm looking forward to our visit."

"You're not driving alone, are you?" she asked, her voice suddenly filled with worry.

"Yes. I have this little card that allows me to be on the road all by myself," I said sarcastically.

"Oh you stinker. Drive safely. Don't make me worry."

"Okay, though I think it's too late for the worry part. I'll be fine. Love you."

"Goodbye, honey, God bless. Drive safe."

I hung up the phone feeling happy and excited. It was the first time in a long time I felt steadied, a new self. I really was glad I was going back. For a long time now I'd been treading water, surviving in NOLA, and now there was a little life raft I could grab onto.

I started packing up my few belongings and planned out my familiar trip with my trusty dog-eared atlas.

Susie came home a few hours later to see my bags packed and by the door. She stood there staring at them, looking sad. "You weren't going to leave before saying goodbye to me, were you? I'm sorry our girls' escape never happened." She sighed heavily. "I did end up getting a gig and was secretly hoping I could get you to stay for it."

"Susie, you know I totally would, but I need to start going in a direction with my life, preferably forward. I have to do this now or continue to feel stuck here."

She smiled encouragingly. "I know. I'm happy for you, girl. I see you're planning on doing just that."

"I was hoping we could go out for dinner somewhere tonight. I'm heading out tomorrow morning to go home."

"Oh my gosh, tomorrow. Dammit, girl, I'm going to miss you. Yes! Where do you want to eat? Wait, hold on, home to California or Ohio?"

"I'll tell you all about it over dinner."

"Oh, a cliffhanger! I love it! So where's the last supper going to be?"

"How about Patois? It's a new restaurant that's just starting out. I've heard really good things from the foodie insiders about it."

"Yeah, support a local and their business. Love it!"

Our last night together in NOLA began as it typically did. The night was steamy, with stars just starting to appear in the sky. The air was heavy and warm, perfect for something appropriately cute and short to wear. Susie and I headed out arm in arm, walking to the nearest streetcar. Of course, we knew there wouldn't be one for minutes or hours; the arrival times were still unpredictable. As we walked down the neutral ground toward the direction of the restaurant, a car pulled up next to us.

"You ladies need a ride?"

"No," I said at the same time that Susie said, "Yes!" I looked at her shocked, and then we both laughed.

"Well, I'm just heading to an On-After—it's an afterparty from a run—and I thought I remembered seeing you two at Mardi Gras," said the man.

"Sir . . . ?" I said, trying to be polite. His blue eyes looked familiar, but it was taking me a minute to remember his name.

"You got it! Great memory!" he said, laughing, and smacked his steering wheel with his hand.

"That's right! Sir Comes a Lot," Susie chimed in, laughing. "Heading off to an afterparty, are ya? Well, that sounds deliciously tempting, but we're off to dinner. It's my better half's last night here in New Orleans, and we need to eat before partying."

"Oh, what a shame to see you go, little lady. If y'all want to meet up, we'll be in City Park. Come find us," Sir said with a wink. He waved and drove off.

"I tell you, Susie, there will be parts of this town I will certainly miss," I said.

"You'll be back, Cole," she said, smiling. "And when you are, I better be the first person you look up."

"No, I don't think so."

"What?" Susie stopped in her step and looked me in the eye.

"I don't plan on losing touch with you, sister. When I come back, you'll know about it well enough to plan another epic time together."

"Yeah, I like that better." She gave my hand a squeeze.

With a new hot cup of tea, I sat preparing myself for my mandatory scheduled me time. I snuggled up to the corner spot of the bay window in my parents' house. I opened the journal I'd started keeping since I'd returned to Ohio four months ago, picked up my dedicated fancy pen to help inspire me, and began to write. I needed to make sense of my life and what had happened. Thinking back to my complicated life in New Orleans was . . . complicated. Everyone I had met during my post-Katrina time there was dealing with some sort of stress or loss or displacement, whether it was small-scale or large, literal or figurative. There weren't any professional therapists around to help process the pain. Hell, there weren't even professional hair stylists around during those early rebuilding years, which was apparent by my longer and messier than usual hair. I grabbed a lock and examined it for split ends. We'd all relied on each other, broken people trying to lift up other broken people. The voids were filled with instant gratification brought on by alcohol or relationships, or both. *What makes me happy?* I wrote. I looked at those words on the page, slowly and nervously tapping the side of the journal with my pen. I didn't know if I could answer that seemingly easy question.

I thought hard about New Orleans. Apart from the friend-ship I shared with Susie, the occasional rush of a good shift at the restaurant, or the few last months hanging out with my dart crew, those three years as a whole had been hard. I wasn't living a happy life. I was a version of me, the survivor version of me. *Okay, self,* I willed myself, *what about now?* I'd been slowly piec-ing my existence back together. I started looking for OB nursing jobs, something a little different than I had done before. Babies made me happy, even if they weren't mine. *Got one!* I wrote down my happy thought. I looked out the window and spotted a robin landing on the grass. Living here at home in a failed state wasn't making me happy either. *I need an apartment.* I wrote down the second bullet point. *Man, I'm on a roll,* I thought.

Mama and I had started to make a habit of meeting Peter with his mother after church. It was something I actually looked forward to, but it made me feel like I was still in high school. *Having a proper date with Peter.* I froze at that thought. Wait a minute, what was I thinking? I erased that sentence from the list. *I'm still a married woman.* I paused, and my eyes began to well up, blurring the words I started to write on the page. I filled in the last bullet point and quickly closed the journal. *Not being married to Nick.*

Over the next few months, I made it a point to try to recognize happiness big or small and add that back into my life. I got a postcard from Susie with a busty woman wearing a slightly see-through tight shirt that said "Wish You Were Here" on the front. I held it in my hand. Such a small gesture that brought me a huge amount of joy. I missed her so much. Trying to catch her for a phone call these days was nearly impossible. She was constantly on the go. I turned the postcard over and read it. *My girl, Cole, I miss my buddy! I had a small gig the other day and there was a talent scout in the audience. I was talking to this hottie after the show and totally ditched him for this forty-something old dude with bad hair but hot connections. Haha! Things are looking up for Susie Star! I hope they are for you too love! Love, Susie.*

She had drawn a star after her name. I so did hope she'd go far in that world. She was so talented, beautiful, and a little crazy. A perfect combo for the music industry. I made a mental note to get a postcard from the Rock & Roll Hall of Fame and send it to her, writing that I wanted to see her outfits in there someday. She'd love that.

The alarm clock woke me the next day, annoyingly. I rolled over and shut it off. It was my day off today from the hospital, but I'd forgotten to silence it before going to bed the night before. I lay there willing myself to go back to sleep but was unsuccessful. My mind jerked to full-speed-ahead mode while the rest of my muscles didn't want to move yet. Reluctantly, I got up and made my way to the kitchen.

Mama spotted me sitting at the kitchen table with some tea as she was heading downstairs carrying a pile of dirty clothes in a hamper.

"Do you want to join me?" I asked. "There's more water in the teapot."

"You know I'd love to." Mama smiled a big smile, recognizing her chance for the "talks with tea," and put the hamper on the floor. She went over and grabbed her favorite mug from the cabinet. Seeing Pork Chop quietly appear from around the corner and dig in the laundry to find a sock, Mama scolded her. "Pork Chop, no! Oh, that little dog. She likes to hide socks on me," Mama said, although I already knew this. She filled her cup with bay leaves and a spoon of sugar. After pouring the hot water, she happily sat down. Smiling at me over her cup of tea she brought to her lips, she seemed to be waiting for me to start, but then said, "I've loved my time with you these days, having you back home, dear." She paused and said gently, "You know you can stay for as long as you'd like, but I do wonder when you're going to go live with Nicholas again. It's not good for the health of a marriage when people live apart from each other." She reached over and patted my hand.

"It's been good for my recovering mental health."

"Oh, honey." Mama's eyes looked concerned.

"Life was all very hard there, Mama. There were things I just couldn't tell you."

She took a sip of her tea and waited for me to go on, but couldn't contain herself. "You know you can tell me anything. I'll always be here for you. What happened that you couldn't tell me?"

"I just didn't want to worry you. It wasn't just the difficulties of rebuilding the house or living there, which was challenging in its own right. Nick and I . . . we're just broken right now."

"Broken up?" she said, shock registering in her voice and face. "I thought something wasn't right when we came to visit."

"No, not broken up, just broken as people. I feel we both have been living a lie the past three years," I explained calmly.

"What lies are you talking about? Has he lied to you about something?"

Not knowing how to broach the subject I just internalized it. "No. Never mind."

"It must have been very hard living there for you two, but now he's living in California. By himself." Mama paused. "So far away," she said sadly, staring into her teacup. After a pause, she looked right in my eyes in earnest. "You must go there and join your husband and amend any differences you may have had, since you're clearly not telling me any details. You need to talk to him face to face. Whatever this issue is between you two won't just go away, Collette. You need to work it out."

I sat in silence, thinking of how pointless this whole conversation was since Mama didn't know the whole story, and I didn't want to tell her either. I wanted this decision, my actions, whatever they were, to be my own.

"Do you think spending time with Peter could be complicating things, unnecessarily?"

"No, I'm happy that I have his friendship right now. I enjoy talking to him. He makes me feel happy." I took a sip of tea, realizing I may have let some feelings slip out that I shouldn't have. "You make it sound as if I don't talk to Nick at all. I still call him, Mama. It's just with the time difference, it's hard to always catch each other."

"Collette, it's natural for marriages to have ups and downs. Your father and I have had some here and there. But we talked it over, grew from it, and moved on. You should consider doing the same."

"Okay," I said, smiling, not wanting to talk more about this subject. "I'm thinking of going grocery shopping today. I want to make a nice dinner for you and Dad tonight. I learned how to develop some good meal pairings while cooking at the restaurant."

"Oh that would be fun!" Mama said, lighting up. Then she continued her thought, not to be derailed. "Maybe you should go and visit him sooner rather than later. This way you don't have to concern yourself about a time zone difference and you can talk it through. I'm sure you'll work it out."

I thought I'd successfully changed the subject, but apparently, I hadn't.

"Right—I'll talk to him about that on our next call. When do you want to eat dinner?"

"Oh, anytime—your father and I can wait if it's a special dinner. I have one more load of laundry to do and some tidying up around the house anyway." She got up and gave me a kiss on the cheek.

I sat there ruminating.

Nick and I did talk occasionally, but it was infrequent and getting harder with my new job working both days and on-call hours three days a week. We'd decided on setting up a standing date of Mondays at 9:00 p.m. Eastern time.

I completed my long day and suddenly realized that it was Monday. I let out an audible grunt. One of the nurses remarked, "Oh, I know that grunt. That's a crap-it's-only-Monday grunt."

I looked at her and smiled. "Exactly. See you tomorrow." I was so tired from working all day, but I didn't want to cancel my call with Nick. Wife guilt: I still had it.

Right on time, the phone rang. Looking at the area code, I knew it was him.

"Hi," I said, trying to hide the obligation in my tone.

"So good to hear your voice," he said.

After some small talk about the weather, the conversation became pointed.

"Look, I really have to ask you a question," Nick said. "I've been thinking about this for a while now. What is *this* that we're doing? This current situation doesn't make any sense to me. It seems as if you're moving on. Are you?"

"I'm not, Nick—I'd be up-front with you about that. I just need some time to figure things out in my head." Maybe I was drifting apart from him. I certainly didn't mind our current situation, and remembered that Mama's suggestion about living apart during the rebuilding might have been a good idea after all.

"How much time do you need? Wait. Don't answer that." He paused, likely realizing that came across sharp. Then through the silence he said, "Why don't you take some time off and come see me and we can talk together, here. It's too hard to have meaningful conversations over the phone. I want to see you again. I can show you around. You've never been here before." He sounded excited to suggest this, hopeful even.

It was a reasonable enough proposition to me, and one that I'd been thinking about anyway since my talk with Mama. It might even help me to have closure one way or another. "Okay. Nick, send me some dates that work for you and I'll figure it out."

"That's great! I'm so happy to hear that! Anytime that works for you works for me! I can buy your plane ticket too, just let me know."

A smile came across my face. I couldn't help it, he sounded like the old Nick I once knew. The one I'd fallen in love with. "I will. Thanks."

We hung up that night and I started to think—I couldn't take off around a holiday, but I might be able to squeeze a Thursday night red-eye through Monday. It would be a quick trip, but without much leave, I didn't have a lot of choice. And really, not knowing what the trip would bring, I'd rather err on the side of caution and not overstay my visit. I felt hopeful that I would be able to figure this out. Maybe the wall I put up between us would dissolve when I saw him. Maybe he'd changed? Maybe he hadn't. Maybe I was too scared to say goodbye.

I sent him the dates after talking it over with the doctors and other staff. I was leaving in two weeks.

Driving home from work late one day, I decided that getting an apartment might be too rash of a move right now. I needed to know what the path I chose for myself looked like after the visit. My thoughts were getting louder and more distracting in my head. I turned up the radio to drown them out. Only a few minutes away from my house a song came on the radio. I immediately switched from dwelling to thinking of Susie. She would have loved this song, so bouncy and fun. I turned it up and my jaw dropped—I was listening to the new single of Susie Star, on the radio! I couldn't believe it! At the next stoplight, I texted her. *I just heard you on the radio! OMG Susie, amazing!*

A few minutes later, I received her reply. *Cole, my girl! It's been a whirlwind! I recorded a few songs and they're playing everywhere! I miss you, we need to talk soon to catch up!*

I pulled into my driveway, threw the car in park and replied, *I absolutely love the new song! I just got home and am free to talk now if you are.*

The three little bubbles were teasing me waiting for her response. *Girl, I'd love to but just about to meet up with my agent. Soon I promise!*

I was so happy for Susie. She was finally realizing her dreams. I gave loving thoughts to the universe for her.

Work was keeping me busy and going great, filling me with both happiness and satisfaction. I loved having growing relationships with my soon-to-be moms. Two weeks passed ridiculously quickly; I couldn't believe the calendar. When the day came for me to leave, Mama insisted on driving me to the airport.

The traffic, combined with the emotional intensity of this trip, seemed too much for her—I could tell it was stressing her out. "I could have taken a taxi," I said apologetically.

"No, honey, I wanted a few more minutes with you." I could tell she wanted to say something.

"Don't be nervous about my trip, Mama. I got this."

"Honey, don't do anything you'll regret."

"I'll tell you all about it once I'm back." I leaned over and gave her a kiss on the cheek. "Love you."

Once on the plane, I nervously twisted my wedding ring around and around on my finger as I thought about seeing Nick again and the unknown of what I was walking into.

"First time on a plane?" the woman next to me said. She was wearing thick glasses that made her eyes seem larger than they were. *Oh man, I don't want to chat for the next six hours with her*, I thought.

"Oh, no," I said with a little exhale, and I reached for my book in my bag. "I was just trying to remember if I put my mail on hold!" I smiled. "I guess I'll find out when I return!"

She chuckled and thankfully didn't ask any more questions. I received a last-minute text: *I'll be thinking of you this weekend. Text when you get back.* It was from Peter. I smiled but didn't respond. What could I say? It had made for a slightly uncomfortable situation when I told him I was going to see Nick, but to his credit he was patient and supportive, which only made me feel more troubled. I didn't want to hurt him, again. We'd only been hanging out as friends, but I could feel there was other potential there too for something more. I felt a stress headache coming on. I needed a drink.

I spent the flight mindlessly turning pages of the book, seeing but not reading the words on the page. Instead I was deep in thought about Nick, Peter, and my whole situation. The words I wrote in the journal kept returning to my mind. *What makes me happy?*

Seeing Nick for the first time in months, I was excited to recognize my person in a crowd of strangers.

"Collette!" Nick waved to me and started to come over to the luggage claim. I still missed the days before 2001, when loved ones were able to meet each other right off the plane. "I can't wait to show you around! How was your flight?" He planted a reserved kiss on my cheek.

"It was fine, long though," I said, unsure of the greeting I should give him. I decided to give him a hug. It was awkward meeting—clearly we weren't sure how to act.

Nick put my things in the car and started driving me around. I looked out my passenger window, watching one gigantic palm tree after another zip past.

"Want to see the Pacific?" he said excitedly.

"Of course! I'd love to see the ocean."

The smell of the salty air filled my nose. It was all so enchanting, but strange to me. Making our way back to his side of town, he was driving me through different neighborhoods, pointing to streets dense with bars, restaurants, and coffee shops. I could instantly envision him enjoying himself here. I wasn't even jealous. I was happy for him to be living in this beautiful area.

"I hope you're not too tired for a nice dinner? I have this restaurant I've been meaning to try," he said as he pulled slowly into the apartment's covered garage, the tires making loud squealing sounds on the painted cement as he turned.

"Sure, that sounds great. This is a really nice area, Nick. I'm glad to see you've settled in so well."

"Cole, I'm just trying to find my way here. I'm happy to look for larger places once you come live with me." He looked at me, waiting for a response.

"I feel like we're dating again. It's a bit uncomfortable," I said, sitting in the car as he turned off the engine.

"Well, we haven't seen each other in a long time. I was hoping we'd be able to pick up where we left off, in Ohio."

"And skip our three-year experience in NOLA?" I said, wondering if our visit was going to be soured by a fight.

"Right!" He smiled and tapped my knee.

It was just like him to think that we could skip over the bad and only concentrate on the good, cherry-picking memories. The heavy feeling in the pit of my stomach came back.

That night we drove up to a circle drive where the valet was waiting for cars to park. I looked at Nick and he smiled a happy, playful smile, raising his eyebrows up a bit. The restaurant Nick chose was beautiful.

"Reservations for Delaney," Nick said to the hostess.

"Yes, right this way Mr. Delaney." We walked hand in hand following the hostess to our table overlooking the beach complete with crisp white tablecloths. I could see outside there was a classy outdoor fire pit where people sat with their dinner drinks and talked on white outdoor cushions.

"Wow, Nick, this place is fancy," I stated, feeling a bit uncomfortable, not knowing if my modest outfit fit in.

"It's known to have the best seafood. I thought you'd appreciate it after working in a restaurant for so long."

"It's nice to be served and not cook. I have a new appreciation for restaurant staff. It was such a cool experience for me, but I am so happy to be back working in the OB ward again." Talking freely to Nick at the restaurant, I was noticing how much I really liked my life back in Ohio. I'd never realized it until I started hearing myself talk.

"I love hearing about your job—you know there's a VA hospital here that you could do the same thing at," Nick suggested.

"Yes, I know." I smiled and took another bite of our sturgeon ravioli appetizer, making sure to scoop up the caviar and beurre blanc sauce. We had a wonderful meal and talked about his job, the new challenges and responsibilities. We took our wine outside after our meal and sat by the fire listening to the ocean waves and watching the sun set and the first stars come out. It really was beautiful. I knew that the night would eventually have to end with the realization of going back to his place and spending the night together. I wasn't ready yet to sleep in the same bed with my husband.

"That was such a wonderful dinner. Thank you," I said as the car's wheels made the squeaking sound again in the garage of his apartment. "I'm so tired," I said. "I think I just really need to crash tonight." I wanted to ward off any expectations he might have, buying myself some time to figure out what I really felt.

"Okay, Cole—I understand. Luckily, we have all weekend together!"

I could tell that Nick was really trying hard to pick up where we'd left off during happier times. I was also aware that my feelings toward him had changed. I hadn't wanted to admit it in Ohio, but I'd really wanted to see if being together would spark that old flame of ours again. But now, I realized that my feelings were telling me otherwise.

The next morning Nick woke up and quietly stroked my long hair. "You are so beautiful, Collette."

I was already awake but was lying there thinking, staring at the wall. I loved having my hair played with and it felt wonderful to be touched again. Not hearing anything negative from me, he shifted his body closer and started to spoon me, gently touching my arm and tracing my body with his fingers. Calmness descended over me. I closed my eyes, enjoying his light touch on my skin. Leaning over to face him, I gave him a kiss on the lips and turned off my mind; I let myself go.

After making love, Nick got up to take a shower. "Do you want to join me?" he suggested.

"No, I just want to lie here a bit more," I said, feeling the euphoria melt away and the anxiety take its place.

"Okay, well think about what you'd like to do today. I'm up for anything—even staying in." He winked at me as he walked into the bathroom.

I guiltily suggested seeing a movie together when I met him in the kitchen for breakfast. He had two mugs of coffee out waiting to be filled on the bistro table.

"A movie? Like a matinée," he said. "I hadn't thought of doing that, but sure, if that's what you'd like, we can go."

It wasn't even anything I wanted to see, but I did enjoy not having to talk during those two hours.

As we were leaving the theater I could tell Nick didn't really want to see the movie but had done it for me.

"How about getting some pizza to go and having it back at my place tonight? We could talk and spend some time together. You only have a day left here. It's going by fast," Nick suggested.

"Okay, sure." It was a reasonable enough suggestion.

"Great!" Nick sounded thrilled. "There's this pizza place here that specializes in all types of artisan pizzas."

We drove over to the pizza place. It was take-out only but still had a line waiting to get in. While standing in line, Nick pointed out the Old Mission that was nearby and the Museum of Natural History. I think he was trying to sell me on living there. It was finally our turn. Nick went first. "Let's do a whole pie and we can split it," he said. "I'll order my side and you can order yours, unless we want the same thing." He laughed and put his arm around my waist.

"I'll take half of the Italian," he told the person at the order window "and half . . ." He looked at me, waiting for my response.

I was scanning the menu. The Italian had sausage, black olives, fresh basil, oven-roasted garlic, and sundried tomatoes. I was trying to find something not so complicated. "Do you offer just a cheese pizza?" I asked the person, who was getting a bit impatient with the time I was taking to figure out my choice.

"We have a Margarita. It's buffalo mozzarella, basil, and house-made tomato sauce."

It wasn't exactly what I was craving. I thought of the plain cheese pizza I got at home, covered with melted regular mozzarella cheese that was just slightly burnt on top, making crunchy spots. "Okay, thanks. Half with that, please."

We returned to Nick's place and I happily placed the pizza box on the table, since it was a bit too warm on my lap in the car.

"This is just like old times, Collette!" Nick grabbed two of our plates we used to use from the cabinet and put them next to the box.

"I have napkins this time though," he said, referring to our last night in Cleveland.

We both grabbed our respective pieces and sat at the table with our drinks. "I've enjoyed seeing where you live, but you haven't told me much about your job. What's it like?" I asked Nick. He went on to tell me about the port and his role with the shipping traffic and security. "I love the responsibility," he went on. "I'm getting lots of qualifications too and going for training on others."

"Is training local?" I asked, realizing that this was the first time he'd mentioned this.

"Some are in LA. It's not a big deal, maybe a day or so away." Realizing what he was describing, he clarified. "It's not as often as it was in New Orleans. There is a mandatory IO training in Yorktown, Virginia though."

"It sounds like you landed in a good spot. How long is the IO training?" I asked him, trying to stay positive but not liking always being second to his job.

"Three weeks. It's important work. I'm glad you're okay with travel sometimes. It's part of what I do."

I took another bite of my pizza, only getting the sauce and basil.

On our last day together, I rolled over on the bed and saw he was already up. I could smell the coffee brewing. I took five minutes for myself and breathed. I knew I owed it to Nick to tell him my honest feelings. I met him in the kitchen—he was staring out the window into yet another perfectly sunny California day with a cup of coffee in his hand. He turned once he heard me.

"I poured you a cup." He pointed to the still steaming cup of coffee on the white tiled counter near the coffee pot and the lone orchid. The sun was lighting up the side of his face.

"Thank you." I smiled. I held the warm cup in my hands for a moment, trying to find the right words to say. How to begin the conversation I'd been replaying over and over in my head? "I'm really glad that I came," I finally said. "I'm genuinely happy so see you fitting in here."

His mouth opened, but I continued. "Please, Nick, let me finish. I have a whole head full of thoughts to tell you."

"Can we at least sit at the table?" he suggested, clearly sensing the heaviness of the conversation that was about to take place.

"Of course." I pulled out a chair and put it next to him to sit in. "I care deeply for you, Nick. I loved living with you in Ohio, surrounded by friends and family. I felt like I was on top of the world, I had everything I wanted. I wasn't sure how I'd feel about becoming a nomad with you and moving every three years, but I didn't want to dwell too much on that part—it scared me. I thought that if we were together, we could do anything. But we weren't together, whether due to evacuations or your job. I had to do so much on my own, without you, my partner in life, to help or rely on." I took a breath. "I had to console myself when I was alone and hurt. Being back home, I've had the time to think about every-thing I experienced and see it in a different light. I survived all of that, myself. I never knew I was capable of handling all that. I feel something's changed between us. With me. And it's not just your infidelity that's bringing all of this on, though I overcame that as well." An audible grunt came from him, and I continued quickly so that he didn't suddenly stop listening.

"Please listen. I know you love me. You deserve someone who will love you back. It's not just what happened in New Orleans, but maybe I needed that to wake me up. I don't want this life of always moving. I need stability. I want a marriage where my husband is around. I want to have the same doctor, drive down the same streets . . . be surrounded by my family. It's not fair for me to hold you back from your career and your dreams. I loved you, Nick, but I can't be your wife."

He looked at me stoically. "You're just still mad about what happened in New Orleans," he said. "I'm willing to talk things through with you *again*, if that's what you need from me."

I shook my head. "You don't get it. We *are* talking, Nick. But you're not really hearing me."

I knew I was making the right decision now. I took a minute, knowing that this situation wasn't easy for either of us. We were both achievers, and not good at accepting failure.

"This isn't an easy decision for me," I went on. "I want you to know I'm not taking this decision lightly. I've been thinking about us for a while now. I was hoping that when I saw you again I'd find that spark between us. But it's not there, Nick." I paused and looked in his eyes. I was unsure if he agreed with me, but he didn't say anything. I continued. "I'm not sure it ever will be. It's only fair that we both start to live. I want you to be happy again. *I* want to be happy again. I can't imagine that happening if I continue to follow you all around the country putting my life on hold and restarting constantly. I want to be in control of my own life."

I stopped talking. He still didn't say anything. He sat there completely still, staring at me. I twisted and pulled off the ring that was unwilling to leave my finger. I held it out to him, and he slowly extended his hand, reluctant to accept it. Placing the ring in his palm, he looked at it, then at me.

"If you've made up your mind, then I can't change it." He sat there holding the ring, not saying anything more. I could see thoughts swirling in his mind. We both started to cry. I cried for the loss of our marriage, for our failures—for our relationship, which hadn't been honest from the beginning, starting with me. I had ignored my heart.

Finally I stood up, and so did he. I wrapped my arms around him and we hugged a strong hug, as if our bodies were physically trying to keep us together while ignoring the mind's decision. One last long kiss was shared. I stepped back, wiping the salty tears from my cheeks. Then I headed to the bedroom and began packing.

Nick drove me to the airport, holding my hand in his for the last time. The last personal levee of mine had come down, the one keeping back the flood of real emotions stuck behind that wall. Our marriage was the last thing we'd lost in Katrina, but now, after having nothing left, we could finally start rebuilding ourselves to become better than before.

When I got off the plane in Ohio, I got my luggage and walked outside, scanning the row of cars in the pickup line. I saw my mother waiting for me. She smiled and waved me over. I put my suitcase in the back seat and climbed in next to her.

"Oh, Collette, I was praying for you all weekend. How was your trip?" She looked in my eyes, searching for reassurance.

"It was good, Mama. I'm good now."

She looked at me quizzically and then down at my bare left hand. She gasped and started to cry. I held her in an embrace and cried with her. "It's okay. It's going to be okay. Things are going to be better for me now."

I started going to church again with my mother, mostly so that we could run into Peter and join him and his mother for their weekly brunches. Brunches turned into frequent phone calls. We were becoming very close friends again.

After brunch one day Peter walked me to my car ahead of the moms, who were still talking about what to plant in their gardens.

"Collette, we're a bit old to be having to date with our moms present. Can I take you on a proper date tonight?"

I laughed. "Dating with our moms? Is that what we're doing?" I grabbed his hand. "Yes, I'd love to go out with you tonight."

Peter's eyes lit up. He leaned in and we kissed. My heart leaped with joy.

"Would you like to take a walk through Cuyahoga National Park? It's perfect weather for it. We can catch dinner afterward?"

"That sounds perfect. I haven't seen those falls in forever," I said, and we kissed again goodbye.

Occasionally I'd see a Coast Guard sticker on a truck while driving around town, and I'd think of the old Nick I'd fallen in love with. I smiled, thinking of our good times. I wished him only the best.

CHAPTER FIFTEEN

REUNITED

I entered the foyer of my apartment building and paused at the wall of silver mailboxes in order to check mine, as I usually did after work. I held in my hand a letter from Susie. I ripped it open, juggling all the other mail in my hand that was far less important. Inside the envelope were two tickets to that year's 2014 Jazz Fest with the note: "Surprise me! Come and watch me perform!"

Susie, you haven't changed a bit, I thought. I couldn't believe that she was performing at Jazz Fest! Of course, it wasn't the main stage, but still a huge accomplishment for a new performer. I ran up the stairs, taking two at a time to my apartment, opened the door, and flung the many bills on the table. Running to my tiny office—the small room that could only fit a computer and chair in it—I put the tickets next to my computer and immediately started looking for flights.

Scrolling through the first page of flight options, I paused at the realization of how Susie and I had come so far in the nine years I'd known her. I thought about bringing Peter with me, but I didn't want to combine complicated memories of the New Orleans of my past with the new happier ones I was making now. Still, I hesitated before clicking one seat. I picked up my phone.

"Hi, love," Peter said. "I'm still at work wrapping some things up, so I can't talk long."

"No problem, I just have a quick question. I'm about to book flights to go to NOLA next weekend for Jazz Fest. Susie sent me two tickets unexpectedly. Do you want to come?"

"Oh wow! That sounds like a blast, but I can't next weekend—I have to prepare for a trial. So sorry—you know I'd love to go."

"Right, I forgot about that. I just wanted to ask you before I booked anything. We can go together next time!"

"Maybe you can ask your friend Olive from work, or your mom?"

"All good ideas, I'll figure something out," I said. "We can catch up on our date tomorrow night, right?"

"Definitely. I'm looking forward to it! Bye, love."

I hung up the phone and tapped my finger on the keyboard. Who to bring? WWSD—What Would Susie Do? I smirked at the silly options that popped into my head. I could hear Susie's voice suggesting all of them—*Make a new hot friend in New Orleans for the weekend; convince the airline pilot, if he's hot, to go with you. He's already in town anyway!* I opted to go alone and sell the extra ticket for drink money. I was sure Susie would approve of this idea as well, though it probably wouldn't have been her first suggestion.

The much-anticipated weekend came after a grueling week at work. Sitting in the cab being whisked through New Orleans to my hotel, I looked outside like a little kid glued to the window. Some things were the same as I remembered. The heat and humidity still wrapped the city like a comforting hot towel you'd get at a fine restaurant, but things were different, too. As we drove through the city, I saw restaurants with signs advertising cuisines different from Cajun and Creole.

"Is that a Thai restaurant?" I asked the driver.

"Yes, ma'am. All kinds of things here, Japanese, Italian . . . almost any type of food you want," he said, straightening his Super Bowl Saints ballcap on his head.

"Wow! That *is* different from when I was here back in the days of Katrina."

The driver nodded. "A lot's changed since then. I can show you around if you'd like?"

"Yes! That would be wonderful, thank you! Could you turn down Magazine Street? I used to work at a restaurant there."

The cabbie nodded enthusiastically and made some turns to get us going to Uptown, all while pointing out the big box stores and new four-lane streets along the way.

"You used to work here?" the cabbie asked as we came to a stop in front of the old building. "It's a nice place." I saw the familiar brick building with the large windows that opened to the street.

"Well, when I was there it was an upscale French Creole restaurant. It looks like it's under new ownership now though."

"Yeah, this place changed hands a few times. Still trying to figure out what it wants to be. Where to now?"

"Let's head to the hotel, but could we go through Mid-City on the way? There's a house I'd like to check out."

"Sure thing. Houses around here have changed a lot too. People got lots of money to raise their houses higher."

He wasn't kidding. Some houses were eight to ten feet off the ground now—based on how deep the floodwaters had been in that part of town.

"Amazing. I don't see any FEMA trailers anymore either."

"Ha!" He laughed. "No, those bandages are long gone too."

We were approaching my old house. "Could we slow down here?" The car slowed to a crawl, then I saw the house. It still looked beautiful.

"This here's a pretty house. Was it yours?" the cabbie asked as we coasted down the street.

"Yes. Lots of memories in that house. I'm proud to say that I helped rebuild a part of New Orleans." The yard looked land-scaped and there were a few kid toys out front. The new owners had also put hanging ferns on the front porch. *I knew those would look good there!* I thought. "Thanks," I said. "We can go to the hotel. I'm good now."

I woke up early for Jazz Fest the next day so that I could sell the ticket near the Fair Grounds. Flush with cash from the easy sale of the extra ticket, I went in and started to walk around all the vendor booths. The official Jazz and Heritage Festival shirts caught my eye.

"Are those watermelon seed buttons?" I asked while feeling the Hawaiian shirt printed in a bright watermelon pattern. The silky fabric felt cool and inviting.

"Sure are. This year's theme is What a Melon."

"How fun! I'll take one men's shirt and one women's dress, please." Peter would love to add this to his Hawaiian shirt collec-tion, and I could match him. I was giddy thinking of being one of those cute matching couples. I snaked my way through the crowds and found the Gentilly Stage. Susie Star was to perform fifth that day, and I unfolded my beach chair and sat down tapping my foot—I couldn't wait to surprise her! I luckily found an open spot in the center, a few rows up so that she'd be able to easily spot me.

I was marking off each performer, and then the time came. Susie strutted onto the stage wrapped in gold sequins, and a large dark blue feather swayed in her hair as she walked. Her set started and it was wonderful. Her music was so fun, filled with a combination of pop, R&B, and soul. Everyone around me started dancing when she sang. I stood there beaming with the type of smile that hurts from keeping it so long. Susie went on singing and strutting, and without missing a beat we made eye contact. Her eyes lit up and she sang "Oh hell yeah!" when she spotted me. Everyone else thought she was getting into her song, but I knew it was because of me.

I went around back to the performers' tent after her set to find her.

"Girl! Come over here!" Susie said, waving both her arms for me to enter. Squeals emerged from both of us as we hugged and rocked each other back and forth.

"It took every ounce of my willpower not to jump off that stage when I saw you!"

"I didn't think you had that much willpower, Susie!" I said, laughing, still in her arms.

"Did you come with anyone?"

"No, you have me all to yourself. I hocked the ticket for beer money."

"Ah, love it!" she said, slapping her leg. "Though you could have brought along a fun side piece with you, just for the weekend." She winked.

"It's so good seeing you. You haven't changed a bit."

"Ms. Star, there's a line starting to form of fans out here wanting an autograph," a skinny, sweaty man said as he peeked in her door.

I looked at Susie. "You shouldn't keep your fans waiting!"

"You goof!" She grabbed a Sharpie and quickly wrote "Susie" in cursive with a star for the dot of the "i" on my chest. "I'm free after I attend to my adoring fans. Let's hit the town after that. Wait for me," she said as she walked out.

I looked at my customized autograph and laughed. "You know I will!" I hollered back.

We spent the remainder of the day together, getting complimentary drinks wherever we showed up due to her rising star status. I felt like we owned the city.

⌒⌒

Returning to Ohio after a weekend filled with proper Susie debauchery reminded me of how happy I was to come back to my familiar stable place, where I felt I belonged. I snuggled up to Peter in bed. He kissed my forehead. "I'm happy you had a great time with Susie, but I'm super happy to have you back here."

I looked up at his flushed cheeks that had the warm glow he got after making love.

"Me too. I love playing house with you."

"When will we play for real?"

I looked at him, searching his eyes. "You know I can't answer that." I smiled and looked away. "Maybe soon, I don't know. I'd like to start my own family and get to hold a baby that's mine."

"I'd love to help with that," said Peter as he kissed my cheek and then lips. Our passion began all over again.

I got up the next morning feeling the cold wood floor under my feet and wrapped my naked body in my fuzzy warm robe. I made two cups of coffee for us and yelled to the bedroom where he was still lying, "Give me ten minutes—I'll be right back. There's coffee on the table!" I walked to the bookcase and grabbed my journal, not knowing why I needed to log an entry today, but drawn by a force to do so.

I didn't think I would ever be lucky enough to write this, but I have a second chance at love. I am falling deeply in love with Peter and I know he is with me. As much as I hate to admit it, what with our mothers' constant nagging about making our relationship official, I can't help but agree. I feel like I'm more settled with my life and not spinning to and fro like a top.

There was a time in my life when the hardest decision I had to make was to have faith in myself, move on, and make my own direction in life. Perhaps I had a little bit of Susie inside me daring me to take that leap. I remember it was so terrifying realizing that at the time. The hardest part was telling everyone over and over again what had happened. Thinking back, I'm glad I did it, allowed myself to hit the restart button. I have no idea what my life would have been like if I stayed with Nick. But spending too much time in the past doesn't allow for living in the present.

I closed my journal, put down my special pen, and tucked the journal away back in the bookshelf. I needed to document a new beginning in my life. I looked around admiring my apartment—the pictures of Peter and me framed on the buffet table, my roller derby skates on the floor in the hallway—and I smiled. I felt whole again, in charge of my future. A happy glow filled me. I paused and allowed it to envelop me like sunshine.

HISTORICAL NOTE:
ABOUT HURRICANES KATRINA AND RITA

Hurricane Katrina made landfall on August 29, 2005, in the early morning, directly striking Southeast Louisiana. Katrina was downgraded from a Category 5 hurricane to a strong Category 3 when it hit land. However, the momentum of the storm carried it over a hundred miles inland through Mississippi, maintaining 125-mile-per-hour winds during its course. The resulting storm surge from Katrina spanned a hundred miles wide and affected three Gulf states: Louisiana, Mississippi, and Alabama.

In New Orleans, the levees surrounding and protecting the city from neighboring waters breached that same day, allowing fifteen- to twenty-foot floodwaters to invade and envelop the low-lying areas. New Orleans was 80 percent flooded, causing catastrophic damage and loss of life. It's estimated that 275,000 houses were damaged or destroyed in the affected states, and over a thousand lives were lost in New Orleans alone. A combination of record levels of rainfall and four levee breaches at Lake Pontchartrain filled Louisiana with water.

People living in the Gulf Coast region were not the only ones affected by this storm. The entire United States felt disruptions to commerce, as two major ports in Louisiana were closed to commercial boat traffic. Major oil refineries were shut down due to serious, extensive damage. Significant environmental damage occurred due to oil leaking from holding tanks and pipelines into the surrounding waters, and hundreds of oil barrels were scattered throughout the surrounding land. Major highways leading into New Orleans were damaged or destroyed, preventing any traffic into or out of the city and surrounding areas. Communication systems lost infrastructure in Southeast Louisiana and Mississippi, compounding efforts to relay information to or from the affected areas. Cell phone towers were down and only texting worked in certain areas.

Hurricane Rita made landfall barely a month later, on September 24th. Similar to Hurricane Katrina, this storm also was a Category 5, which was downgraded to a strong Category 3 at the time of landfall. Rita remarkably impacted much of the same areas in New Orleans that Katrina did, delaying efforts to drain the already flooded city. Floodwaters in New Orleans finally receded forty-three days after Katrina's initial landfall.

As of June 2024, Hurricane Katrina is considered the costliest hurricane and natural disaster in United States history, with estimates of over a hundred billion dollars in damage, mostly the result of levee failures. Due to the extent of damage, restoration efforts and repopulation of the city was slow. The city recorded 51 percent of its population returned by 2006. Basic services for the area—electricity, gas, public transportation, schools, hospitals, and grocery stores—were at less than half of pre-Katrina capacity after the storm. In 2006, a year after the storm, restoration efforts had barely begun, leading some neighborhoods to rebuild on their own or with outside assistance. Economic disparities were made evident, as many people had no or inadequate insurance, which confounded timely rebuilding efforts and recovery rates. Recovery was slow throughout New Orleans. In 2007, two years after the back-to-back hurricanes, tens of thousands of households were still relying on FEMA assistance. By 2016, New Orleans still had only 81 percent of its pre-Katrina population level.

The United States Coast Guard (USCG) was the first to respond to the aftermath of these storms. A three-tiered response occurred from air, land, and sea. After the storms, floodwaters were inundated with raw sewage, and toxic components composed a mixture of oil, natural gas, and chemicals. More than nine million gallons of oil leaked from storage tanks, refineries, pipelines, and marine facilities. This created environmental damage not seen since the *Exxon Valdez* spill of 1989. The Coast Guard assessed the condition of over two hundred refineries and processing plants, and recorded an additional one hundred oil and gas platforms in the Gulf of America (formerly the Gulf of Mexico) missing or damaged due to the storms.

USCG air crews alone led an extensive effort in rescuing more than twelve thousand stranded people who stayed in the city. Simultaneously, USCG boat crews contributed to rescuing over twenty-one thousand people. The total lives saved from rescue operations were calculated at 33,735 during Hurricane Katrina alone. Over five thousand Coast Guard men and women served in Katrina and Rita relief operations. Of those who were directly stationed at Sector New Orleans, 582 Coast Guard men and women lost their houses during Katrina and another sixty-nine lost theirs during Rita. Despite shouldering tragic personal loss, their unwavering duty to the mission remained first priority.

The people of New Orleans who returned and rebuilt their

lives exhibited resiliency that has remained strong throughout. Those who came back to rebuild have improved on their homes and, likewise, their city. A particular highlight for the city and its people occurred in 2010, when the New Orleans Saints football team won their first Super Bowl in the history of the franchise. The people of New Orleans kept their tenacity through their faith, culture, sports, and food—all of which are unique, proud, and endure to this day.

SOURCES

Facts obtained for this historical summary can be found on the following websites made available for the public and published papers.

- US Department of Commerce, "Hurricane Katrina August 23–31, 2005," https://www.weather.gov/media/publications/assessments/Katrina.pdf

- R. W. Kates, C. E. Colten, S. Laska, and S. P. Leatherman, "Reconstruction of New Orleans After Hurricane Katrina: A Research Perspective," *PNAS* 103, no. 40, October 3, 2006, https://doi.org/10.1073/pnas.0605726103

- Scott Price, "A Bright Light on the Darkest of Days: The U.S. Coast Guard's Response to Hurricane Katrina," https://media.defense.gov/2024/Jun/21/2003490008/-1/-1/0/DARKESTDAY-001.PDF

- National Oceanic and Atmospheric Administration, "Hurricane Rita, September 18–26, 2005," https://www.weather.gov/lch/rita_main

- Encyclopedia Britannica, "Hurricane Katrina," last updated May 9, 2025, https://www.britannica.com/event/Hurricane-Katrina

ABOUT THE AUTHOR

ALLISAN BECK is a seasoned marine research scientist, publishing numerous peer-reviewed scientific journal articles throughout her career. This work of fiction is her first novel. She has traveled all over the United States with her husband, who proudly served in the United States Coast Guard for twenty years, resulting in a total of eight PCS moves. The military life gave them both the opportunity to travel, meet people, and participate in different cultures of each new city where they were stationed. Throughout their years of service they experienced many hurricanes, the largest and most damaging of which was Hurricane Katrina. They can both take credit for rebuilding a part of New Orleans. These days, Allisan, her husband, their two children, and their fluffy dog still love to travel, but now enjoy packing for vacations instead of permanent moves.

9 781966 629566